Any references to historical events, real people, or real places are used fictitiously. Names, characters, and places are products of the author's imagination.

Copyright © 2023 by David J. Neumaier

All rights reserved. This book or any portion thereof may not be reproduced or used in any manner whatsoever without the express written permission of the publisher except for the use of brief quotations in a book review. For more information, address: dneumaier@hotmail.com.

Printed by Kindle Direct Publishing, in the United States of America

First hardback edition February 2023

Cover Design by Matthew P. Smyser
Edited by Alisha Dahl, As the Page Turns Editing

ISBN 979-8-9875739-2-1 (Hardback)
ISBN 979-8-9875739-1-4 (Paperback)
ISBN 979-8-9875739-0-7 (Kindle)

www.davidjneumaier.com

For my late grandparents, who never had a chance to read it

PREFACE

GREETINGS. I write this to prepare you for something within the contents of this book. My children, born as they were, were then separated. Though this was not my intention, it has made their story a strange one to be told. As such, I have allowed them to both take their turns in narrating it. I will introduce them the first time before they take over, along with any other narrators who may have a part to play, then denote their narration with their first initial. With my newest children, I will introduce how they experienced their creation, for they remember little of it. Let them tell their own stories. It's for the best. *Hacre ite mare imu manio.*

Guardians of Aranor: Rebirth

PART 1: PATHS

DAY 1

A YOUNG BOY FLOATED PRONE with his head facing an incomprehensible direction. He could not determine what was up or down, left or right. He couldn't move his frail arms, trapped inside a cast of wind binding him into his current position.

Before he could think of breaking free, he heard the howls and whistles of the wind as it circled around him. It seemed to whisper in his ears, but he could not make out the words. The wind's grasp tightened around the boy, and he had no choice but to endure the pain. A cyclone of wind appeared before him. It spun simply for a few moments, raced and coiled itself around him, then finally decided to accept him—falling into the boy's throat.

After suffering momentary breathlessness, he was set free from the grasp of the mysterious wind. Still, he continued to float. His eyes changed to a cloudy gray and wind stormed in his mouth, then a strong, continuous gust forced itself out of his body through his eyes and mouth. This boy would be known by the name of Horus.

H

I woke to the sound of the wind as it rushed into my ears. It filled them with everything around me from the leaves and the birds to the sky. I opened my eyes and saw all that the wind spoke of, there was beauty in this world that my senses could simply not resist. The air smelled and tasted sweet. The sun was warm, and the cool breeze pressed up against my body. I felt I was a part of this world, yet something told me I was not.

"Welcome, Horus," a voice whispered.

"Where are you? How do you know me?" I asked. My voice seemed so strange to me, while equally as natural.

"I am the wind around you, I am the guardian of your life," It replied.

"How are you alive?"

"I am feeding off of you, in a sense. A parasite of your energy."

I tore violently at the air around me in an attempt to remove it. "Get away!" I screamed, backing away from nothing. I had no clue of what it was talking about, but something feeding off me could not be safe.

"It's no use, Horus," It whispered. "I am a part of you. I am here to keep you safe and guide your life. This world has become rather cruel to your kind, so it is my solemn duty to keep you alive, not to harm you. You have immeasurable energy from the life of this world pulsing through you. It is in so much excess, in fact, that I was born of you to feed off of that energy to keep you from being overloaded with power. A helpful little parasite if you will."

My breath slowed as I calmed back down, "Is that so?"

"Indeed," It claimed slowly.

"So, if I am not of this world, then what am I?"

"You, Horus, are an Arinthian. The first pure born in hundreds of years to this world. To them, you are a myth. A being of pure energy, magic energy."

"Why am I here?"

"This, I do not know. I did not create you. Perhaps this world has need of you."

"So, you will always be around me?" I asked, in confirmation.

"Should you need power for a spell of sorts, I can return some of the siphoned energy back to you, causing me to temporarily dissipate. It is dangerous to attempt, but it can be rehearsed. I suggest we not attempt this foolishly."

I gritted my teeth and agreed, hoping it must never be done. I didn't want to lose my lifeline. I looked behind me and noticed what appeared to be an old, abandoned structure surrounded by a court of cobblestones. I noticed that in some areas of the court the stone was splitting away from the tower. I looked closer and saw tunnels underneath. I approached the one nearest to me, just to my right. The moment I stepped into the tunnel, I retreated at the sound of a howl from the beast within. The growling continued and I backed away slowly.

"Where exactly am I?" I quietly wondered to myself.

"I believe it is called the Arcane Ruins here," It replied rudely. "If I were you, I'd find some clothing soon. The people in this world would find you strange, fully grown and naked as a newborn, especially if they found you in this area. This is where their myths say your kin are born." After a pause, he muttered, "They now hate those who brought magic to them, what an ungrateful lot."

I wandered around the center tower looking for an entrance. There were no doors or low windows. The facade was too smooth to even think about climbing, but it seemed like there was a possible opening on the roof of the tower. I had no means of getting up there, so I turned around. "It's clear," It said.

"What do you mean?"

"The coast is clear. Head to the roof, you can reach."

"What?"

"You have magic, use it!" It said sharply.

"How?" I asked, equally annoyed with It—well, technically with myself.

It sighed. "Close your eyes," I did. "Open your mouth," I obeyed. "Now, repeat after me, *Icerepin*..."

"*Icerepin*."

It continued, "*Ilatteve*..."

"*Ilatteve*."

"*Icounten*," It finished.

"*Icounten*," I repeated. The wind howled around me, I began to feel weightless, I felt out of control, and panicking made it worse. I didn't know what to expect, the ground beneath me grew ever distant as my feet and arms flailed trying to grab a hold of anything that might keep me stable.

"Calm yourself," It ordered. "Breathe..."

I took a deep breath, closed my eyes, and slowly let the air out of my nose. I began to feel more stable as I spread my arms as if they were resting on a chair, but I remained upright. The calmer I became, the more control I had over my position. I was flying. I looked down for a moment and noticed that the ground was a little too far below me. Panicking once more, I immediately lost control and plummeted down to the earth. However, the moment before I hit the ground, he caught me.

"Remember," It said, "remain calm. Do not be afraid." I tried again, this time making sure not to look down and I arrived above the tower. "All right," It whispered, "now say '*Iveeno.*'"

"*Iveeno,*" I echoed. I began my controlled descent above what seemed to be a trapdoor. By the time I landed, I had a new appreciation for the being, and a new appreciation for solid footing. I bent my knees and knelt on the roof for a moment before it ordered me to get up. "What should I call you?"

"That is up to you entirely. I was created by you, so it only seems fit that you name me," It said.

"That makes sense," I agreed. I pondered for a moment when the name suddenly came to me, "How about Eyvindr?"

"It sounds fine, I have no objections," Eyvindr said shakily. "Now can we get inside the tower before someone sees you? I sense... something... let's get to cover."

I agreed and reached for the handle of the trapdoor. It was heavier than expected, so much so that the handle slipped through my grasp and slammed shut again. I began lifting it again, this time I made sure to grab the underside of the door the moment it came up and I shoved the door out of the way only to see another drop into the tower. It was much shorter than the last drop, but it was still longer than it had to be.

"I'll handle the fall this time. Simply jump down." I closed my eyes, placed my feet into the opening, took a breath, and leapt into the tower.

The wind whirled around me as I raced toward the bottom, and I was gracefully slowed to a stop. The interior of the tower was rather messy. I saw a variety of objects scattered around the room and what appeared to be cut trees forming spaces to contain them. "Ah, there we are," Eyvindr said. "Check inside those tall 'cut trees' as you call them. Here they are known as cabinets. There should be clothes in there for you to wear."

I checked the first cabinet, discovering nothing but some sewn-together cloth, and elected to ignore it. However, as I turned around, Eyvindr said with a hint of the exhaustion I felt in him before, "Turn back around, those are what you need. Put them on your body, there should be holes in them to fit your limbs through." I did as I was told without a word. The clothes were long and seemed to be mainly one piece of cloth, but it was the color of the sky that I so admired.

A thought then occurred, "Eyvindr?"

"Yes?" It replied, then as to answer the question before It was even asked, "I will get you out, just hold onto your new belongings tightly."

I wrapped my arms around my chest, locking my arms in place as I lowered my head and closed my eyes. Then, without a moment lost to thought, I was flying up and out of the very hole we came in, followed by a rather quick descent I was glad I had my eyes shut for.

"That should be good enough," It said.

I reopened my eyes and agreed with him, "But what now?"

Eyvindr exhaustedly explained, "I have used up so much of the little energy I siphon from you that I believe I must remain dormant for a short time until that energy is returned. You should ... rest ... too ..."

And just like that, I was alone again. With the clouds above me, casting shadows and blinding the stars, I found a spot above one of the tunnels, rested my back against the base of a tree and shut my eyes.

"STOP! PLEASE!"

A flame was nearing the boy strapped to a wooden chair. As the boy clenched his eyes and gritted his teeth in fear, the flame then flickered and dissipated. After a few moments of expecting to have his flesh seared, but it not happening, the boy reopened his eyes and relaxed his teeth to reveal flames trickling down his face; soon they began to cascade out of his eyes and mouth in torrents. The fire seared his legs causing him to shout in pain. As his voice grew louder, the flame grew stronger, extending straight, creating a column of flame. The empty abyss of a room lit up with the bright flame protruding from the boy's body.

Afterward, the flames began to weaken and return to their fluid state, but never again touching the child's legs, before receding into his eyes. The fire burned in his mouth and eyes until he collapsed. His eyes closed, he was unconscious, and the flame was gone. His mouth shut in sweet bliss. The outcast. The ranger. The flame wielder. Firelord. These are the names given to Drocan.

D

I was burning. The agony surrounded me in flames, searing my flesh but refusing to kill me. I tried rolling on the ground to remove the fire, but it refused to die. I looked at my charred arms as my flesh began to boil, pus flowing from the blisters, soon followed by blood. I screamed in frustration and pain, my vocal cords aching from my cries. I couldn't contain it. I couldn't control it. It lashed out around me.

"Hello," I heard a voice say. It sounded as if It was coming from me and the flames around me. My world flamed around me, and I couldn't see anything. I assumed the voice came from beyond the flames. "I am the fire around you."

"GET AWAY FROM ME NOW!" I ordered, trying to regain a sense of control of my voice.

"I cannot, I am a part of you," the voice sternly informed me, "You and I are in this world together. We are inseparable!"

I gritted my teeth and closed my eyes, "I will destroy you."

"I would like to see you try," It mocked.

I repeated, "I will destroy you."

"I would not recommend it," It advised. "Without me, you would die."

"I will destroy you."

"Did you not just hear what I said?" It asked. "Without me, you will die! You could get used to the pain, or you could be a complete and utter fool and kill yourself!"

"I will destroy you. I will stop this pain. I will survive," I grunted.

It scoffed at the thought, "You can't get rid of me. I was created by and for you to keep you alive! Do you really think it would be possible to defy nature as you so pitifully attempt? You are a fool."

I clenched my jaw until the pain of it surpassed the flames. I opened my eyes, and while they began to burn in the thick flame, I felt the words come to me, "*Icerepin ictusfie gous!*"

"What!?" I heard It question. "That's impossible!" Its confusion turned into outrage, "How do you know those words!?"

I answered simply with, "I am destroying you!" But I wasn't entirely correct. Its body began to dissipate, yes, but It was not going to be destroyed. Its knowledge and essence became magical energy, and my body absorbed It. I felt like I was drowning; my brain was overflowing with the knowledge of the world, the atrocities that the people of this world had committed. The only thing that remained yet unclear was why I had been created, but pain soon directed my mind away from the thought.

I held my throat but soon felt the need to hold every single inch of my body. I recognized I had the body of a young man, every last part of it ached. I coughed and puked on the ground near me, and a flaming sludge spilled from my mouth. With my newfound knowledge, I determined that it was my concentrated magical energy. I learned my name was Drocan and that the fire surrounding me was a "gous". How those words came to me before was still a mystery.

I felt sick. I tried to stand, and stand I did for a brief moment, before I fell onto my hands and knees and continued to vomit. Flames were pooling up beneath me. I tried to stand again and move back. As I moved back, I noticed

I hit a wall of sorts. I felt the structure of it, and it felt rather weak and moveable. I feel like I almost broke it.

I turned to face a nearby wall made of large stone very smooth bricks; the wall seemed nearly seamless with the exception of the section that I now faced. There was a thin break in the wall surrounding roughly twelve bricks. I tried to push the bricks; they felt moveable but were too heavy for me to budge. I backed up, keeling over my stomach as I held it, but I was determined to break this wall. I had already killed the unkillable, time for me to break the unbreakable. I charged toward the wall with my shoulder, slamming into it only to rebound off the wall and fall to the ground.

Looking up at the sky from the ground, I saw that what I was trying to break into was a tower. I turned my head to the left and noticed a forest around me and some passages that lead off into the distance. I looked to the right and saw an echo of what I saw to the left. I sighed and looked back up.

My throat filled again with the magic energy. I could feel myself producing it as fast as I was expelling it. I had to find a way to compress it even more, suppress it somehow... or use it. I then saw something move high in the air and it definitely was not a bird - I knew that much. It looked a lot like me.

"How could someone like me fly?" I thought aloud.

I then heard a clamor from the inside of the tower. I had to see what had just landed; I had to know who that was. I pressed my hands against the wall, fighting back the vomit, and pushing forward muttered, "*Icerepin ipare.*" The bricks began to move under the force of my will and soon I had pushed through the wall of the tower and fell on top of the bricks I just broke through.

Suddenly, the bricks began to move from underneath me and reformed the broken wall hiding the entrance from unwanted visitors. I saw a few rays of light peeking through cracks in the wood from which the otherwise-pitch black room I found myself in, a shadow occasionally eclipsing them as something passed over. To be sure that whatever was above me did not know I was here I whispered the command, "*Icerepin ingnis icounten*" A small flame protruded from my palm, and I was able to see that I was surrounded by many books, a singular wooden chair, and one cabinet.

I made my way towards the cabinet; life without clothing would be risky in this world, and I would need to blend in. I opened the cabinet and found some old, dark, orange robes; as I closed my hand to extinguish the flame, I felt the vomit come back into my mouth. I slipped the robes on. They fit perfectly, feeling silky on the inside with a rough cloth on the outside; these would do nicely in this world.

I began to skim through the books around me. There were all kinds of books about the history of this world, but I felt I already knew all of it. I knew of the atrocities that the race of this world had committed against my kin. It didn't matter what side they were on; it made no difference. Both sides of every war had enslaved my kind and forced us to use magic for them, draining our bodies of what energy we had then beating, whipping, even executing us for so-called treason. I hated the people of this world, but they were also my best chance of survival. They had the resources I needed. I may be a fountain of knowledge, but I am not a fountain of iron.

Sitting in the chair, I heard a whirlwind from above shoving a powerful gust from the wood planks above me and the shadow that occasionally moved was gone. I stood up fast and vomited again. I keeled over and tried to look up, but I could not raise my head and my eyes strained as I struggled against my body. I stumbled over to the one opening in the sets of bookcases and repeated the phrase I said before, "*Icerepin ipare!*"

The wall did not budge. I tried again, but it still refused to move. I tried and tried and tried but the wall no longer had any loose bricks. I slammed my body against the wall repeatedly, vomiting flames the whole time. The flames didn't spread and died out after a few moments and, fortunately, were not very bright. I screamed in frustration and fell back down to the ground. I was trapped.

I crossed my legs and closed my eyes to calm myself. I took a deep breath and the need to vomit passed. I could not tell whether it was because I had expelled enough of the concentrated energy, cast enough spells, or if I had finally learned to suppress the magic. I set my hands on the wall I had entered through and concentrated as much of the magical energy into my hands as I could and forced the wall forward and without even saying the words. After a few moments, the wall collapsed. I reopened my eyes and looked at the open brick. It was dark now, so I would be able to move unseen at this time, but the monsters would be rampant, so I elected to stay near the tower, but not in that room.

When I opened the door, I felt drained beyond belief and wanted to collapse from exhaustion. I leaned against the walls of the tower and watched it reform again, sealing the entrance. I followed the wall and encountered the being who I saw fly earlier leaning against a tree. I sensed a strong presence from him, not as strong as mine, but I had killed the thing that would keep me hidden and restrain my magical output. He was asleep, or at least pretending to be. I reached for him but felt the wind bite me.

"Stay back!" something ordered, though Its voice was wispier than the roaring sound I heard when the flames surrounded me.

"Who are you?" I asked It. "And who is this?"

"I'd like to ask you the same..."

"I asked first."

"I am the wind around this being."

"Who is he?"

"Not important," It answered, "but I am known to him as Eyvindr."

"Interesting name..." I said, "As a courtesy, I will tell you mine," I paused, "I believe my name is Drocan."

"What do you mean 'I believe'? That sounds like an Arinthian name, and I can sense the immense amount of energy flowing through you, but it is more than any single body could withstand, so you can't be an Arinthian. What *are* you?"

"I am an Arinthian."

"Let me speak to your gous, then."

"You can't," I said with a smirk. "It's dead."

"What?" Eyvindr asked as I reached once more to wake the man before me. "That's impossible."

Then I was blasted by a wind and the lights in the sky disappeared.

DAY 2

H

THE SUNLIGHT ASSAULTED MY EYES before they had even opened. I tried to open my eyes, but with the rising sun right across from me I could merely squint.

I groaned tiredly, "Good morning, Eyvindr."

"Good morning, Horus!" Eyvindr replied.

Jokingly, I thought to mock him, "You seem eager, anything I miss?"

Eyvindr hesitated then quickly stated, "Nothing, but we should just get moving. Can you stand?"

I stood and stretched my arms above my head, "Where to?"

"A city called Haven."

"What's there?"

"Good people," Eyvindr said hopefully. Then after a brief pause, it commanded, "Start walking toward the sun, and don't change course; that's the fastest way to Haven."

I took a step forward and collapsed to my knees overwhelmed by pain. *Why couldn't I walk?* My legs and stomach ached. *What am I missing?* I gripped my stomach.

"You are hungry," Eyvindr said. "To your left are some berries. Grab and eat them."

I followed his orders and ate as many berries as I could. The berries he showed me were a mix of blue and purple, each exploding sweetness into my mouth, but all insubstantial and nowhere near enough to satisfy me.

"You should be fine for a little bit. Let's keep moving until we can find something more suited to fill you."

My legs still felt weak, but I pressed on. The distant sun was a bright orange ahead of me, perfectly illuminating the path ahead. As I walked, I played a little bit of a game with myself trying to run from my shadow, it was entertaining and helped me move further with each step.

The trees around me stood tall and magnificent, echoing the sounds of the birds and creatures scurrying in the brush. With each step, the ground I walked seemed softer and the wildlife more vibrant. The trees clumped closer together, inhibiting most of the sun's blinding light to the point where I could barely see.

"Be careful," said Eyvindr. "This area has not been touched in ages. The animals here will not recognize you as predator, but as prey."

The forest grew dense. I began to slow down; the brush and thorns of the vegetation around me started to scratch and cut my legs, stinging me as I pushed through the branches of the trees around me. Occasionally, I would spot a small lizard scurry beneath my feet. The crunch of dead leaves and twigs was loud, echoing across the endless forest. The path I was to follow was relatively clear in terms of vision, but the forest fought me with all its might. I struggled against vines pulling them forward until they eventually broke.

"Remind me again," I asked Eyvindr, "what's so great about humans? You *said* they would try to kill me."

"Humans are fearful, violent creatures," he replied. "They do what they believe is necessary to survive. Their instinct tells them that you are dangerous; instead of trying to learn about you, they continue to massacre your kind..."

"How does that make them good?"

"What makes them good is their natural kindness towards one another. Humans are naturally empathetic and will feel your pain of being lost. As long as we don't do anything to act out of the ordinary, they will gladly assist you. Humans want humans to survive, but nothing else is certain."

The cuts in my legs stung with each step and I started to slow down more. Noon quickly passed, as did the evening. Soon, it was pitch black.

"This is not optimal. Get low: we'll stop for the night," Eyvindr quivered. I obeyed and went prone with my chest to the ground and my arms in front of my face, but I couldn't sleep.

I began to notice the damp softness of the ground. The earth and the air felt frozen, making it impossible to go a moment without the cold touch of night chilling me to the bone. But that wasn't the only thing that froze my blood. The monsters around me began to move, and I turned my head to the left and watched them.

"Don't worry about them. As long as you don't move too much, they shouldn't notice you," said Eyvindr.

The beasts themselves were rather spectacular in the night. The trace amounts of moonlight that reached them glittered off their reptilian skin, and their eyes shone a bright red. They crept carefully through the tall grass, looking for prey – foolish animals that did not or could not hide early enough. A lizard-like creature on its hind legs began to approach me. It didn't seem to have a neck or even arms, and its mouth was vast, allowing for a large amount of food to be consumed at once.

"That's a *lacerine*, one of our biggest concerns here, but the better question is, where are its friends?"

I turned my head again, to see if I could spot its "friends."

"Don't move."

Stupidly, I ignored Eyvindr and turned my head again to see the lacerine's eyes meet mine. They grew a brighter red, then it sniffed me. Its jaws began to separate, and its drooling mouth and jagged, sharp teeth threatened my very existence.

"Hold. Still. It's trying to scare you."

The lacerine's breath smelled terrible and caused me to gag. It kept its mouth open for a couple more seconds before snapping it shut. It stepped on and over me and seemed like it weighed a ton with just a single foot and its long, slimy tail dragged over me.

"Thank Arinth, you listened for once."

I'm sorry, I thought back.

"We need to move now."

Wait, why? Didn't you just get on to me about moving too much, just with my head?

"Odds are, that lacerine is likely just looking for its friends before it eats you and definitely has you marked in this spot. After all, you do smell terrible."

Ok, do you have a backup plan if this goes south?

"Exactly."

What? I thought we were going east?

"There's a pond to the south. It's probably where that lacerine was going. Start crawling to your right."

Eyvindr, what happened to your sanity? There are going to be more of them! Isn't that a problem?

"They can't see behind them and, when alone, have pretty poor eyesight." A shriek was heard in the distance. "And they found some food. Let's go now. If we can get you to the pond, we can wash you of your scent. They will be too busy chasing their food."

But the pounding steps of the heavy beasts were getting louder. The lacerines were running toward me, not away.

Oh no, Eyvindr and I thought simultaneously.

"Quick," he urged, "Get up that tree to your left."

I stood up and bolted to the tree and reached for the lowest branch with both of my arms, grabbed it, and pulled myself up as the lacerines caught up and snapped at my feet. I pulled my legs over the branch and continued to climb. I arrived above the tree line just in time to see the birds scatter from the treetop. As they flocked east, their feathers shone in bright, bluish silver. The tree shook.

I looked down, the lacerines were desperate for me. One of them had sunk their teeth into the base of the tree. The tree shook, again. The lacerines took turns biting the base of the tree.

"What do we do? Eyvindr?" I asked, nervously.

"Be patient," he replied, "They are at a disadvantage."

The lacerines surrounded the base of the tree, biting it from all angles, chipping away at the trunk – sending fear down my spine.

"How so? They are completely surrounding us, we can't go up, and they want us to come down, and obviously, we don't want to."

"Exactly," he stated, "When the tree falls, it will land on a few of them and crush them. That will be our food – they aren't cannibalistic."

"Ok, but we go down with it, and will still be outnumbered."

"Give me control."

"What are we going to do? Fly?" I asked hopefully as I eased my mind and control.

"Nope," he replied. I tensed up again. "Trust me. Remember, if you die, I do, too."

I hesitated and looked down, then back up. The moon was sitting peacefully above us, yet below was a violent gnashing of teeth. I counted five lacerines.

"All right." I shut my eyes and handed control over to Eyvindr. "Here goes nothing."

"Oh, this will be something all right," Eyvindr said. I felt weightless for a moment before Eyvindr caught my body as the tree crumbled and fell right onto two lacerines.

"*Icerepin ilacroe lacerine!*" I heard my body shout as Eyvindr placed my hands between myself and the remaining lacerines.

They opened their mouths and raised their heads to let out another shriek, but before they could, their body and legs were sliced apart by what seemed like nothing. He handed control back over, and I felt exhausted.

"What was that?"

"A laceration spell, one of the stronger wind-based spells."

"When will I..." I said as everything turned black and my body crashed into the dirt.

D

I AWOKE IN A CART. It was moving at a rather steady pace, and I was surrounded by a bunch of sleeping, beaten up, dirty humans. The cart smelled terrible on account of the unclean people and lack of proper waste disposal. The tarp above us didn't help it to air out, either. One other man, who looked cleaner than the rest, was near the back of the cart and noticed me awaken and greeted me with a harsh stare. I furrowed my brow and stared back; I was evidently more threatening as he finally looked away.

I climbed over the people, about twelve of them, made my way to what I perceived as the front of the cart, and lifted the tarp just a little bit to see if I could see the driver. They were dead. The cart was driven by a pair of skeletons. In front of the horses pulling the cart were more carts. The area around us was dying, if not already dead. The branches of the trees looked weak and wilting. The occasional spotting of yellow grass among the red dirt signaled the existence of some life in this area, but it wasn't moving. Making my way to the back of the cart, I was less careful in my maneuvers and woke up a few others with my own weight.

"Who are these people? And where are we going?" I asked the man. He replied with a finger held to his mouth and a deathly stare. Suddenly, the cart stopped. I heard the clattering of shields and swords make their way to the back of the cart, and the tarp was lifted. Finally, some fresh air, or so I thought. The air outside smelled rotten and dead, making me wish for the smell of the humans' body odor.

At the cart's tail stood two skeletons that were roughly the same height, but definitely shorter than me.

The skeleton on the right pointed its sword at my neck.

"Quiet!" it demanded. "And you will be allowed to serve the great King Ubel!"

I took the time to look around, commanding my senses to absorb the surrounding area as fast as they could. I now knew it was not a great time to act. The road was surrounded by flatlands, with the exception of a few dead trees, so I could easily be chased if not killed by the sheer number of skeletons I had noticed. I stood straight up to stretch my back.

"Sit," snarled the other skeleton.

"May I ask that you keep the tarp open?" I stated firmly. "It is awfully stuffy in there, and I won't exactly get far even if I get out."

"No. It closes," said the first skeleton as he withdrew his blade from my neck.

"Ubel demands," sneered the second.

"Very well," I said and sat back down. They closed the tarp over me and sealed it again. I waited until I had heard the clatter of their weapons move back to the front. After the cart started moving again, I uttered, "*Icerepin ingnis icounten*" and the same spell I had used to illuminate the tower revealed itself in my hand.

I pressed my hand against the tarp and burned a hole through to allow for more airflow then quickly whispered, "*Iveeno*," before I could be noticed. The air itself did not smell any better than before, but it was still better than the stench of dirty humans.

The expressions on the faces of the few awake humans changed once they realized what I had done. One woman stared at me with wide eyes and turned away when she noticed me looking at. I just created airflow for them so it would stink less yet they are still more frightened than thankful. I felt someone touch my shoulder from behind.

"Are you an Arinthian?" the old man whispered.

"Depends on who you ask," I replied. "To some, I am an Arinthian and to others, I am neither human nor Arinthian."

The old man was frightened now but pressed on with his questions, "Are you a flame wielder?"

"Obviously."

He was now excited, "Could you burn these caravans?"

"You would die, too," I reminded him.

"Oh, yes," the old man said as sadness struck his face. Why do I feel pity for him? Probably because I wanted out of this likely slave trade as well.

"All right," I said. "I have an idea."

The old man's face lit up. "Yes?"

"I need you to be loud," I turned to the rest of the cart. "I need all of you to be loud. Then on my signal, you will all run in different directions."

Most of the cart was listening, and others were trying. "That will get us killed!" shouted the woman. The cart stopped again.

"Perfect, I'll handle the guards." I moved to the back edge of the cart ready to pounce on them as soon as they opened the tarp. I heard the clatter of their weapons and bones, but they were both on one side, stopping earlier than before. Suddenly, a blade struck through the cart and impaled the woman, her last breath sighing softly out as she died. They pulled the blade back.

"What we tell you?" the skeletons said. "QUIET!"

One of the younger men shouted in fear. The skeletons thrust another blow through the wall of the cart. The whole cart was in shock, refusing to speak or acknowledge what just happened. The passengers kept their lips sealed as we watched the dark red blood spill from the woman and the man. Shields, swords, and bones clattered once more to the front and the cart started moving again.

Now I had a different plan. I got as close to the driver skeletons as I could and asked, "Is there any food we could eat?"

"Eat her," they said.

"And if we don't?"

"You starve."

"I'm sure Ubel won't want weak slaves, will he?"

The skeletons growled, "That why eat her."

"But eating her would make us sick."

"You all soon only bones."

The skeletons were clearly annoyed now. I heard the one seated on the right unsheathe its blade as it tried to stab me. I narrowly dodged the blade and grabbed the sword's edge as it passed me. The blade cut deep into my hand, but I grabbed it with my other hand and pulled as hard as I could.

The instant the blade came loose from the skeleton's grip, it shouted, "Stop the carts!"

I grabbed the handle of the blade and cut through the tarp longways, pushing it over the edge and standing up in one fluid motion, riding the stutter of the cart's stopping with some trouble but remaining upright, nonetheless.

"Now!" I shouted to the caravan. An arrow scraped me and struck the side of the cart from about three carts back. "MOVE NOW!"

The remaining living humans scrambled from the cart and ran off in different directions.

"*Icerepin,*" I began as another arrow whizzed by, "*ricopros revisnuus ingnis icounten,*" and I was enveloped in flames.

The flames stung my body but did not hurt as much as my gous. I charged at the cart behind mine with the blade in my left hand.

"Get them back here!" shouted a commanding voice. "I'll deal with this Arinthian myself!"

The commander rode his horse from the front to my location and dismounted. He was clad in full, black armor, a dull plate that seemed to absorb all the light that hit it. This skeleton was different in many ways from the others: its eye sockets lit red by some evil light, and he wielded a halberd on his back. He pulled his weapon in front of him and put his left foot back, preparing to strike. I readied myself and put my right foot back, mirroring his footwork.

The commander swung his halberd up and brought it down in a sweeping motion. I dodged and tried to get in close to hit as I knew I would not have long if I was burning this much energy all at once. The commander saw through my plan and had already pulled his halberd back, ready to spear me. I saw the thrust coming, but I was too close to be able to avoid it. The tip pierced through the fire that coated me, and I began to bleed a blue blood. I gasped for air, shaken from the pain but still standing. Another figure, clad in dark red armor and a dragon helmet, approached from the front, stood next to the commander, and whispered something in his ear. The commander withdrew his halberd and placed it on his back again.

"Congratulations. You have just been spared by the mighty Ubel," he said, clearly disappointed.

I knew the longer I kept the commander and the new dragon-helmeted figure close to me, the longer it would take them to regain all the slaves they had lost.

"Oh, come on," I slurred through the pain. "I can still fight."

The figure in dark red armor whispered into the commander's ear again, "Let them all go!" the skeleton in black announced. "Ubel only wants this one!"

My vision began to fade as I lost more and more blood, my coat of fire finally dying as I fell forward, face down. but still conscious.

"Turn him over!" the figure in dark red armor commanded. "I want him alive."

"But M'lord, Ubel!" protested the commander.

"Don't question me!" rebuked Ubel. "He's worth more alive as Arinthian than dead as a skeleton."

Then everything blacked out again.

DAY 4

H

I OPENED MY EYES. I was on something as soft as a cloud, but saw I was close to the ground. "Well, good morning," said a soft voice that clearly did not belong to Eyvindr.

The ceiling above me was a sea of marble reflecting the nearby torchlight around me. I turned my head to search for the source of the voice. "Where am I?"

"The royal palace," Eyvindr informed me.

My eyes settled on a young, black-haired woman in white robes lined with gold fabric, kneeling next to my pad. "King Justain's castle," she told me. "A few merchants found you near dead on the side of the road near a bunch of dead lacerines. You're lucky to be alive right now." She dabbed a sponge on my forehead and wrung it out.

"She's right," Eyvindr stated.

"It was your fault," I said aloud.

"Excuse me?" she asked, very confused, replacing the sponge on my forehead. "What is my fault?"

I hesitated, "Nothing. I'm sorry. Who are you?"

"I," she hovered her hands over my chest, "am the king's healer, but you may call me Lady Erione." Her sky-blue eyes were intensely focused on the task before her, disinterested in anything else.

I tried to sit up, but a pain pierced through my back like a spear, and I fell back down to the comforter.

"Who told you you could move?" Lady Erione said. She moved a braid that barely reached her elbow behind her. "Turn over. I have to make sure your back is fixed." A thin, golden circlet surrounded her head and, in cooperation with her braid, managed to keep most of her hair out of her face. However, a few strands on either side escaped their confinement.

I attempted to roll over but was stopped again by the pain. "I can't," I grunted. "It hurts too much."

"That's what you get for moving before I told you to, I wasn't done with even your front side yet. Now I have to fix much more."

"Sorry," I said through my teeth, fighting back the urge to cry from the pain.

"How long have you been here?" I asked Eyvindr.

"I only recently reformed after all of that energy we expended," Eyvindr said. "I've been around for as long as you have been awake."

Lady Erione again thought the question was for her, but luckily this wasn't as weird of a statement as the last, "I've been here for a few hours, tending to your more minor wounds from being bounced around in the back of that merchant's cart. You had many small cuts and splinters from the wood. I am honestly surprised that you don't have any deep gashes from the lacerines." Then she commanded something under her breath and a white glow appeared above my chest as the pain slipped away from my back.

"She must have Arinthian blood in her," Eyvindr said. I looked at her very puzzled and she noticed before I could take my stare back.

"One sixty-fourth," she said with a sigh.

"Arinthian?" I confirmed.

"What else?" she asked bluntly.

"If you're an Arinthian, why aren't they hunting you?"

"Because I'm useful in a war and situations like this. They always left the Arinthians with healing magic alive for the sake of keeping themselves alive. But I will say it is nice for me," she said.

"How so?"

"I'm the royal healer, so they keep me here in the palace near King Justain, should he ever fall ill, and the room they have me in is much nicer than this ugly room you're in."

I looked around the room and only saw beauty in the finely crafted pillars and the portraits of the king's lineage, "This is ugly?"

"Not really, but it is compared to the rest of the palace. Now turn over."

She helped me roll over onto my stomach and once more hovered her hands over my body and muttered under her breath the same spell. I could hear it more clearly this time.

"*Icerepin,*" I heard her say, "*aiman revisnuus ioaxuli.*" The pain in my back felt like it was being spread throughout my body, then it faded into nothingness. "Now you may stand," she instructed me.

I sat up and was relieved to feel no pain this time. Placing my hands on either side I pushed myself up and into a standing position.

"Feel free to walk around a little bit. Just don't break anything. I'm going to tell the king you are awake." I turned away from her and started looking at the king's portrait, or one of them at least.

"Why does he need to know?" I asked, still admiring the art. I heard no response. So I turned around to look, and she was gone. All the portraits had one thing in common – a golden crown with a sapphire gem embedded at the front. The kings all looked relatively similar: brown hair, a long, brown beard, and ocean-blue eyes.

The castle was nearly empty. Aside from the high-up portraits, there were a few standing sets of armor, but mostly just emptiness filled the room. The armor sets appeared bulky, made of shining silver with a gold dragon emblem on the left shoulder. I lifted one of the helmets and set it on my head. The helmet fit snugly on my head, and the golden face divider barely inhibited my vision. I removed the helmet, placed it on the ground, and tried on the rest of the armor set. It all fit perfectly and was surprisingly lightweight for how thick it was.

I heard the footsteps of the caretaker returning and frantically attempted to return the armor to its post, but she saw me placing the helmet back on the stand.

"That specific armor set hasn't been used in years, if you want it, the king will likely let you have it." Her voice was already becoming familiar to me.

"What's so important about me?"

"You are an Arinthian," said a man who must have been the king as he strutted forward from the hall accompanied by one spear-wielding guard and another armed with a long, wide, straight silver blade. Both of them were adorned with heavy golden armor.

"Oh, no," said Eyvindr. "We need to get out of here."

The king, seeing fear on my face, said, "I have no intention of harming you, I simply have something to ask of you."

I stared him down, making it clear I was still suspicious.

"You see," he continued, ignoring my disinterest in the conversation at hand, "I have been at war with a madman named Ubel," he looked at me to check if I recognized that name. I did not react. "We've been in a stalemate for what feels like a lifetime. He is truly evil. Marching his hordes of skeletons upon my cities, with no regard for the living. We are both equally matched, but you..." he paused, "you could be the very thing we need to tip the scales. Join my Crown Guard and you shall be spared."

"Don't ans—" Eyvindr started.

"And if I don't join?" I asked.

He smiled, a truly terrifying smile, "I have a hunch that you already know."

Eyvindr told me, "I was afraid of this very thing. People like him are the exact reason you are the last of your kind."

"So, I am to die on the battlefield if I do, or die here if I don't?" I clarified.

"Yes, sadly," the king stated, with little remorse.

"What can you promise me if I do join you?"

"Your life, a roof, weaponry, food," he paused and looked at Erione, "and anything you could ever want."

Lady Erione looked down with shame.

Eyvindr said, "I don't think we have a choice."

I now shared the same shame Lady Erione felt – wishing I could do something but knowing I could not. Unless… "I will join your guard and accept everything you have to offer..."

"Perfect," the king began, "I will introdu—"

"On the condition," I interrupted, "that Lady Erione is free of any obligations she has to you."

"You don't have to do that," she said. She looked worried, but I wasn't sure about what.

"How about a compromise?" the king offered. "She, too, is a valuable asset to my army. So instead of attending to me, she will attend to the squadron I intend on having you lead."

Lady Erione was still worried.

"Will Lady Erione be treated the same as she is now?" I asked. "Free of the 'ugly rooms?'" I mocked.

"Of course," he said. "She will continue to be treated as royalty when in this castle. But outside of these walls, I leave that up to you."

"And what do you say of this, Lady Erione?" I asked her.

"The king has offered me so much protection from the other attendants he has. If you believe you can offer the same, I will accept the order to attend to your squadron."

"I believe that I can," I confirmed, but I only saw doubt on her face.

"Then it is settled," the king announced. He turned to his guards, "Sir Jerum, Sir Petrus, lead..." turning back to me, he asked, "What is your name?"

"Horus," I stated.

"Very well then, Horus. Sir Jerum and Sir Petrus will lead you to your room. Erione, fetch him some of the finest linens and clothes we have to offer."

The king's personality had shifted back toward benevolence as the knights whisked me away to some forgotten place in the castle.

D

WHEN MY CONSCIOUSNESS RETURNED, I found myself on a table. My stab wound was being covered by a young-looking woman with white hair streaked with black and olive-green eyes. "Where am I? How long has it been?" Her long black robes had a red dragon embroidered over her chest, and lines of red decorated the borders.

"You've been out for a little over a day, which, by the way, is impressive for how harsh the commander was with you. Welcome to Ubel's castle."

Skeletons surrounded me. The woman with white hair was still tending to my wounds when a figure clad in red armor tore through the crowd, dispersing them. Whoever they were, they were not large enough to be Ubel.

"How is he, Lyss?" the figure asked. They had a relatively high voice, but I still couldn't see them clearly. I assumed it was another woman.

"I am doing fine," I answered, attempting to sit up. My attempt was met with a sharp pain in my gut that reminded me why I was almost dead in the first place.

"Clearly not," Lyss said. "Ubel," there was that name again, "must have really liked you to not chop off your head and limbs. Very few things make it into these walls alive. But to be fair, you were mostly dead."

"My father said you were an Arinthian," the figure in red stated, "but you are certainly a strange one." It was certainly a female voice now, and the red of her armor was closer to that of cherry than of the dark red of Ubel's. "He told me," she started, "you don't have a gous."

I tried to sit up again, "I think we have established that." I collapsed again in pain.

"But how?"

"It was killing me. So I killed it," I said through my teeth. "I absorbed it to stop it from burning me alive."

"They are designed to not kill you," Lyss said, as if I was a child.

"To be fair," I forced my head up and echoed Lyss' tone, "maybe it was not killing me, rather searing my flesh as fast as my body could heal it. It was constant torture."

"That was it keeping you alive," she shouted. She placed her fingers onto the bridge of her nose, clearly disappointed in me for something, "the gous is exactly what heals you. That is why this is taking forever. Because you killed it, that stab wound from Commander Treynar may take weeks if not months to heal on its own!"

"I stand by my choice."

"And you are an idiot for it," Lyss interrupted. "Without a gous you might as well be dead the moment Ubel puts you on the battlefield."

I coughed and it pained my gut, "Who said I would fight for Ubel?"

"You are not fighting for Ubel, you are fighting for his mercy," stated the woman in red armor, "under my direct command."

"And just who might you be?" I asked, knowing the moment the words left my lips that I shouldn't have.

Lyss chuckled and accidentally, or at least I hoped so, jabbed me where I had been stabbed, causing me to wince again. "She happens to be heir to the throne of Ubel, daughter of the king, Princess Bellona."

Bellona had a smug look on her face. She pushed her long scarlet hair to the side, awaiting my praise.

"All right," I shrugged. "And if I don't want to serve you?"

"Lyss?" Lyss immediately stopped tending to my wounds, took a step back, then in that moment the pain grew fiercer and fiercer. I felt like my stomach was burning with more intensity than when I still had my gous. I started with a hiss of pain before letting out a scream of dismay. It felt like an eternity before Bellona barked, "That's enough." And my pain ceased.

I was sweating heavily. "What did you do?"

"It is more of what I stopped doing," Lyss explained. "I do not have healing magic, but rather I am descended from an Arinthian of Death. Granted, I have a mere fraction of what they are capable of, and I can really only kill small animals and birds. Hence I am here instead of the frontlines, but for you, I was 'killing' all the pain receptors around your wound. Making it so you did not feel the burning sensation of getting stabbed."

"If you do not obey my orders by the time you are well enough to stand," Bellona started, "she will let you experience a slow and torturous death that we are so kindly sparing you of right now."

"Your father would never allow that," I replied. "I heard him say I am better to you alive than dead."

"Although true, he has left you in my command. I am confident I can win this war without you. You are merely a catalyst to accelerate my plans," she paused and looked at me in the eyes. "You have until tonight to consider your loyalty." With that, she turned. Her black cape trailed slowly behind her as she strolled away all high and mighty. The skeletons soon followed after her. I guessed they were her personal guard.

"Lyss? What do you think?" I asked.

"It's 'Princess Lyssandra' for you. No one calls me 'Lyss' except Bell and my father."

"Fine." I started again. "What do you think I should do, Princess Lyssandra?"

"Listen to her," she said. "She does not actually want to kill you, and we can spoil you here. With an undead army we have plenty of food to spare. The King of Haven would hunt you down if he knew there was another pureblood, but Ubel merely requests your service."

A loud and heavy clash of metal against the nearby steps rang through my ears. I turned my head to the source of the sound and gazed once more at the powerful dark red armor and iconic draconian helmet that the king himself wore. He had a large sword the size of a claymore yet resembled an elongated falchion hanging from his waist on the left side that was just barely too short to constantly cut into the ground beneath him. Some of the ancient letters that appeared on the walls in Arinthia were engraved on the blade, causing it to glow with a faint dark red.

"How are you?" Ubel asked. His voice was deep, loud, and commanding.

"Dying," I said flatly.

Ubel let out a brief burst of air from his nose, "I see you at least have some humor left in you. But I was not talking to you. Lyss?"

"I am fine, father." Princess Lyssandra's concentration broke, and I felt the searing pain of my stab wound begin to fire up again. She bowed as I began to hiss again. "But he isn't," I screamed again, crying in pain, reminding her of why she's been so focused on me. She finally refocused and my pain ceased once more.

Ubel removed his helmet to reveal hair matching the same dark red of his armor. His face was fair, and though he had a tired expression in his black eyes, his mouth cracked the faintest of smiles, surrounded by a few days of stubble.

"Now you," he directed his attention toward me, and the smile faded. "What you did was damn near suicide, setting yourself on fire like that. However, I commend you on your bravery. But why would you even attempt to sacrifice yourself for them? There hasn't been another pureblood Arinthian ever since—" He stopped himself. "Their lives were going nowhere. If anything, they would have been better dead and serving as members of my army than starving themselves on the highways and hiding in the forests filled with monsters. Those people were trapped in the Arinthian forests where I found you, I rescued them. They could have willingly served me and would have been well-fed, but instead, you forced them back to the wild. Why?"

"If anything," I mocked, "it was for my own nose they stank so bad. I asked your minions for some fresh air, and they said no, so I decided it would be better for my own sanity to get them as far away from me as they could."

"Funny," he did not laugh. "Did you consider how many of them may run to the nearest town and tell of you, the man who stood up to me and wields fire?"

"Not exactly."

"If you step foot outside of my walls, outside of my protection, I won't hunt you down, but the kingdom of Haven will. That's a promise."

"You seem a lot more reasonable than Princess Bellona," I said jokingly. "Her best option was for me to serve directly under her command."

"I wish you wouldn't talk about my daughter that way, but that would be the situation if you stay. In return for your protection, you would serve in my daughter's command taking orders from only her, Lyss, and myself."

"Well, I don't like listening to dead people, that's for sure."

"Who said you haven't been already?" Princess Lyssandra interjected. Her gaze shifted to her father.

"You don't look dead at least. I can work with that."

Ubel smirked again, "Thank you." He looked to Princess Lyssandra, "Lyss, you can give him the potion now."

"The what?" I asked. Princess Lyssandra smiled.

"All right." She reached behind her and pulled out a small vial filled with a bright red, somewhat translucent liquid and pulled out the cork. "Are you sure?" she asked for confirmation.

"It will be worth it."

She placed the vial at my lips, it smelled sweet and tasted just as such. Instantly, any sense of pain I had before vanished from my stab wound and I was able to sit up with ease.

"You were holding onto something that could have fixed me that fast for how long?"

"The whole time," Princess Lyssandra said. I finally got a better look at her now smiling face, content with the prank she just pulled.

"We had to be sure you would take our side before we used anything of value on you," Ubel said. "As long as you are loyal to me, I shall do my duty to protect you."

Let's end this war quickly then, I thought.

"Welcome to the Undead Army."

DAY 6

H

"AGAIN!" Sir Jerum Wolfsbane of the Crown Guard barked. I attempted to stand from my defeated position in the training field just outside the castle. Using the remainder of my physical strength, I pushed myself against the grass and forced myself to stand. It was just past midday.

"I only have four more days to train you," Sir Jerum said. "So I need you to improve before you get yourself killed."

"Wouldn't the king be the one sending me to die?" I asked, half-joking.

"I suppose you're right on that," Sir Jerum smirked, "but let's make sure you don't die here first."

Sir Jerum backed away until he was about twenty feet from where I had been knocked down. He turned around and placed his dull training sword (a considerable downsize to his familiar, wide claymore) evenly in front of him. He gripped it tightly and straightened his arms. Then he moved his right foot back and pulled the sword to his right side, keeping the blade skyward. He turned his head and looked dead into my eyes.

"He's going to—" Eyvindr started.

"I know," I interrupted aloud.

Sir Jerum smiled, confident in his ability to beat me. He was in his full shining armor that bore the emblem of the king's dragon: a golden symbol of the ruthless king's "divine might." I was lucky enough that today was cloudier than usual. Otherwise, I would be forced to struggle with the clean reflection of the burning sun off of the knight's shoulder guards. Sir Jerum saw no point in training without full armor, yet he allowed me to stick with a lightweight leather set. Maybe it was torture. Maybe it was mercy. I would never be sure. He felt it was necessary to know your own speed while fully equipped. He was also generally against wooden swords, an opinion he had made very clear over the past few days.

I prepared myself and mimicked his exact motion to begin, but instead of keeping the blade upright, I leveled it to be parallel with the field. I double-checked my stance then looked at him.

"Ready?" He asked.

"Ready," I stated. The smile never faded from his face. In an instant, despite the heavy armor covering his body, he dashed forward covering the entire distance between us. He raised his sword behind him for a heavy downward slash, but I was prepared. He always slashed inwards, aiming for a direct blow to the main body which caused me many pains on my shoulders, so I dodged to my left and dropped the blade beneath me preparing for an upward slash.

"He beat you again," Eyvindr told me. I was confused until I saw for myself the sudden shift in Sir Jerum's stance as he turned while the blade that was doomed to miss changed its fate and followed my dodge with great force. The edge of the blunt blade slammed into my back and knocked all of the wind in my lungs out of my chest and sent me face down into the dirt.

"You moved too soon," Sir Jerum said. "You stepped before I had committed to my slash. Wait until the very last moment before you even think about moving. I'm going easy on you. No one in a real fight will ask you if you are ready or would give you the courtesy of attacking the same way each time."

"You say that every single time."

"Then why haven't you figured it out yet?"

"I'm trying."

"I know, and you still move like a sack of rocks."

"Only because you won't let me use everything I have available. I can easily beat you if you let me use my gous," I said, rolling over to be on my back. I hated looking directly at the sun, but it was certainly much more comfortable than eating dirt.

Sir Jerum offered his hand to my bruised body, "Then we'll do that." I clasped his hand, and he grabbed my arm to lift me back up to my feet. "I'll prove you wrong."

Once more he backed away and prepared the same ready stance, but this time, he closed his eyes, taunting me with his confidence.

"Eyvindr, do your thing," I muttered. I closed my eyes and let Eyvindr take over as much of my body as possible. I felt the wind surround me and instantly felt refreshed and faster. I opened my eyes again and shouted over to Sir Jerum,

"Ready!"

"Very well," he said, opening his eyes and a crude simper reformed on his face. He seemed to move slower but was still faster than I would have expected.

Again, he raised his sword above his head. Eyvindr had still yet to move me, he raised me a little off the ground so that Sir Jerum would not be able to see any footwork. Just as Sir Jerum's blade was about to strike my head, Eyvindr forced my body in a rush of wind around to Sir Jerum's back, but I was instantly met with the broadside of a sword. I felt the impact even through the barrier Eyvindr prepared for me. Combined with how fast I was already moving and the strong impact from Sir Jerum, I was flung to the ground beneath me about ten feet away.

"How did he even do that?" Eyvindr asked. "You should have been moving faster than he could see."

"You and your gous are both predictable." Sir Jerum said. "Both of you think the only way to beat me is to get behind me. I'm used to fighting surrounded. I'm not called Wolfsbane without reason. So, as you can see, that won't work."

"Then what will?" I turned over, once more lying on my back.

"You need to have complete control over what you do. Your gous can move you faster, sure, but it still doesn't know how to fight. You moved at what you thought was the last moment, but I had not committed my strength to the strike yet; I was still able to move the blade behind me to catch you. You keep making the same mistake of watching the blade instead of me." He walked over and reached out to me. "Let's try it again, just you this time, no gous, but I will give you a hint, do not watch the blade." I grabbed his hand and stood up once more.

"All right, then what?"

"Watch my eyes and my feet."

Sir Jerum backed away again and prepared a somewhat different ready stance. He wanted to give me some variation, but it was a move he had done before. The ready stance he held now was lower and he held his blade in front of him parallel to the ground like I had done before. He was going to go for a thrust or an upward slash.

"Ready?" he asked. He refused to smile this time.

"Ready!" I confirmed. I focused in on his eyes; he looked straight back into mine. I turned my attention to his feet. His left foot pointed toward me, and the right held him stable, perpendicular to his left. He charged forward and pulled his blade behind him to thrust, but something was off. Just before the thrust his footwork stopped short of where he would need to be for the tip to even tap the outermost layer of my armor. I waited longer, not even preparing myself to parry or dodge as I normally would.

That's when I saw it: his gaze shifted from my eyes to beneath my left arm, and on the final step before his thrust, he bent his knee, bringing him even closer to the ground. He then leapt into the air, spinning and having the blade follow a vertical path, ready to slam down into me. It was a quick and powerful move. I had to react fast now that he was in the air, but I waited a moment longer for the spin to complete until I dodged and thrust my sword to his neck as if threatening his life.

He had not given up, though. Sir Jerum's footwork shifted from his landing stance to the same one I used to attempt my upward slash. He dragged his blade up from the ground pulling from his lower left to his upper right. I dodged toward the slash's origin point, forcing him to commit to the slash. He refused to give me an opportunity as, the moment the motion was complete, his stance shifted to a level stance, spinning to keep his momentum flowing. Our blades met an instant later, causing a metallic ring to be heard for miles beyond the training yard.

"Finally," he said. "You forced me to block." He almost sounded tired. Sir Jerum stood up, dropped the training sword to his side and offered me his hand in congratulations. "Good job." I dropped my own blade and grasped his hand firmly. "We can end here for the day," he said, letting go of my hand. "Go get some rest. I'm sure there's someone who would like to see you." I followed his gaze toward the barracks behind me and saw Erione standing patiently, but certainly annoyed.

I started to walk toward her as Eyvindr began to heal my more basic injuries and general aches from dealing with the heavy weight behind Sir Jerum's blows.

"Lady Erione," I said.

"Sir Jerum must really be going easy on you for you to still be standing," she said.

"Of course, I was!" Sir Jerum interjected from across the field.

"In a real fight, you would still be dead in an instant," Lady Erione reminded me.

"Eyvindr?" I asked him.

"Nothing too serious, you have another fracture in your lower spine and that's the worst of it," Eyvindr replied.

"Probably from all the dirt I was eating."

"What?" Lady Erione asked, clearly confused with what I had just said.

"He says I have a fracture in my lower spine, and I'm sure there are other bruises he has not gotten around to fixing quite yet. Nothing too serious," I repeated.

"On the ground," she ordered, "on your stomach."

"Not again," I groaned. "I just got off the ground."

"Too bad," she claimed. She placed her hands around my lower back and began her healing spell once more, "*Icerepin aiman revisnuus ioaxuli.*"

"Thanks," I muttered.

"Excuse me?" she asked. "I couldn't hear you."

"Thank you, Lady Erione," I said, trying to keep my voice genuine only to have it come out as even ruder than before.

"You're welcome."

D

"YOU ARE BY FAR ONE of the easiest people I've ever had the displeasure of training," Ubel said.

"I'm honored," I joked. Deciding to take a short break, I set the longsword Ubel had given me for practice to the side. I made my way to a nearby rock, set my weight down and took a deep breath.

Ubel followed suit and sat on another nearby rock. He removed his helmet and set it between his feet on the dirt beneath him.

"Do you know why I want to train you myself?" He placed his usual sword beside him. It was hard to tell because it had a constant red glow, but it seemed to be made of some white metal that reflected little light, if any.

I pondered it for a moment and relatively sure of my answer replied, "So you can keep a close eye on me to be sure I don't run away."

He laughed. "Something like that. I want to be sure I can trust you on the battlefield: that you would be able to have my back – to stand in my place. Whether you like it or not, you will be one of the most valuable soldiers I will ever have." He moved his helmet to the side of the rock and slid down so he could lean against the rock. "The fact is, I'm less worried about myself." His head dropped, revealing the sweat around his neck. "I'm worried more about Bell."

"She seems like she's a great soldier. She's confident, that's for sure," I said, removing my own helmet he had given me and setting it at my feet.

"Aye," he said, lifting his head back up. "That's for sure." A smile appeared on his face for only a brief moment before his tiredness and concern took back over. "She's too confident. She leads some of my best soldiers, the ranks of which you will soon join, but she has no patience on the battlefield, and I think it is going to get her killed. She's so sure of her ability to best anyone in combat, but that leaves her vulnerable to pride."

"I think you can trust her," I said. "The Princess' confidence could be the very same thing that saves her." I reached behind me to remove the black chest plate, relieving the straining weight pulling me toward the ground. "If she is not sure of what she is doing, but commits to it anyway, that doubt will certainly lead to mistakes. On the other hand, if she is confident in her choice, even if it is a bad choice, it would be executed without doubt and fewer mistakes."

"Any doubt is bad," he agreed, "but if she makes that wrong choice, who knows what could happen."

"I think you can leave that to me." The sun directly above me warmed my skin as the breeze from the nearby mountains cooled and refreshed my entire body. I closed my eyes and slipped down the rock as Ubel had and relaxed against it.

"Thank you," he stated. We sat in silence as the clouds passed slowly overhead. The place he had brought me to train was just below the cliff behind his massive castle, constructed from the bones of a long-dead dragon, giving some sense to Ubel's helmet.

My mind wandered to Ubel's army as we sat near the bones.

"How do they work?" I asked. "The skeletons, how are they moving? Do you control each one of them?"

"They are moving on their own, autonomous with the magic imbued upon the bones. As long as the bones can collect themselves together, they will always come back, so I don't have many losses."

"Then why do they listen to you?"

"They understand, and many have witnessed, that while I give them their own wills, what I have given, I can take away just as fast. Death magic moves life, *Aiman*, from one thing to the next, and it does not take much life to animate some bones.

"I myself am an interesting case. I died long ago. Yet when life was moved back into me because it was done so quickly after my death, I maintained my ability to generate and use magic."

When Ubel finished speaking, the conversation fell silent.

After about an hour passed by, the sun had passed. Ubel rose from his seated position. "Are we going again?" I asked.

He put his helmet back on, "Yes. Now," he paused, "on your feet. Let's do this."

I stood up and picked up my chest plate and strapped it back on. The weight did not feel as intense after that break. I reached down for my helmet, and just as I was about to grab it, Ubel kicked it away, and while he did, he brought his blade over his head to come crashing down upon me.

"*Savu*," I swore instinctively in Acelin. My sword was still a good distance away, but I risked it anyway. I dove for the longsword, and the moment I grasped it and rolled through, I turned around and stood back up, ready to fight without a helmet. "That was a little rude."

"You think Haven's soldiers will play nice?" Ubel asked. "Come on, it isn't like you used that thing anyway. You need to be ready at any time for an attack," he smiled, "and good on you for not getting hit."

"I'll take what compliments I can get." We paced in a circle around the barren wasteland that was our training grounds, each waiting for the other to make a move. Ubel took a step into the ring and began to charge at me. It amazed me how he could wield such a massive sword without needing a second hand, especially considering he never used a shield. I decided not to let him have all the fun and stepped into the ring as well.

I charged at him, fully prepared to have my blade meet his, but he opted out of the regular clash that would have forced our blades to meet. Instead, he gripped his sword with his second hand and lowered his entire body to sweep at my feet. Luckily, I saw his shift early enough to jump over the sweep. I freed one of my hands from my longsword, pushed myself off of his head to vault over his low body and went for what would be a killing blow but stopped my blade just short of his neck.

"You can read me like a book."

"We have been training for a couple of days already. Is there anything you haven't shown me?"

"I may have a few tricks left up my sleeve," he smiled, waiting for me to ask for him to show them off.

"Well," I asked in anticipation, "let's see them."

He considered it for a moment and seemed quite happy, "I would very much like to not kill you."

"I would hate to die," I said, "but I would also like to see you try."

"I will show you one of them," Ubel confirmed. "Make sure you use everything you have."

"I'm sure I won't need it."

"I'm sure you will," he said. "Now back up, let's do this." I walked a good distance away and set myself into a defensive stance so I could block any direction he came at me. I saw his lips move underneath his helmet and his blade instantly started to grow brighter and brighter, the faint red glow that once surrounded his blade was now near blinding.

"That's all you have?" I asked mockingly. "A blade that glows a little brighter?" He made me eat those words. In the blink of an eye, the blade was at my neck, glowing brighter than before. "How did you even do that?"

"I used to hunt Arinthians for that king in Haven," he said. "This blade will be an heirloom in my family for generations, it responds to magic produced and uses it to enhance the wielder. I figured I would show you this one as this blade is not unique in its ability. I want you to be ready for this," he withdrew the blade from my neck.

"So, you can use magic then?" I asked. "You're Arinthian?"

"My grandfather," he held the sword parallel to the ground in front of him, examining it carefully, "was a twisted man. He took some of the Arinthians he was meant to kill and kept them as slaves and concubines. My father was also one of his soldiers. My mother was a child of one of the slaves. So as a result, I am one-quarter Arinthian. More Arinthian than most these days, that's for sure."

"How were you given that sword then?"

"I claimed it, and another, for Haven from the forges in Aranor," a look of regret washed over his face. "And when I agreed to hunt Arinthians for the rest of my life this blade, Mil, was mine," he gritted his teeth. "I'm glad I stopped."

"As am I."

"The fact is I still hunted throughout all of my younger years, and for far too long," he said finally letting the blade rest at his side once more. He seemed more defeated now than ever. "Let's try again," he said as the glow returned to its normal state. "Now that you know what's coming, hopefully, you will be ready for it. I want you to use a spell before you start vomiting flames like you did yesterday."

"Fine," I said. "But how do I beat that? Would my spell not enhance you even more?"

"It would," he turned to face me after walking a fair distance away, "but not as much as you can enhance yourself. The only reason this blade was able to do its job is because it only had to work once. Some Arinthian would cast some magic in the sword's direction, it would absorb it and enhance it to the point where no Arinthian in the area would be able to survive the enhanced user. I've never had anyone escape that I didn't want to, you are the first Arinthian to witness and survive the deadliness of this blade. If I wanted an Arinthian to live, I would not use this blade. As for how to beat it, I'm still trying to figure that out myself."

"So, your intention is to almost kill me until I get it?"

"That's about right," he confirmed. "Just remember to try something, realistically anything." He quieted down and his lips began to mutter the same spell as before.

I had to think, what could I do to beat something moving faster than the eye? Time slowing spells did not exist, or at least my gous had not known about them. He said that the blade enhanced him, but it seemed like it only gained a fraction of the magic used.

Screw it, I thought to myself. *Time to burn again.*

I took a deep breath and began to chant as I had before, "*Icerepin ricopros revisnuus ingnis icounten.*" Once more I felt the sting of the flames burning around my entire body and before I had a moment to think, Ubel's blade was once again at my neck and the brightest it has ever been.

"Not that kind of enhancement!" he shouted. "Stop being stupid! Do you really think none of them tried that before? It increases how hard you can hit and get hit, but that does not matter! This blade will absorb that and cut right through you."

"*Iveeno*," I ordered the flames. "Then what?"

"Again!" he ordered. "We'll keep doing this until we get it, or we collapse."

DAY 8

HER LIFE WAS FOR THE KING. That was all it ever was for her. She was born to be a healer and nothing more. Her life had been spent mastering a few words passed down over generations so that she could one day pass them on to another while she lived to serve and heal the king. While she remembered little before she was whisked away to the castle to begin her training, she had been born poor, and had a deeply generous heart for those who reminded her of her own family.

She clung to a few happy memories of her former family that only made the recently developed threats of disobedience all the more substantial. Her kind heart could move others, and though she was born for the king, she hoped to serve others. Erione, servant of the Kingdom of Haven, was now obliged to a new master underneath the king, hoping she would find kindness in him as there once was within the king.

E

In the late afternoon, once he had finished his training with Jerum, I approached Sir Horus. Once again, I accelerated the healing of his injuries and walked with him for some time.

"Thank you again, Lady Erione," he said.

"My pleasure," I replied, not intending the hint of sarcasm in my voice.

We arrived at the road in front of the castle that connected the main city and the castle. The castle itself sat upon a hill and the city encompassed the area to the south. Haven was surrounded by walls that climbed up the hill and around the castle, forming a strong defense. The castle's torches were beginning to be lit in preparation for night. Though the sun was still high enough in the sky, storm clouds had mocked the joy of light. Darkness loomed over the city though everyone knew it would soon pass once the rain came crashing down.

I started to walk toward the city in spite of the coming storm when I heard him call out to me and ask, "Are you not coming inside?"

"I'm not worried about it," I said. "I just have a quick errand to run down there, and I think I will be back before it really starts to come down."

"I'll come with you," he insisted.

"There's really no need, you worked hard today, get some rest. I can handle it," I brushed him off and waited for him to turn around. I had hardly any time away from the service of the king and his guard and wanted some time with the people. He stayed where he was. Was he really not going to let me go on my own? I sighed and started walking. He started following me.

"What exactly are you going to do down there?" he asked.

"Well, it is *we* now, isn't it?"

"Yes."

Sir Horus was a lot of work and still couldn't block many hits from Jerum, forcing me to work harder than I had when I was directly under the king. He was kinder, but I was still wary of his choice to free me from the king's service.

"Well then, *we* are simply heading to the city to check on the people. You've been living a life of luxury up in the castle, but others suffer more on a daily basis than you do in a week of wounds."

"And you- I'm sorry, we- are going to heal them? Even with this storm coming?"

"It is precisely because of the storm that I'm going," I said. "I want to make sure they are ready for it as best as I can. I heal who I can and comfort the rest." Then I stopped, turned to him, and gave him a puzzling look. He couldn't even heal himself properly without me. "And no, only I am healing, you are just coming along."

We arrived in the slums of Haven. No longer were there paved roads or lanterns to be lit. I worked quickly, healing minor cuts and wounds and ensuring everyone was under some form of shelter. The people here did not have much, but every ounce of help I supplied, every day I healed a wound, every day I cured some kind of sickness in them, likely meant many more months of life.

The shelters were varied; some had homes of stone and others simple shacks of wood, the least fortunate were forced to share small tents made up of four tall poles and a piece of fabric. Many already felt the cold bite before the storm's fall and were rightfully concerned about being dry. The people with more grounded homes had opened their doors to allow as many people as may fit in, but plenty more were still left outside in the tents.

The first drop of rain sank into my robe. Then the rain got harder and more frequent. The storm was upon us whether we liked it or not. A distant flash of lightning was met with the crack of thunder a few moments later. Sir Horus and I were still in the middle of the street. I pulled my hood up to protect myself as best I could from the rain, but it was of little aid, and I was quickly drenched. He rushed over to me and did his best to cover me underneath his cape as well, but it was not doing much either.

"Eyvindr!" he shouted over the crashing rain. "Any suggestions?" He would sometimes do that, but I learned that Eyvindr was the name of his gous, so sometimes it would seem he just talked to himself.

I noticed him looking around intently. He pointed to a corner and guided me to it while I continued to hide underneath his cape. "Now what?" he asked.

"I don't know! Why don't you tell me?" I responded.

But it seems he wasn't speaking to me.

An upward wind answered his question, ripping the cape from his grasp and bringing the rain with it as a shield of wind protected our heads from the hard rain. Though the wind was loud at first, it ultimately quieted, and we could actually hear each other breathing. The previously harsh storm now seemed like a calm rain with the occasional crash of thunder.

"What would you have done without me?" he said, half-joking.

But I realized if he was not talking to me earlier, he must have been talking to his gous. So I corrected him, "What would I have done without *Eyvindr?*"

"Fair enough."

"Thank you for coming with me today," I said while trying to stay out of the rain. Consequently, getting out of the rain meant getting close to him and I found myself feeling as though I was blushing. "It was nice to have an extra set of hands."

"They seem to really like you here."

"I'm here every week, sometimes more if there's a storm. They really do need help organizing and setting up for a storm, not to mention the guards around here can get a little rough with the people."

"You're a good person, Erione," he said. I think it was the first time he had not included any formality with my name.

"Thank you," I replied.

After a couple of minutes standing in the storm, I began to squirm and strained myself to stand. As strange as it was, I felt it better to rest on his armor even more, it wasn't warm, but it was at least warmer than the air.

"Give me a moment," he said. He walked around me and put me directly in the corner. I looked away, his very size daunting me while he wore his armor. I heard him undo the chain on his cape, but then, much to my surprise, he set it on the ground, tapped me on the shoulder and motioned for me to sit. I graciously accepted the seat, and he helped me sit down, holding my hand while I used my other to brace myself and manage my robe.

"Thank you," I said again. He continued to stand, giving plenty of room, but it felt wrong. It seemed strange to me that he would be so kind, considering how little he knew of me. I patted a spot on the cape, inviting him to sit. "Horus, it's awkward if you keep standing, or do you need Eyvindr to explain that too?"

"Very funny," he replied dryly, feigning a frown. He set himself down next to me along one of the walls. With how much armor he had on, he may as well have been a third wall.

I then had a thought. He seemed sturdy enough and had no issues with how close we were earlier. I needed to rest, so I set my head on his shoulder and he stiffened up a little bit.

"That's better," I said. I closed my eyes to rest them, but now his shoulder felt much less comfortable. I kept trying to find a new spot with my eyes closed, but it proved impossible. "But you do make a terrible pillow," I groaned in defeat before lifting my head up again.

"What is it like?" he asked out of nowhere.

"Your shoulder? Metallic and hard." I answered. He laughed lightly. "What is what like?" I asked back.

"Serving the king, or rather, what was it like?"

"I still do serve him; it is just my focus is no longer as his primary healer. It was fine enough while I was younger, before strange men waking up in Haven for the first time tried to free me from my bonds by entering the service themselves as well. The king is a good man, everyone knew that... or at least they used to. He's lost a lot over the recent years, and he's changed just as much. His methods have changed, but he's always had the same goal of serving the people. It was just a matter of how good of a job he's been doing.

"Life was comfortable here in Haven, especially in the castle and for a Life Arinthian like myself, I enjoyed that luxury for very little cost to myself. I would accompany him to the few battles that would take place, skirmishes really, beyond Aranor in the wastelands. However, now we are in a full war, it seems, and he won't risk stepping foot outside of the castle, so life got boring. Then you came around."

"I made your life interesting?" He tried to make it sound as if I was completely thankful.

"I would not go that far," I said with a smirk to tease, "just not boring anymore."

"Oh, I see."

The rain did not stop until well after nightfall, and the two of us had completely lost track of time. Once it had stopped, he stood up and groaned about how he had forgotten what it was like to stand. Sir Horus helped me stand up, then bent down and picked up his cape, resting it over his shoulder. "Hopefully, the king does not mind the dirt."

"You might just get a new one, it's not like you are supposed to wear it into battle. There are plenty for ceremonial purposes."

"And if not?"

"Then I guess you'll be cleaning it," I suggested with a shrug. "It'll help you with your training somehow. I'm sure Sir Jerum could find a way to make it count. Or even Sir Petrus." I paused before mocking Sir Petrus Ramsguard's voice in a rather pitiful attempt, "'Scrub harder and put your back into it! This will build your strength! A knight is not just a warrior but a noble representative of the kingdom!'" I laughed at my own failure of an imitation.

He laughed as well then gave an attempt of his own, "'If you can't maintain something as simple as a clean cape, what makes you think you can maintain yourself on the battlefield.'"

"Eh, not as good."

"I'd be interested in what Sir Jerum thinks of what I said."

"You won't tell him because then he'll tell Sir Petrus, and then we'll both be a load of trouble. Sir Petrus does not take too kindly to mockery." But I did not tell him I mocked Sir Petrus every chance I got. It was always more fun.

"Noted."

We finally started walking back toward the castle, following what few torches were still lit. The large, metal oil torches that burned at every outpost and over archways struggled to illuminate the area. Though the storm had subsided, the clouds still blocked the moon and stars. He held me underneath his left arm, and I gave him directions through the slums back to the castle. Even after the castle was in view, I did not separate from underneath his arm. It felt nice.

We walked underneath the cloister until we came to the hall where my room was, and I pulled myself out from underneath his arm.

"Sleep well, Lady Erione," he said, reintroducing the formality and, with it, the reminder of our relationship merely as servants of the king. I did not know why, but part of me hoped it would not stay that way.

"And you as well, Sir Horus," I said with the faintest of smiles.

I never wanted to ask him to join me again, and it seemed I would not have to. "Anytime you want to go down there, I will go with you," he said. "Regardless of your invitation."

I thought that could get a little annoying but found it slightly charming as well. "As you wish," I said. "Good night." I shut the door and felt my heart at war.

DAY 10

H

AFTER AN EARLY MORNING OF TRAINING, and a quick demonstration of that training, the king had asked to meet with me and Sir Jerum briefly to discuss where I was to go now. It was rather swiftly established that I would be leading the charge to Aranor, and Sir Jerum would be with me as a second in command but more as a supervisor. He had overseen my training and was the one who deemed me ready to be a leader. If anything, it was almost a test for Sir Jerum. I sensed a little bit of hostility from the king when he assigned Sir Jerum to train me and later when he said he was to come with me. Once the king was done speaking with me, however, he dismissed me for the day.

"You leave tomorrow morning at dawn, I expect great things from you, Arinthian."

"Yes, my lord," I agreed. "I won't let you down."

"Sir Jerum... Wolfsbane..." the king started, menace manifesting in his voice, "make sure he follows his orders."

"Of course, my lord," Sir Jerum said, cringing slightly. The two of us bowed to the king and waited patiently for him to leave our presence before we stood up straight again.

I walked over to pick up my greatsword, ready to resume training when Sir Jerum placed a hand on my shoulder. "We aren't going to resume training?" I asked, confused.

Sir Jerum laughed, as if I was the one who was insane for asking such a question, "No!" he wiped a tear from his eye. "Of course, we aren't! It's your last day here before we have to go on an expedition! It would be a disgrace to not go to The Dragon's Fire!"

"Why? I could use a little bit more work on my bladework."

"You can hold your own with me now... I'll still beat you," he interjected the latter statement with a hint of doubt in his voice and even more on his face. "But that means you'll be able to handle anything that Ubel would throw at you. Trust me, I've been there. Not like we'll be able to break the gates anyway, but that's for later."

"Fair enough, I guess. Shall we get going?"

"Not quite yet," Sir Jerum said, moving away from me and back toward the main castle. "I'm going to get Petrus and Erione. It's kind of a tradition."

I waited patiently near the archways of the training area for Sir Jerum to return with the others. Soon enough, he returned, and we made our way down the hill toward the main city of Haven. The ground along the path was littered with flowers. As we approached the main street, flowers were found in organized ceramic beds helping to beatify the otherwise monotonous, gray cobble of Haven. Sir Jerum then led the way through the various avenues to reach a tavern with a pair of guards posted out front. He greeted them with a grand smile, and each of us followed him inside.

"Welcome," Sir Jerum said, "to the happiest place in Haven!" He spread his arms out wide, gesturing to everything he could. The din of an indoor archery hall, bar conversations, the multitude of ongoing drinking games being played, and stories being told by the hearth flooded my ears. A small band of bards played light music that could barely make itself heard over all the other noise.

"It actually seems quite dull," Eyvindr said. That was partially right, the people inside seemed happy and loud enough, but the environment was definitely boring. There were no grand windows or paintings; it was really just an over-glorified wooden shack at best.

"Home at last," Sir Petrus said with a smile on his face, something that was not even there when he greeted the guards posted out front.

"Well, well, well," Lady Erione taunted, "who's this excited fellow?"

"You don't have to make fun of me for it every time we come here."

"Then don't make it so easy," she said with a laugh. "You need to lighten up before we get here, then we can talk about you not being made fun of."

"Neither of you are even going, so you two are here on my good graces," Sir Jerum said.

"Who said I wasn't going?" Lady Erione asked.

"I can't have you come with us, Erione," I said before catching myself. "I'm sorry, Lady Erione." She did not even seem the slightest bit disturbed by my mistake, but I suspect it was because she did not really care. "It is just too dangerous."

"What is the point of me being a combat healer if I don't even go near the combat?" she asked.

"She'll be able to handle herself," Sir Petrus said as he guided all of us to a table, finally taking some role of leadership over the rest of us. "I know I am staying behind for the first time in what feels like years. It will be nice to have a break. Though, really it will just be boring guard duty while I'm here."

"I'm sure the king will be able to keep you entertained," Sir Jerum said. "He does like you the most." His voice was clearly mocking him, almost accusing him of being a pet.

"Maybe that's because I've never failed to follow orders," Sir Petrus retorted, meaning no harm. But Sir Jerum's face grew dark and remorseful, remembering something painful. "Jerum, I'm sorry, I didn't mean..."

Our table fell into an isolated silence.

"Don't worry about it," Sir Jerum said after he snapped himself out of his trance. "We're here to have a good time, not to remember the past, or anticipate the boring future!" His mood seemed to change almost instantly. But it was good to see Sir Jerum in a happier mood, his joy always spread to be my own.

"So, what exactly do we do here?" I asked.

"This really may be a historic moment," Sir Jerum said happily, looking to Sir Petrus.

"It really could be, it is a first for sure," Sir Petrus continued with a smile. Then he and Sir Jerum both looked to Lady Erione.

Lady Erione caught both their glances and sighed, "They both know I can out-drink them. Ever since I started working for the king, when they first invited me here, almost as a joke, they wanted to see if they could out-drink each other, and I wanted in. They laughed me off at first!"

"And that was a mistake," Sir Petrus interjected.

"That it was," Lady Erione continued. "So anyway, the two of them start drinking and I join in knowing the rules, loser, or rather losers, buy the winner's drinks, and needless to say I beat them both."

"Combined," Sir Jerum said, going wide-eyed.

"No way either of us could really accept it, turns out she cheated too!" Sir Petrus said.

"By being born?" Lady Erione said, faking offense. She sighed again, "Arinthians can just drink more. I don't know what it is. Probably has something to do with our blood liking to heal and clean itself, but who really knows?"

"We do!" Sir Jerum said. "You are living proof of whatever it is that makes it work!"

"Anyway," Sir Petrus said, "we were curious if it was just because she is a Life Arinthian that her blood has that effect or if it was Arinthian blood in general. Also, it could be quite impressive to see a full blood Arinthian get drunk..." his pause was emphasized by an epiphanic expression on his face. "If that is even possible." He gave me a seriously inquisitive look that startled me, begging for an answer.

I put my hands up and shrugged, "I have no idea, never had a drink."

"Well, we are about to change that aren't we?" Lady Erione said.

Sir Jerum called out, "Barkeep!" then held up four fingers. The barkeep chuckled for a moment then nodded. He brought over four pints of ale and set them on the table. "You know the drill, right?"

"New competitor I see. Yeah, I'll keep 'em coming, and I'll keep the tab going," the barkeep said with a wink.

Sir Petrus counted down, and the drinking game began. I hated the taste of the ale, but it was fine enough as long as I did not drink it alone. The taste alone was almost reason enough for me to stop, but I had to keep going. Sir Petrus was the first to stop drinking, citing that if he had even one more sip, he would lose his liquor. Sir Jerum, unfortunately, encouraged him to go for that last sip, saying it was too early to give up. However, the moment the mug hit Sir Petrus' lips, he belched and fell onto the table in defeat, groaning miserably after about ten drinks. Sir Jerum was next to fall to the alcohol. He gave up about four drinks after Sir Petrus. Lady Erione kept her same pace as last time, drinking another fifteen after Sir Jerum Wolfsbane belched his way to defeat.

Even though the others were down and out, they wanted to see just how long I could go. I reluctantly agreed, not wanting to drink any more than I really had to. Their drunken insistence was admittedly adorable as they slurred their words, trying to convince me. Once they had, the endless chanting of "Go!" was ironically slower. I was able to keep drinking, but we never quite found my limit before the barkeep cut me off because he said he worried I would drain his barrels of ale.

"In truth, I'm stoppin' ya' not 'cause I'm out but because the tab's gettin' to be a little high and you've already proved your point," the barkeep whispered in my ear after my eightieth drink.

"Fair enough," I whispered back. Then I pat Sir Petrus on the arm that still loosely held a mug. "All right, you heard the man. I'm done. You need to settle the tab now. I won."

"Definitely in the blood," Sir Petrus said.

"Cheating, stupid, train... ee..." Sir Jerum slurred himself into a drunken nap.

Even though Lady Erione was drunk, she was more lucid than the others. She still slightly slurred her words, "They are such terrible losers, aren't they?"

"Absolutely, is this how it went last time?"

"Almost exactly the same, just this time their remarks are directed at you instead of me," she laughed. "Come on, get up you," she said in an attempt to shake Sir Jerum awake.

"I'm going to have to settle the tab, aren't I?" I asked.

"No, no, no..." the groggy Sir Jerum said, "we got it, it's no big... deal..." Then he fell asleep again.

"Looks like I am." I walked over to the bar and placed down a sack of coins. "I hope that's enough."

The barkeep looked at me strangely, "You don't get it do ya? Sir Petrus is paying whether he likes it or not. I know the rules too. I'll deal with him later." I picked up the sack of coins and returned to the table.

Lady Erione was staring at me on the way back with an interesting look in her eyes.

"Dance," she begged with both of her arms held up. The band of bards was now playing a jauntier tune, so I lifted her up out of her seat and we walked to an open area where many were up and dancing drunkenly. She was definitely unbalanced as we walked, but soon enough we were dancing until she was tired, which did not take long at all. She seemed ready to fall asleep as she leaned on me the whole way back to the table.

"How are we going to get them back?" I asked.

"Well, you could get some of the other guards to help you," Eyvindr suggested.

"Wait for us to sober up!" Sir Petrus suggested.

It took long enough, but later in the night, they were sober enough to walk on their own. I led them back to the castle, herding them like cats and picking them up once they'd fallen down. I led Lady Erione back to her room after I almost had to shove the others into their quarters.

"Thank you, *Sir* Horus," Lady Erione said, purposefully slurring her words and smiling softly at me. "I hope you had fun."

"Believe me," I smiled back, "I did. You are all so very entertaining when drunk."

"Good to know," she said as she slipped into her room, smiling.

D

"ICEREPIN," I began, *"ricopros revisnuus itomum ingnis icounten."* My breath left my lungs the moment the blade came slicing through me. I only had one second to get it right; the sword Ubel was using got brighter than it ever had before. He was faster, but no matter the strength of the wielder, he was left wide open as he cut through what would have normally been my body. This time I put my own blade to his neck as he finished his swing and said, *"Iveeno."* I had my body back.

"That was new," Ubel said, staring at the steel that teased his neck with its razor-sharp edge.

"I'm just glad I timed it right," I said, dropping the blade back to my side. I was breathing heavily trying to restore air to my lungs after the near suicide I just attempted.

"What exactly was that? I felt significantly stronger passing through you than I ever did stopping at your neck."

"I believe," I said panting, "I temporarily made myself a gous." I felt so weak, so ready to drop to the ground, but I persevered and stuck the sword into the ground beneath me to lean on it.

"You brought yours back? A gous has never been able to defend against the blade."

"Far from it, I became a gous," I clarified, slowly regaining my strength. "I manifested my entire body to become fire, so that you would have nothing to cut through but magic." I decided it would be best to take a seat, sitting on the same rock as I had before. "I thought of it last night. I tested it on my forearm, and it seemed to work just fine. But that," I paused for a moment to recognize my own stupidity, "was the first time I tried it on my whole body."

"What did it feel like?" he asked me.

"I think I understand why no Arinthians ever tried it. I felt... dead," I answered. "I don't really know how else to describe it. When it was just my forearm, it just felt like for a moment my arm had disappeared and was weightless. When it came back it felt like I had been sitting on it for far too long. But when I did it to my whole body, I felt, well, dead. I had no lungs, no heart, no brain, nothing was left as my own. I felt my consciousness fade and with the last second, I stopped the spell before I think I would have been gone forever. So, I think I became a gous without a body to attach to. I don't know if I can ever do that again."

"You'll have to be able to, because that's the first time anyone has come close to beating me, much less actually doing so," he said, making his way over to his own rock to rest on.

The sun was only just now breaking over the cliffs above us, it was barely morning and my stomach groaned with hunger.

"You did eat?" he asked.

"I had a large breakfast, but now I feel like I could eat it all again," I said. "There has to be another way to beat you because if I'm destroying all of the food in my stomach and exhausting myself within one second, I would not be able to last a fight."

"That's true but if that one second wins you the fight, you wouldn't need to keep fighting," Ubel said while removing his draconian helmet.

"In a one on one, true, in a battle with another person like you, perhaps even stronger, but with the same weapon, who knows if I'd be able to last." I loosened what little armor I had left that remained unscorched. "It also does not seem practical for armor, heavy armor limits me too much and lightweight stuff just seems to get burned."

"Lyssandra might be able to manage something for that, a lightweight magic-based armor. We'd need some hide of some kind of Arinthian creature, but I'm not sure what."

"I think I'll just have to keep working through more solutions."

Ubel pondered with me for a moment before he asked another question.

"You said you tested this with just your forearm, right? Have you thought about just applying the spell to the area that would be damaged?"

"I don't think I can cast that fast."

"Do you have to cast aloud?"

"To my knowledge, it has to at least be a whisper," I said. Ubel smiled as if he knew something critical.

"Try just making a fireball without saying a word."

I tried for a moment, thinking as hard as I could with my hand held out, concentrating without making a sound. I thought to myself, *Icerepin ingnis icounten*. Nothing seemed to happen. I made sure for myself and said it aloud and the fireball instantly appeared in my hand. *Iveeno*, I thought, and the fireball stopped.

"Do you understand it yet?" Ubel asked. "If memory serves from when my mother would cast, there's only one thing you have to say aloud."

I finally understood what he was getting at. I tried again to start the spell, "*Icerepin*," I said aloud, then thought to myself, *ingnis icounten*. Instantly the fireball reappeared in my hand and now I was smiling as well, proud of the discovery we made. *Iveeno*, I thought to stop the fireball once more.

"*Icerepin*," Ubel reminisced, looking back through his memories, and gazing up at the sky. "It was the only word my mother would let me hear. My mother was only half-Arinthian, but she had learned from her mother how to use spells because there was enough Arinthian blood to allow her to do so. Not much, certainly nothing on your level, but small stuff like killing rodents or forcing a tree to die to make it easier to chop for firewood. She never used her power beyond that, though I am sure she could do so much more. It was the only Arinthian word she ever said aloud. I have to say them aloud because my Arinthian blood is too weak," he explained. Then he lowered his head and stared at me and said, "Now try to change your forearm to flame, then your leg without saying anything but that word."

"*Icerepin*," I began. *Ricopros rabicmach itomum ingnis icounten*, and my arm became flame. It still obeyed my will, but it felt gone. I was tempted to say the final word and stop the spell, but I persevered. I stood up and examined my hand as I pushed through my mind the next part of the spell as the words came to my mind, *itumo ricopros rucs*, my arm was restored to flesh and my legs left the world and were replaced by flame. I did it! My smile grew even wider with excitement at this discovery. Ubel and I laughed briefly in shock and joy.

"Yes!" he shouted. "We can practice with that! We can make you faster in mind and in body and you will be unkillable."

Iveeno, I thought to myself to end the spell and my leg was restored to normal. "But for now, may I go eat again?" I pleaded.

"Let's. Even I'm getting hungry again." We grabbed our armor from beside us and walked back through a nearby tunnel to the depths of Ubel's castle. After stopping by the armory to return what I had borrowed for the day, despite not having a face, the skeleton working the armory seemed displeased with the scorch marks on some of the best lightweight armor they had to offer.

Ubel and I entered the throne room where skeletal servants were waiting for orders, Ubel commanded them to fetch Princess Lyssandra and Princess Bellona for another meal. He required their presence, not for them to eat.

By the time all of the royalty had arrived, a banquet was set in the throne room and chairs placed beneath a gorgeous table in the long hall. Princess Bellona was the last to arrive, but she looked like she was in a hurry.

"Relax, my daughter, it's only a meal, please sit," Ubel said. Princess Lyssandra did not need that request and was already sitting while she waited for her sister.

"You're having a meal now?" Princess Bellona asked.

"Didn't the guards tell you?" Ubel replied.

"I came here of my own volition," she said. Her eyes were fierce and ready to fight, with murderous intent she said one word, "Scouts."

"What about them?" I asked.

"A party of scouts was spotted along the Aranorian border," she replied, excited for what she was going to say next. "They're coming for another battle."

"A little sooner than expected, but I'm sure you'll be able to handle it, Bell. Now, could you please take a seat."

She was disappointed and made it well known as she sighed, "Fine."

I started to eat to my heart's content as I had done before for breakfast, but I was the only one eating, so I stopped. Ubel was staring at me.

"In one week," Ubel started, "you will join my daughter Bell on the frontlines of Aranor. But before that happens, Lyss, I need you to make something for me, or rather for our friend here. I need you to make Arinthian hide armor for him."

Princess Lyssandra seemed shocked, she turned to me and asked, "Are you okay with this?"

"Why wouldn't I be?"

"Because I'll need your blood," she said, "and a lot of it."

I turned to Ubel, and he nodded.

"I don't think I have a choice," I said.

Princess Bellona was startled for a different reason, "Why so soon? The last recruits you trained for six months, and they all died within the first battle while not even fighting on the frontlines. You train him for six days and you think he's ready?" she asked. "Have you gone mad?"

"No, my dear, he is ready," Ubel said smiling. "In fact, just before this meal, he bested me in a match. So, I hope you'll trust me on this. Oh, and I should mention," he drank from a goblet in front of him, "I was using Mil."

"Impossible," Princess Bellona said.

DAY 12

H

IT WAS QUIET, of course, with the exception of the clamor of metal on the hard ground. A scout familiar with the forest guided Lady Erione, Sir Jerum, my new troops, and me through the dense forest. Any form of life scattered at the sound of footsteps and broke the peace of this forest.

"How much more?" I asked the scout.

The scout paused for a moment and looked intently at some of the nearby trees. He told me earlier they were marked with white and red paints to give a relative idea of a trail to follow but were often hidden high up or in awkward locations to prevent the trail from being followed by soldiers of Ubel's army.

"We are still quite a way away from where we will camp for the night, milord. Would you like to take a break?"

I looked back into the single troop of soldiers the king had granted me for the mission. The ones in the front were exhausted from carrying their armor and weaponry, it was written all over their faces. They were ready to die but forced to march on in the king's name.

"We'll keep going," Sir Jerum commanded. Then he looked to me, almost disappointed. "We don't have any time to waste, the king is impatient and expects results soon." Sir Jerum resumed marching forward and pushed the scout a little bit to prompt him to move again. I looked through the leaves of the trees and saw it was roughly mid-day and turned to Lady Erione.

"It is not worth arguing with Sir Jerum," she said. "You know that." She was the only one allowed a horse for the journey. King's orders.

"It just seems unnecessary for them to all press on like this. It is about time for a meal anyway," I said.

"They had one already. Besides, we only packed enough food for light meals twice a day, we do not have the rations if they want to eat now," Sir Jerum shouted back. He was almost out of sight, veiled by the trees.

"You're sure we can't take a break? Not even for a moment?" I shouted to him, but he refused to listen. I hesitated for a moment, fixed my posture, and turned back to the troops that drew closer and shouted as loud as I could,

"Men! Take a short break and we will move again in a few minutes. Drink something and sit down!"

I heard a large sigh of relief come from the two-hundred-some soldiers as word of a break spread to the archers in the back, but I also heard a greater sigh of annoyance come from Sir Jerum. He walked back to talk to me, "It isn't worth it," he said. "They'll be able to rest plenty before the battle itself."

"That would leave us vulnerable to a surprise attack, and if Ubel's army is as ruthless as you say they are, they will find us and they will take advantage of our rest."

Sir Jerum was upset with my decision. "I promise you," he said, "it won't make a difference." He looked to make sure the scout was not listening to him then whispered, "Truth be told, this is a suicide mission. Most of these men will die, you and I will be lucky if we even survive. Most of these soldiers are just former criminals, their lives don't matter to the king."

"Then we will aim for a draw, but seize victory if we can," I assured him. "Regardless, I am leading these men, I will decide how we move. So, you will listen to me."

"Very well," he said, holding back the anger in his teeth, "as you command."

"If you'd be willing," I told him, "I would like to strategize with you and Erione for what we do when we actually get there. I know nothing about Aranor, and I think we should plan now rather than later."

"I'll get the scout," Erione said. She moved her brilliant white horse a few yards to where the scout was and invited him back to our conversation. When she returned with the scout, Sir Jerum gave her a weird look for not simply calling him over.

"What is your name?" I asked him.

"Abaven, milord" the scout replied. "It was the only name ever given to me."

"Now, Abaven," I said, pulling out some parchment, ink, and a quill from the royal blue pouch lined in golden fabric on the saddle of Erione's horse, "I want a map of our side of Aranor leading to the city. I need as many accurate details as you can give me, every ditch, every hill, and every tree. All of it."

"Right away," Abaven said. He took the parchment from my hands but left the ink and quill alone. He placed his hand above the parchment then he began, *"Icerepin nauga ramoiem icorbs."* The thick parchment was marked with water and created an incredibly detailed map in an instant. Towards the left side of the map was what I assumed to be Aranor, and around it was a vast empty chasm with a thin land bridge that would grant us access to the city. One way in and one way out.

"Amazing," I said, dumbfounded. "Thank you."

"Basic water magic, it is the only thing I know how to do, milord," Abaven said. He pointed to the edges of the map. "This entire section is long enough to have just one line with all of our soldiers, but the bridge can only fit about two-wide at a time. Advancing into the city will be a challenge on its own."

"Sir Jerum," I said, "How many archers do we have?"

"About fifty or so, but their arrows won't be able to reach the walls. Not from the edge of the chasm at least."

"I won't need them to," I said, smiling. "How many do we have with tall shields, or really any shields?"

"Including some of the archers, we have about one hundred shields, most of our men are using two-handed swords."

"We are going to need about twenty soldiers with shields and we will form a two-wide formation with shields above and to the side. I will stand in front and defend the front of the formation." I trusted Eyvindr to protect me from any potential hits and knew my armor was dense enough for arrows to reflect right off of it. My armor was also bright enough to blind anything that dared to look at it on a sunny day. "I'll only need about four archers to follow the formation closely behind and take cover with the others as they nock their arrows."

"How do you intend to take down that city with only twenty-five men?" Abaven asked, and I started to reply but Sir Jerum spoke for me.

"He doesn't," Sir Jerum said, smiling now as well. "He will use this first group to take out the ranged defenses on the wall and allow the rest of us to charge in without too much of an issue."

"That's the plan," I confirmed.

"What if more of them meet you at the gate?"

"That's what our archers are for," Sir Jerum explained. "While we march forward the archers whittle down their numbers on the wall and at the gate, and if they meet us at the bridge, we can supply volley fire from the mainland while our own men remain protected by all the shields."

"Of course, this means a few men will have to give up their shields as they charge in, but we will make our way into the city and seize control of the gate in no time," I clarified.

"However," Sir Jerum doubted, "most of these men are untrained, how do you expect to pull off this kind of formation anyway?"

"I will practice with some of them before we are fully done with the march," I said. "I suggest that you go through the troops and see which of them would be best suited for this kind of job. The thinner they are the better because it means our archers are more likely to fit between them, even if it is just for a moment."

Sir Jerum begrudgingly obeyed and began his search as the water-made map began to fade. It was starting to get surprisingly warm, even with the shade of the trees. "Let's get moving," I told Abaven. "Sir Jerum can conduct his search while we march."

"Yes, milord," Abaven said as he made his way forward once more.

I shouted back to the rest of the troop, "Break is over, we are moving again, grab your stuff and let's go!"

The men seemed much more refreshed now and ready to fight. Luckily, they would not need to for a while.

"Where did you come up with that idea?" Lady Erione asked me. "Because I will still be surprised if it even works, especially with you so open in the front of the formation."

"Is that an insult?" I asked, but she was smiling, so I knew it was a joke. She had seen me fight and knows that I can hold my own. Eyvindr could always protect me from any mishaps.

"Yes," she said with a straight face this time. She rode forward to ride next to Abaven and spoke with him for the remainder of this day's journey.

After about two or so hours of marching, Sir Jerum returned to the front and told me, "I have found some men that I think will be suitable."

"Oh?"

"They have shields on the larger end, short swords, and the archers I've chosen were former outlaws known for their aim," he said. "But Horus, I believe it would be best if you did not lead the charge. It would be bad if the troop lost their commanding officer."

"If I don't lead them, Sir Jerum," I said, "who will? I will lead by example, not by cowering in a tent from a safe distance. If I'm gone you will take control of the troop."

"Understood," he said.

It was the middle of the afternoon, and we still had another day to go before we would reach the outskirts of Aranor. "As for the men you found, have them meet me up front tomorrow morning for breakfast, I'd like to meet them all." Sir Jerum left me once more to go gather the chosen few for battle.

"This plan is still suicide," Eyvindr said. "I do not think it will be possible to coordinate outlaws to be a cohesive group in a matter of days. A month is a maybe, but there is no way you will be able to do this. You'd be better off just going in yourself. I could protect you and move you to dodge everything."

You and I both know nothing about who or what resides in there, I thought to him. *If there is even one skilled soldier over there I could get easily overwhelmed, and I'll trust anybody if it means they will be fighting alongside me.*

"I just hope he's not there," Eyvindr said.

Who?

"The other one."

D

AFTER A RATHER UNEVENTFUL MEAL the other day, Ubel and I resumed training. He had me practice shifting the locations over and over again to the point where I did not even have to think about it. It would still be my last resort as it drained immense amounts of energy, but becoming flame was now second nature. I have not lost a fight against Ubel since.

"Come on," I heard from over my shoulder, it was Princess Bellona. "It is almost sunset, that's when we move." She was putting on one of her arm bracers, the last piece to complete her scarlet armor.

I grunted and pushed myself up from the chair, "Has she finished it yet?" I was exhausted from all the blood taken from me in the past couple of days.

The princess looked me dead in the eyes and stated unnecessarily seriously, "Of course she has." She turned to the doorway and yelled into the hallway, "Lyss! Bring the Arinthian his armor."

"I have a name," I said.

"Arinthian will work fine," she said, ignoring me. She looked into the hallway, "Here she is."

Princess Lyssandra rushed into the room with some light armor that looked very similar to what I was using before but just... red.

"Did you literally just cover my old armor in my blood?" I asked, very confused about what was special about this armor.

"That was most of it," Princess Lyssandra said, almost embarrassed, "but there's more to it than just being doused in blood. This is Arinthian hide, it was already made of lacerine leather, and now it is specifically yours."

"I would hope so, it was my blood."

"And that's just the thing," she continued, "the armor will only work for you, it will act as another layer of skin whenever you transform during spellcasts."

Ubel stepped into the room and explained, "So now, instead of letting them tear through the armor we need for our other troops and burning it every time you decide to set yourself on fire, or rather become fire, the armor will change with you. Outside of casting, it will serve as adequate light armor for all other combat."

The armor itself was surprisingly fashionable. It was tanned very, smoothly and the red was as dark as Ubel's, but there was no helmet for it. I put on the chest plate first: it fit comfortably and did not impair my movement at all but felt thick and sturdy. The shoulder guards, the bracers all fit perfectly as well.

"Here," Princess Lyssandra said while handing me a black cloak. "It is not specifically for you, but it should keep you a little warm and help you hide better at night."

"I'm not sure I'll need it to keep me warm," I laughed, "but I'll take anything to help during the night." The cloak complimented the armor well, its midnight black supplied a perfect enough contrast to the dark red of the hide.

All that was left for me was to grab a sword. I reached for my favorite sword to practice with. It was lightweight and strong, but Ubel stopped my hand just short of grabbing it. "Not that one," he said. "I had one of my blacksmiths craft you a special weapon, two actually." He handed me the hilt of a sword with a small crossguard, but there was no blade. "It operates off of your magic. The more you channel into it, the longer the blade and the more durable it is."

I took the hilt and held it in front of me. "*Icerepin*," I said. I felt a strong connection to the blade, it was begging me for magic, so I thought the rest of the words, *ingnis tabuasnits ictusnor icounten*. Flames burst forth from the blade and flickered into what appeared to be a solid blade that glowed with a bright orange. Then, without my knowing, Ubel grabbed my old training sword and swung it against the blade of my new flame sword. My old sword broke in an instant, proving the strength and durability of my new sword in a fight.

"Looks like it is working perfectly," he said. "Use it well. It won't be as burdensome as this old thing." He flung the remainder of the broken sword to the ground, casting it aside as useless.

"And the other weapon?" Princess Bellona asked for me, eager to see what was next. She always seemed more interested in magic than anything other than war, and this was just a combination of both of her interests, I figured.

Ubel called into the hall, "This one is a little harder to conceal." A skeleton brought in an unstrung short bow. It was thick and pure black. "It's made of wood from trees at the base of the volcanoes and, like the sword you just got, is infused with a drop of your blood."

"I don't know how to shoot," I admitted bluntly.

"I know," Ubel smirked. "But I intend to teach you on our way up. You seem to learn fast enough that I don't think it will be a problem."

I placed my hands in a basic position I had seen the other archers in his army take when they would draw their bows and I repeated the same spell I used for the sword. A fiery bowstring and arrow appeared in my hand. I pulled the flaming bowstring back and pushed the bow limbs forward to maximize the strength of the draw and then released without thinking. The flaming arrow shot forward and landed in the wall and remained for a few seconds before fizzling out of existence.

"See?" Ubel said. He chuckled and was leaning to one side as I had evidently almost shot him, "All I have to teach you is how to aim."

"Amazing," Princess Bellona said. She was clearly fascinated with my new weapons, but also frustrated with her father, "Why did you not make us any of those?"

"None of us have the necessary power to fuel them, or strong enough blood for that matter. These weapons will work for at least him, at most I would expect that maybe a half Arinthian could use it, but any less than that, and they are just a piece of metal and a nice-looking stick."

"This bow is amazing, but where am I supposed to keep it?" I asked. "I can't exactly sling it over my shoulder because well," I gestured to the lack of a string.

"Didn't you notice the pair of leather straps on the back of your armor?" Princess Lyssandra asked. "I originally intended for you to put a sword there, but it should work for your bow as that fancy sword of yours should just fit as part of your belt now."

I slipped the bow limb into the straps on my back that I did not know about before, it was a little bit of a tight fit, but I guessed that made it secure because it did not move.

The skeletal commander from the day of my capture walked into the armory where we were preparing. He knelt down and said, "We have two battalions standing by and ready to go your majesties."

"We'll only be taking one," Princess Bellona boasted. "It's only fun if we fight them on even numbers, the enemy only has one troop, so we will bring the same. We leave the moment the sun drops below the volcanoes."

"Very good, my lady," he looked to Ubel for confirmation. Ubel granted his daughter's wish with a simple nod and the commander left the room.

"Wouldn't it be easier if we had more troops?" I asked. "A sheer numbers advantage could be enough alone to dissuade their attacks."

"Not really," Princess Bellona said. "The courtyard of Aranor is so small that only one troop can even realistically fit, with two in there, there's almost no room to swing a sword."

"So, what do we do when the enemy troops arrive in Aranor?" I asked.

"They won't even make it to the gate," she smiled. "The path is just barely wide enough for two soldiers at a time, and they always just come at the gates charging blindly as if they want to die. All they end up doing is fortifying our defense with their corpses."

"What if they do something different this time?"

"They never have, and they never will," she said confidently. "They only ever send prisoners with no tactical training, so it is really easy to annihilate their forces every time. I'm not sure if their king even wants Aranor as much as he just wants to get rid of criminals while boosting his image for giving 'failures a second chance.' He just makes me sick."

"Humor me then," I said, the last ray of light faded from the sky behind the volcano, it was time to move. "What is our plan if they do make it?"

"Then we fight them head-on," she said like it was obvious. "No one has bested father or me in combat other than you, and now that we have you, we probably don't need to bring anything other than archers for our outer defenses."

"That still does not sound like a plan to me."

"It's more of a plan than what we need for those mindless criminals who will be fleeing at the first sign of death."

"Ubel," I turned to him and asked. "Do you agree with this?"

"I leave everything about the defense of Aranor to my daughter, she has not failed me once. She reclaimed the city for me and has not lost it since."

"But I have a feeling there's going to be something different about this one. There might be a person like me on their side, but I have no idea where this person is."

"There's another Arinthian?" Princess Bellona asked.

"I think. Let's just hope he's not on their side. It would be foolish, after all, to side with the people that want to kill your entire race."

"Let's hope," Ubel agreed.

"And if he's there?" I asked.

"We kill him first," Princess Bellona said, smiling grimly.

DAY 18

H

I HATED THE IDEA OF leading a suicide mission, but somehow it was the only chance I had at survival. It had been a little over two weeks since I entered this world and now, I was prepared to die in it. After a full day of relentless practice with my twenty-four men, I was still unsure of my plan. If even one arrow managed to hit the front, it would mean total chaos for the rest of the company. During early practices on occasion, one of them would trip, and the entire formation would crumble. We just had to hope it didn't come to that.

One archer seemed unconcerned with the mission. He was skilled enough to consistently hit targets and would shoot down birds during our breaks. During practice, he wove quickly in and out of formation to fire his bow. He was likely our best hope of making the whole thing work. I was not sure, but I thought I heard him echoing my commands from the back for those who could not hear as well, all the while never claiming any sense of command.

"Remember, men," I said, as the soldiers I had been training with gathered with their shields into ranks, "take it slow and steady. The entire battle depends on us getting through, so if even one of us falls, it's all over. Look out for one another." I raised my greatsword high in the sky and cried out, "To victory!"

The response was more of a concerned whimper than a cheer. Morale was low and I was just as concerned, if not more, for the success of this mission. Our shields were far from uniform leaving tiny gaps that could allow for an arrow to slide through and pierce the entire formation, I just had to make sure that could never happen.

"Are you sure you don't want me to lead them?" Sir Jerum asked. "It is far too dangerous for the entire troop to lose their commanding officer."

"And it is far worse," I replied, "for a king to lose his trusted retainer. Remember, you are to take over if anything goes wrong. Lead them justly."

The sound of hooves grew louder behind me. I turned to see Lady Erione on her horse. She rode proudly with perfect posture, and her staff mounted to some straps on the side of the saddle. "I'll be waiting for your return or for your signal to join you in the city," she said, smiling. "Don't disappoint me."

I jokingly bowed and said, "As you command, Lady Erione." Before I returned to standing, she had already retreated deep into the treeline of the forest, far from any danger. Her responsibility was tending to any of the wounded that had to retreat, not to the frontline. Sir Jerum followed her into the forest to join the rest of the troops.

I did not intend to return to her with so much as a scratch, but I also knew there was no way to reasonably take this city as long as we only had one entrance.

I gestured to my men to follow me into the open clearing that stood before Aranor. The twenty warriors and four archers were about as excited as I was. I heard during practice yesterday that all the king had done in the past, or at least the commanding officers, was to order the criminals to charge in and hope one of them made it to the gate. Apparently, I was the first to ever think of something other than group up and charge until we are out of troops. Over the course of the march, we lost maybe thirty men to desertion, but I was still not too concerned. Our odds of winning this did not depend on numbers but on execution.

Once we were in the clearing, I had them form behind me with shields above their heads and to the side to form a shell like a tortoise. The four archers nocked their arrows and stood closely behind the rest of the warriors; they were ready to take their first shot once we were within range.

"Remember, men," I reminded them for what seemed like the thousandth time, "slow and steady. One step at a time, and we will be within those walls in no time." That was a promise I knew I could not keep. Each step was a chance for a new opening in the formation, so we had no choice but to take it slow. I also knew that this would take a while, and there was no guarantee of us making it within those walls.

"I'll keep you safe, but I promise nothing for these... fighters," Eyvindr said.

If you are doing one, I thought to him, *then you are also doing the other.* Eyvindr remained silent for a little while after.

"Sir?" I heard one of my men ask me.

"Yes?" I replied.

"Can we start moving? It is hard to hold this position," he complained.

"Of course," I acknowledged. I pointed my sword forward and marched in place. "Forward!" I commanded. I continued my marching and on every fourth step took a step forward with the rest of the company. We were on our way into Aranor.

The clamor of our march and footsteps alerted the army inside the city as they prepared their defenses. Skeletons began to arm the ramparts along the wall and a beautiful woman with dark red hair stood just above the gate barking orders at the undead. I saw her raise a sword high in the air.

"Halt! Ready yourselves, men!" I called back while ceasing my march. "They are sending the first volley!" The moment the words left my lips the sky turned black with arrows blocking out what little sun had been peeking through the clouds. The arrows that hit landed with a heavy thud into the leather shields that made up most of our formations, the other arrows whistled by our ears or bounced off the metal shields.

I turned back to look at my men, we survived the first volley. "Forward! Double time!" I resumed my marching, but on every second step we all moved forward. It should take them time to reload. We moved forward quickly, but still not fast enough as there was still what seemed like an eternity left for us to cross when the woman raised her sword again.

"Halt!" I called again. "Tighten up!" The second volley came down upon us just as overwhelming as the first.

With this many arrows in the sky, I thought to Eyvindr, *then there can only be so many skilled swords inside the city. I think if we make it inside, we might have a chance of winning.*

I turned back again to check on my men. They all survived. I resumed facing forward and saw for a moment what I thought to be a flaming arrow, but after I blinked it disappeared, so I thought nothing of it. We resumed marching at twice the normal pace. We were now about three-quarters of the way across the bridge.

"Archers!" I yelled back. "Take aim and start knocking them down."

"Aye!" I heard from the unconcerned archer; he was always the first to act. The archer stepped out of the defensive formation to make sure he could have a clear shot. Using his bow hand as a temporary quiver, he fired three arrows in quick succession with deadly precision that split the skulls of three different skeletal archers. The other three archers each only fired one before returning to the formation to nock another arrow and take a breath. Of the six arrows fired, only the three he had fired and one of the other arrows hit their mark. The others passed pointlessly through the ribs of the skeletons.

"Fire at will!" I heard from in front of me. We were now close enough that the woman commanding the skeletons could not rely on volley fire to take us out. "Focus on taking down the archers in the back!" she ordered, frustrated. Then she disappeared below the ramparts to order some other troops, I assumed, to brace the gate.

The arrows started flying at us unceasingly. The noise as they slammed into the shields was too much for me to even hear my own thoughts, but I had to maintain order. "Keep the formation tight and keep walking, trust the rhythm you can feel in the ground!" I commanded. "Keep our archers safe!"

"Aye!" I heard from the entire troop this time, they were excited, I assumed. It was the loudest response they had ever given me. Was this the farthest any group had gotten since Ubel took Aranor? I refocused the moment I felt a burn against my cheek, but when I touched the sharp pain, I saw no blood.

"Eyvindr?" I asked him. "What was that?"

"I'm... not sure, I've been reflecting all of the arrows that could hurt you, but something must have somehow gotten through," he sounded scared out of my mind. He continued to manipulate the wind around me forcing arrows that would hit me off the side of the land bridge.

Meanwhile, behind me, the men were roaring as they marched forward and the archers continued to fire at the same pace they had before. The unconcerned archer continued to fire arrows with perfect accuracy and precision into the skulls of any skeletons that would line the ramparts before retreating back into the defense of the warriors to reload his hand and his bow.

After another round, he called out, "I'm out, sir!"

"What about the arrows on the ground?" I shouted at him over the sound of the arrows that seemed to be slowing down in terms of pace.

"They are too damaged to use," then he let his pretentious side get to him, "and quite poorly made."

"Well, find some!" I ordered.

"That's not very simple when under pressing fire like this!" he refuted somewhat humorously.

I groaned and shouted another order back, "Archers, give that man some of your arrows so he can keep firing." Frustrated as I was, I whispered to myself, "He'll make better use of them than the rest of you."

We were drawing close to the gate and fewer arrows were leaving their walls with every twang from our archers' bows to the point where it actually seemed manageable without Eyvindr. The gate must have been at least twelve feet tall as it towered over anything that approached it. Luckily, no one had fallen when we got to the gate.

"All right, men!" I called out. "Let's open up these gates! One! Two!" We all wound up and braced ourselves to push with our combined might through these gates, "Three!" The gate fell open without much of a push, and the city's main courtyard was flooded with skeletal soldiers with bows, a considerable amount with swords, but in front of them all were three figures. The farthest to the left was the woman with red hair. In the middle was a large man in red armor and a draconian helmet. Lastly, to the right was a figure clad in blood-red armor and a black cloak with nothing more than a bow without a string hanging on his back and a bladeless sword hilt in his hand.

D

UBEL WAS AN AMAZING TEACHER; either that or I was a natural. Within the short breaks on the trek to Aranor, Ubel had taught me to shoot any target within twenty feet as if it was right in front of me. Anything further out, I was still somewhat accurate. I could, at the very least, scratch the target.

That was all with a normal bow and rather poorly made arrows. With my flame bow, I could control the arrow as it flew through the air to a minimal extent making my shots even more reliable. The flame bow doubled, if not tripled, my effective range.

I practiced my aim with my flame bow by taking a shot then backing up for another one until I could hit the edges of a tree about eighty feet away. The red-haired princess spectated my progress in the main courtyard of Aranor.

"Very good, Arinthian," Princess Bellona taunted me. "Not bad for a day's work of practice."

"It's better than good, really," Ubel assured me. "It is honestly impressive, but with how long it takes you to fire, I don't think I can put you on the ramparts quite yet."

I nodded but did not agree with his decision. I took a breath, closed my eyes for a moment as I focused my mind and prepared the spell to fire the bow. I had to prove him wrong. I was not going to just wait for the enemy to break in.

"*Icerepin!*" I ordered the bow and finished the spell with my mind, I shot immediately and ordered again, "*Icerepin!*" I fired the second shot before the first could hit its mark. Unfortunately, Ubel was right, I had not mastered the speed combined with accuracy, both shots flew wide and hit stone walls near the tree I had been practicing my shots. I was only thirty feet from the tree.

"Should the moment ever come where we need to fire at will," Ubel began, "supposing they even get close enough before they are slaughtered on the bridge, you would be a waste of space on the ramparts." He said it bluntly, but he did not mean to discredit the effort I put in. "I will let you participate in volleys, and in the unlikely case they can even hit our soldiers, you will be in the last reserve for the ramparts, but let's hope for the best."

"Thank you, Ubel."

"I don't think that's your call, father," Princess Bellona said, very annoyed. "I thought I was in charge of the defense of Aranor."

"That you are, Bell," he confirmed. "Just make sure you don't need him on the ramparts and my decision will mean nothing." He was grinning. Ubel seemed to smile a lot for someone who was dead, but at least the smiles were genuine.

"That's right, Bell," I taunted her. "Maybe you won't need me at all."

The princess was immensely frustrated and stormed over to me and in one smooth motion placed the point of her bastard sword at my neck, "I won't," she started, "Arinthian." I could feel the anger seethe through her teeth. She put the sword back in its sheath and took a deep breath as if she could ever be calm.

"My lady, Bellona!" I heard the commander that had struck me down nearly two weeks ago call over to her. If he had lungs, he would have been panting from how fast he ran in his heavy black armor. "A small company of twenty or so humans have started marching toward the gates. It is time."

"Thank you, Commander Treynar," she said. With that, Bellona was taken away to the far side of Aranor where the Haven army would be approaching.

Ubel walked over to me and heavily laid his hand on my shoulder, "Calling her 'Bell' may have been a bit much," he joked. "Now," he said hoisting his shoulders up to allow his armor to settle properly again, "let's go to the gate."

As I approached the gate, Princess Bellona's sword was already raised and the skeletal archers were aiming at the sky, ready to fire the first volley on the poor souls that were suicidal enough to approach the gates of Aranor. "Fire!" she ordered while letting her sword fall in front of her. The number of arrows in the sky was a true spectacle to see as it completely darkened the sky.

"Nothing can survive that," I thought aloud.

"Ready the next volley! Two-hundred feet!" Princess Bellona ordered. We were supposed to fire within a range of twenty feet of her marker.

I was confused. How could anything survive that first volley? The commander had said there were only twenty of them, and we fired over a hundred arrows at least. Regardless, I held my flame bow up to the sky and uttered under my breath, "*Icerepin.*" I was standing center with the gate, so I could just fire up and forward. And trust my magic to hit something. The flaming bowstring and arrow appeared in my grasp, and I pulled it back to max strength.

"Fire!" the princess ordered once again. The arrows all let loose at once and blacked out the sky once more this time with my flaming arrow accompanying them. After a few moments, she flared up with anger, "Dammit!" she shouted.

Then four of the skeletal archers on the wall were shot in the head, their skulls shattered from the force of the arrows. She turned back to face the army and ordered the foot soldiers to prepare for close combat, but not to brace the gate. As for the archers, she commanded that they prepare to fire at will without any more volleys.

"That's strange," Ubel said, donning his iconic helmet and walking closer to the gate to gauge the situation with his daughter. The princess noticed her father approaching and stepped down from the ramparts to meet with her father and make room for more archers on the wall. "What's happening up there?" Ubel demanded.

Princess Bellona looked down and ashamed, "They are getting too close. They've made some kind of shell with their shields and the one in front doesn't even have a shield, but it seems like he can't be hit."

"What does he look like?" I asked, concerned that it could be the other Arinthian from the tower.

"I can't tell," she replied. "He is wearing a full helmet and heavy armor." Then she turned back to her father, "I have the archers firing at will, but the humans managed to get a few good shots in their formation, and they are gradually whittling down our own archers. I've turned our focus on their archers to stop the bleeding so to speak."

"That's the best we can do for now," Ubel agreed. "I will lead the main army and Drocan," he started to turn toward me, "I want you on the wall until they get to the gate. Stay low and fire your shots carefully. Don't worry about the archers they have: I need *you* to test the defenses of that soldier in front. Once they get to the gate or you find out if you can hit him, fall back and join the rest of the army and stand by my side. This could get bad."

"Very well," I obeyed. I rushed over to the wall we were defending as fast as I could, then climbed the ladder to the ramparts just above the gate itself. I kept myself low and barely let my head show above the wall. I saw what the princess had mentioned, a man with large, heavy armor. Even I could not tell if he was who I thought he was, but I began the spell to fire an arrow. "*Icerepin*," I started. I readied myself before looking over the wall. They were moving rather fast and roaring with excitement. This was the farthest they had gotten in years, according to Ubel, and their cheering proved it.

The soldier's armor was incredibly bright and daunting to look at, and his helmet hid his face. I had no idea how he could see out of that thing. My own cloak impairs so much of my vision that I have to take it off for close combat. That was my target, within twenty feet of the gates now, I looked over the wall and pulled the bow back and fired my shot. It flew wide and to the side as if pushed away by a strong wind.

"Impossible," I said in disbelief. I knew I was a better shot than what I just demonstrated. I ducked beneath the ramparts again and prepared to fire again. "*Icerepin*," I said.

I took a deep breath and aimed carefully at my shining target. This time I would try to keep the arrow flying straight with my own magic instead of relying on it to shoot straight. He was even closer now, so I aimed directly at the center of his helmet. I loosed the arrow and focused on controlling the flaming magic to maintain its straight path, but it was still slightly pushed to the side. It grazed the side of his helmet but definitely burned him in the process. I saw him pause for a moment and check his burnt cheek with his hand. It was not much damage, but it was definitely something.

"There has to be something pushing the arrows to the side," I thought aloud. The last thing I heard from the front gates was some argument about arrows as I dropped down from the walls and regrouped with Ubel. I thought for a moment that it might be that Arinthian I met at the tower whose gous blasted me away, but this wind seemed weak compared to what I felt that day, so I dismissed it.

"I can't stop them either," I told Ubel as I placed my bow in the leather straps on the back of my armor.

"There's something protecting the man in front," Princess Bellona asked.

"Yes," I confirmed. "A wind, a strong wind, though not felt from where we stand, knocks all our arrows to the side. They are continuing to advance."

"It's possible they are using an enchantment much like my blade, though I would doubt it. I am probably the last one, aside from you of course, who can read Acelin." Ubel thought for a moment then asked, "Are they at the gate or did you find a weakness?"

"Found a weakness, but it is probably both by now, they keep gradually increasing their pace. Magic control, or anything heavy enough to get through a strong wind, should be able to break through that defense of his."

"Will your sword work?" Ubel asked.

"Definitely," I said while pulling the sword hilt into my right hand. "Yours will, too. The wind seems strong, but I am sure my arm is stronger. I'm sure he's just another average soldier."

"Good," the princess and Ubel said simultaneously.

The gate crashed down in front of us, but we were far enough back to show the strength of our numbers and not have a single soldier fall under the weight of the door. The enemy fanned out and extended their line but kept their archers behind everybody else. Most of them dropped one shield, but some of them dropped both and pulled out their primary weapon. They were a mixed bunch, some with short swords and others with great axes, but there were only twenty-five of them, and only one of them seemed ready to face an army.

H

We fanned out our line and the warriors prepared to fight to the last breath, dropping any shields that could get in their way during the fight. Our four archers stood close behind me in the gateway and nocked arrows ready to fire, but patient enough to not draw to fire yet.

"Mother Arinth," I heard Eyvindr curse, "it's him. The other Arinthian."

"There was another one?" I asked.

"Yes, and he managed to kill, or rather absorb, his gous. He is incredibly dangerous," Eyvindr said. "I had hoped to never see him again."

"Who are you talking to?" the skilled archer asked from behind me, concerned for my sanity.

"Nobody," I said in short reply. I had not realized I was speaking aloud with Eyvindr, but I quickly changed that and thought to Eyvindr. *Why is he on their side?*

"I can only imagine torture," he replied.

The hooded Arinthian removed his cloak and tossed it to the side to free himself up for the impending fight. Then he said over the distance between us, "Be quiet, Eyvindr! I'm here because I'm not crazy enough to side with the people who tried to exterminate my kind." My men were confused as to who Eyvindr was, but I was more concerned with the fact he could hear us. He took a single step forward and called out to me, "I thought it could have been you, but I hoped it wasn't. You don't have to fight for them. They will discard you the moment they get what they want from you! You're a traitor. How could you side with them?"

I hesitated for a moment and my men looked scared of me now. One of them asked with fear, quivering his voice, "Who are you?"

"Nobody," I answered. Then I replied to the other Arinthian with hardly a wasted breath, "I can't join you. There's... There's someone I have to go back to. But we can keep this bloodless."

"I see no way to," he refuted. "If you continue to fight with them, you will continue to be a danger to me. And honestly," the hilt in his hand ignited and became a full sword, "I would prefer to live."

"Wait!" I shouted. "A duel. The winner gets to stay in Aranor." The Arinthian looked at the figures in dark red armor, asking for confirmation. After a nod from the draconian skull, the Arinthian lined himself up with me and nodded.

D

I smiled grimly, "We will accept your terms," then I looked behind the Arinthian at the archers in the back of the gate and back to him. "I, of course, have a couple conditions myself. First, obviously, there will be no interference from anyone. If there is," I looked into the eyes of the archer that had been shooting our skeletons with unbelievable accuracy, "they will die."

"Agreed," the other Arinthian replied.

"Next," I started, "I would like to know the name of who I am about to fight."

The reply was instant, "Horus." Seems like Eyvindr protecting his name back in Arinthia was useless.

"Drocan," I responded as a courtesy. "Any conditions that you would like to add? Magic usage?"

I heard the whispers of the wind as they spoke to Horus as Eyvindr gave him advice, but I was not listening as closely as I had before when they assumed my reason for fighting for Ubel. "Everything is on the table, so anything can be used," Horus said while moving his greatsword to a more ready position for a duel.

"Ubel? Bell?" I asked my companions. Ubel shook his head quietly and Princess Bellona just scowled at me, forcing a chuckle from my mouth.

"Stand back," Horus told his troops while dropping from his stance. "When I win this, I will need you all to be alive. Do not even think about interfering."

His troops shuffled backward with a fearful, "Yes, Sir." All except the archer I was staring at earlier.

"And what is your name?" I asked. "Assuming you don't mind."

"My family is Calidan," he responded without a second thought. He finally returned his arrows to his quiver and slung his bow over his shoulder.

"Stay back, Calidan," I told him. "I don't want your pride to get you killed."

Horus whispered something to Calidan, and he nodded then ran back onto the bridge. He was definitely agile and the fastest-moving of the bunch that followed Horus. "Are you ready?" Horus asked me. "Because I would prefer to wait a moment if you would allow it." The skeletons behind me started chanting for blood, but Ubel calmed them with a wave of his hand.

"What did you tell him to do?" I responded. I was willing to be patient as long as he did not run from me.

"I told him to get Lady Erione," he replied as he shuffled his feet to test his footing in the stone courtyard, "just in case."

"Where did that confidence from earlier go?"

"It's still there, but I'm equally cautious."

"Fair enough," I shrugged. A moment later a young woman in white riding a similarly colored horse raced through the gates followed by Calidan shortly after. "Is this Lady Erione?" I asked. The young woman glared at me as she dismounted from her horse.

"Yes," Horus replied, "give me a moment to speak with her."

"As you wish."

H

"What in Arinthia are you doing?" Lady Erione asked while walking toward me, this was the most worried I had ever seen her. The only other time that even came close was when I joined the king's army.

"Giving everyone here a chance to live," I said, stopping her from walking by grabbing her shoulders. I let go with one of my hands and took my helmet off to show her I was sincere. "I need you here just in case something goes wrong, but I have no intention of needing you."

She rushed in for a quick hug and whispered, "I hope you won't," before quickly backing away again. It was strange for her, in most circumstances I would have assumed she would just try and hide everything behind her veil of sarcasm, but it seemed even she realized how poorly this could go.

"I promise, I will come back alive," I assured her as I turned to face Drocan once again. Then I whispered under my breath, "I would never be able to forgive myself if I died here."

"It won't come to that," Eyvindr said in an attempt to comfort me. "When we worked together, we were able to match Sir Jerum. I severely doubt a ruffian like Drocan would be able to beat Sir Jerum Wolfsbane."

We still shouldn't underestimate him, I thought to Eyvindr. I felt the burn I received on the bridge and thought, *He was probably the one that hit us.*

"That is likely," Eyvindr said as he strengthened the wind around me, he would accelerate my movements for me by reducing any resistance and pushing my movements to faster than I could sometimes even control.

Drocan must have noticed the magic in the wind around me as he dropped into his own ready stance, his blade was in his right and in front of him with his left leg was back.

He confirmed, "I take it you are ready?" His short hair stood still as it resisted the winds Eyvindr was forcing through the city.

"I am," I told him, chuckling as I was reminded of what Sir Jerum had told me in my training. "I thought you'd never ask."

D

The stance I took was equally offensive as it was defensive. It allowed for quick movements to either side for dodging or even quick parries and counterattacks. Ubel had trained me mostly using magic for the past few days, but I had not forgotten how he taught me to remain light on my feet. Light feet meant faster attacks without sacrificing too much strength.

Horus, on the other hand, seemed to ground himself into the courtyard with his stance. It was low, and he held his sword to his right side with both hands parallel to the ground beneath him, a purely offensive position that Ubel used frequently.

This should be easy, I thought. If I charged him before he made a move, he would be finished in an instant.

"*Icerepin,*" I began aloud then thought the rest so Eyvindr would not know what I was doing. *Ricopros rubicmach itomum ignis.* I held off on completing the spell as to not show my hand before I needed to. After all, it was my biggest failsafe. I leaned forward to start my charge, but at that moment, Horus beat me to the punch and was moving faster than I expected for someone in armor as heavy as that. I smiled at the thought of the challenge, leaned back, and defended with the flat end of my flaming sword, bracing it with my left hand.

The flames stung my hand a little bit, but I knew I would be fine. He clearly did not expect the flames to withstand steel as he continued to push down with presumably all of his might. The wind also pressed me down, but it was still much weaker than anything Ubel had hit me with, so I was able to stand my ground. I feigned a momentary weakness and let him push further down as I dropped, and with that, my opportunity presented itself.

Horus had lost his footing, so I took advantage and pushed his greatsword back up and to my right to give him an awkward handle on his sword. As he stood stunned for a moment, I moved to the left and kicked him in the chest to try and knock him over, but he only stumbled backward. He was more resilient than I thought.

H

"He's strong," Eyvindr said. My gous was worried. Drocan was amused to say the least. It was as if he was playing with me.

Stronger than expected for sure, I agreed in my thoughts to Eyvindr. I needed to conserve my breath. *Even Sir Jerum has struggled recently to deal with our speed and strength.*

"Is that all you have?" Drocan taunted, opening himself wide for another attack. "Because I've been in duels with skele—"

But before he could finish, I charged again. However, I would not make the mistake of challenging him to a test of pure strength this time by pushing his block. I feigned an attack from above, as Sir Jerum often did with me, and instead swung low at his feet. He backed up just in time. I continued to press the attack and forced myself toward him again, not worrying about attacks being blocked. I looked each moment for a potential opening, but he was able to match each attack.

I made another mistake. Somehow, Drocan managed to parry one of my horizontal attacks, throwing me immensely off balance. I staggered with my feet too close together. I almost had him at a wall due to the flurry of attacks. However, in my staggered state, he reached forward, grabbed my arm and body with his left hand, and tossed me as if I was nothing more than a stick against the wall.

I was still in the process of recovering, leaning against the wall, when he came up and kicked me to the floor. He stood towering over me and pushed his foot into my chest. I tried to grab his foot and push him off, but even with the strength of the wind on my side, the foot would not budge.

"Please," I heard a voice beg quietly in the distance.

"For how cautiously you were preparing to fight me," Drocan started, somewhat surprised, "you sure are impatient." He used the tip of his flaming hot sword to push my helmet off. The heat from his sword caused me to sweat through the cool winds Eyvindr was pushing through.

"And for how rugged you are," I said, "you sure are fast."

"Thank you. Anything you would like to get off your chest? Other than my foot, of course," he said sarcastically.

"Just... I'm sorry," I said, looking over to Lady Erione as she held her hands to her mouth. "I'm sure you know who to tell that to."

"Of course," Drocan replied sullenly. He raised his sword back to thrust it into my chest.

"Please stop!" the voice cried out again. It was Lady Erione. She dropped to her knees and begged through the tears that began to fall from her eyes, "Please." Drocan's sword dropped from its position for a moment.

"And why should I?" Drocan threatened. His eyes were normally calm, but now they were burning with rage. He refused to look anywhere else but me and raised his sword again.

"Because," Lady Erione pleaded, "he made a promise."

"That's none of my concern," Drocan said as he thrust his blade down toward me, but something pushed it to the side, causing it to pierce the ground to my right. The Draconian skull stood over me. His blade was the force that stopped Drocan; it was glowing an incredibly bright red.

"You already won," Ubel said to Drocan. "There's no need for you to break someone else's promise. Let him go back." Drocan hesitated for a while, then loosened the pressure on my chest, reminding me how easy it was to breathe before that.

"Fine," Drocan said in a pyrrhic tone. I pushed myself up and propped my bruised and somewhat bleeding body against the nearby wall. "Take your army and leave. Next time we meet, I won't be as lenient." I nodded and coughed in understanding.

Lady Erione came running over and embraced me, as if to verify I was still alive and not just some kind of spirit. "Thank Mother Arinth," she began quietly. Her normally smooth voice was raspy from her continuous crying, "You're alive."

"Thank you, Lady Erione," I said, but the pain from fighting Drocan left room for no more words.

Through her broken voice, she started to heal my wounds, "*Icerepin revisnuus ioaxuli.*" Even after the healing, everything still hurt; Drocan must have hit harder than I even realized. Then she begged me, "Please never do that again. Don't ever break that promise."

"As you command, my lady," I said, trying to dispel some pain with what humor I had left.

D

"I don't understand why you said I should spare him," I said through my teeth. "He is the biggest threat to any of us. To all of us." I was struggling to control my anger as I used my arms to gesture to Horus, then everybody in our army.

"Because, Drocan," my king began, "I don't want you to become like me, and there is no guarantee he will turn out as I did. Unlike myself when I worked for the kingdom, he seems to already have a code of morals." Ubel looked over to Horus with some sense of admiration, then turned back to me and asked, "Do you think if he won, he would have tried to kill you too?"

I remained silent because I knew the answer was likely not. I looked at Ubel and said, "You realize under the terms of our duel, I have to kill you, right? You interfered."

"Good news," he started with a smile in his voice, "I'm already dead." We chuckled at the fact for a few moments, but those from the kingdom were both confused and somewhat terrified.

"Lady Erione, was it?" Princess Bellona called from behind us.

"Yes?" She responded.

"Would you and Horus like to join us? We can promise your safety," Princess Bellona said with an off-putting amount of compassion in her voice.

"We- I..." she started, her tears having dried up at this point, "I can't. King Justain holds too much power over my family, over my hometown. If he found out that I, one of the last healers in his kingdom, abandoned him, he would surely raze my entire village."

"Unfortunately," Princess Bellona said, "I cannot promise their safety."

I thought so. Lady Erione said, "I knew it was too much to ask."

Calidan finally interjected into the conversation, "What will the king do when he finds out we did not capture Aranor and we all survived?"

"I can fix one of those things," I said jokingly, but everybody in Horus' company, including Lady Erione, was suddenly really defensive. I clarified with a sigh, "I'm not going to kill any of you." Everyone relaxed a little bit, but Lady Erione was still on guard.

"We may as well be dead in his eyes since nothing was accomplished and nothing was lost," Calidan stated as if he knew these fears first-hand. "He has no sense of peace or reason, but that is exactly why we are all stuck with him."

I pondered for a few moments what I could do to not have our duel and Ubel's sparing of Horus' life in vain, then it came to me. "I have an idea, but it will need to wait until all of you are back outside of the city, or at least the ones that don't want to join us," I said. Everyone fell silent and started listening to me. "We destroy the bridge."

"That's ridiculous!" Princess Bellona exclaimed, then she approached me to explain her reasoning. "That's our way into the kingdom, we can't just destroy our entrance."

"Can't we?" I responded. "It should be easy enough to build a substitute for what we lose."

"Why?" Horus grunted in pain through his teeth. "Why are you helping us?"

I sighed, "So it isn't all in vain." Horus seemed to understand the answer and went back to dealing with the bruises I left through his armor.

"Shall we get moving then?" Lady Erione asked for Horus' command. He nodded and Lady Erione helped Horus onto his feet and walked him over to her horse.

"Commander Treynar!" Princess Bellona called. The skeleton was clad in full black heavy armor, a stark contrast to the blinding silver of the kingdom's ranks. "Help Lady Erione, will you?"

"Yes, Princess Bellona!" Commander Treynar responded. He dropped his weapons and rushed over to help support Horus and lift him onto the unfortunate horse.

"Thank you," Lady Erione said.

"It's only right," Princess Bellona said, dismissing the need for gratitude.

H

It felt strange to ride a horse after walking for days to get there, but I was grateful. It was a bloodless battle with a clear victor, but I knew going back was going to be risky. I could not stay with them either, though I imagine the offer was mostly for Lady Erione anyway. I tried to sit up on the horse but failed horribly.

"Drocan," I said with all my might. He looked at me, still somewhat frustrated. "I hope we meet again on better terms."

Drocan smirked for a moment then looked to the darkening sky, "One can dream," then looked back at me and said, "and we can only hope. Can't we?" With that remark, Lady Erione led the horse and, consequently, the rest of my men back to where Sir Jerum and the rest of the army was. The skeleton known as Commander Treynar escorted us to the gate, or rather what was left of it and, once we were all through, he stood in the gateway with his arms crossed to make sure none of us turned back.

"I'm sorry," I muttered to Lady Erione. "I'm sorry that I worried you so much. I just thought—"

"It doesn't matter what you thought," she stopped me without turning back. "It matters that you are just alive right now, you can win later. Apologizing is useless," I heard her voice crack again, "so please, just, don't."

"All right," I acknowledged while fighting the urge to just sleep and slip to unconsciousness.

"What in the king's name happened in there?" I heard Sir Jerum ask, but I couldn't bring myself to look up at him. "Why are only you injured?"

"I..." I struggled to speak. "I failed."

"You got in, didn't you?" Sir Jerum asked. "That's farther than any other group that's been sent before."

"I came back alive with nothing," I clarified, with pauses between each word. "The king can't know that we made it at all."

"Why not?" Sir Jerum inquired. I suppose he was not as firm in the king's grasp as some of the rest of us were. But either way, it would be clear soon enough.

"Because," I echoed the thoughts of Drocan, "otherwise, it would be in vain."

"That makes no sense! I need a better explanation than that. I need a good reason to lie to the king," he disputed.

"Our lives are in danger otherwise," Lady Erione answered for me.

"Fine," Sir Jerum said. "I'll keep quiet. But I still want to know the full story," he looked at me, "once you have... fully recovered." Sir Jerum looked far behind me, then asked, very confused, "Wait... what is that?"

D

When I saw them having a conversation on the far side of the chasm, I knew it was time for my plan to commence. I stood above the gateway, facing the bridge. "*Icerepin icemmenntur ingnis icounten,*" I ordered my magic. Between my hands, a small ball of fire formed and started to grow rather rapidly. In a matter of moments, the fireball was larger than what could be contained between my hands. I could feel it draining a substantial amount of energy from me, and my knees grew weaker, but I could not give in quite yet. It needed to be larger still. It burned bright and lit up the now darkened sky.

"Incredible," Princess Bellona whispered in awe, "that is... unbelievable."

"I don't know how much more of this I can handle," its diameter was larger than the height of the gate at this point; I felt the weight of the fireball actually pushing me down. "I have to let go," I gritted through my teeth.

"Do it," Princess Bellona ordered.

"*Iveeno,*" I sighed in relief as I pushed the ball forward to the bridge. The fireball moved slowly through the air toward the center of the bridge. The impact of the fireball left a twenty-foot-wide gap in the bridge; the pieces that were blown off fell into the chasm below. It was finally over. "Don't die," I said, panting and looking over to what I could see of Horus' silhouette, "not yet."

"We will leave a single company here," Ubel barked to the city, "the rest of us will go home, back to Dracadere." That was the first time I had actually heard the name of his castle.

DAY 24

H

THE JOURNEY BACK WAS FILLED with the agony of knowing the coming wrath of the king. He could accept failure at the price of death, but never in any other situation. That became clear the moment he saw my face, walking through the throne room's gigantic doors alone. I had mostly recovered from the injuries Drocan had given me, to the point where none of them would show to the king, but I let my head hang low in defeat.

"I expect good news," the king stated drearily but with a hint of hope that my expressions were lying to him. His voice was low and understandably disappointed, yet somehow frightening all the same.

"I am afraid I bring none," I admitted, my voice weaker than I remembered. "We could not capture Aranor."

The king stood up and began to pace around the throne. He took a deep breath to calm his impending rage. "What are our losses?" he asked without a hint of sympathy in his voice.

I attempted to strengthen my voice in my reply and firmly said, "None, my lord."

The king's eyes flared up in a moment of pure rage when he asked with all the power and force of the air in his lungs, "Then did you even try?" He was rash, I knew that, and he seemed to value the city over the life of those beneath him. One of his advisers rushed to him and tried to calm him by leading him back to his currently empty throne. He brushed his adviser aside and took another deep breath before finally asking again, pointedly pronouncing each word, "Did you even try?"

"Yes, my lord," I replied, attempting to keep my voice steady as I presented my lie, "but when we arrived, the bridge leading into Aranor was completely destroyed, it had crumbled to pieces, and the gap was too large for us to cross. We could not make it to the city. My guess is that they saw us coming and destroyed the bridge before we could get there."

The king pinched the bridge of his nose with his fingers and sighed heavily, then, with the words coming from the back of his throat, said, "They've never destroyed the bridge before."

"Sir Jerum said that too, but it happened, my lord," I said.

"How?" the king asked, anger seething through his teeth.

"I'm sorry, my lord," I said. "How what?"

"How did they destroy the bridge?" he replied with a booming voice as he began to get out of his throne again. Repeating himself in mockery and anger, he asked, "How?!" He became increasingly frustrated and, sitting back on his throne again, said, "You saw it happen, didn't you?"

"No," I lied. "It happened before we arrived, but the entire middle section of the bridge was completely destroyed." I had to lie so that Drocan and I would not be hunted down. So that the lives of the men I fought with, Sir Jerum and Lady Erione, could be spared, as well.

The king sat quietly in defeat for a few moments before he began again, exasperated, "We will simply have to build a new bridge."

"Please excuse my rudeness, my lord," I said, "but how do you propose we do that?"

Finally, he smiled, but, as his smiles always were, it was terrifying, "With you, of course." He got out of his throne calmly for the first time since our meeting and walked down the steps to where I was kneeling. "We will use your wind magic to build a rope bridge, then a stronger bridge across the gap that was made."

"My lord, that would be suicide for anyone who tried to build it. What if they just destroy it again?" I suggested, but he clearly was not listening as he began to pace around me.

"We will use wood to support the underside of the bridge as well to make it stronger. Either we build a bridge large enough for an army, or you go in alone. It will be your choice," he said deviously. "Well?"

I forced my head lower and responded with a regretful, "We will build the bridge, my lord."

"Good," he nodded smugly. Then he returned to his throne and sat down for one last remark. "Should there be another Arinthian, you are to kill him on the spot. They are far too dangerous for us to ignore." He reminded me of what Drocan had said before Ubel had stopped him. How this man's power was ever recognized as authority baffled me.

"As you command, my lord," I said after a few beats of breath.

"You are dismissed," the king commanded.

I stood up and walked out of the room. The moment I was free from the king's gaze I finally let myself think to Eyvindr, "What is good about that king? I thought these humans were supposed to be *good*. Helping each other survive, not sending them to their deaths and being disappointed when they come back alive." Eyvindr did not have an answer.

"He used to actually go into the streets, give alms to the beggars and invite them in for a feast," Lady Erione replied, noting the frustration on my face and the anger in my breathing. "I do my best in his stead, but ever since he lost Aranor years ago, it has driven him mad, and now he does not even seem to know who he is anymore. Years ago, he would regularly go to Aranor himself to inspire the soldiers and occasionally lead a battle; it is why I was even needed. I was there if a stray arrow so much as scratched his beard, but the fall of Aranor into Ubel's hands forced him to become like this."

"So reclaiming Aranor would make him a benevolent king again?"

"I'm not sure about that," she replied. "The pit of greed is hard to escape; someone may just need to remind him of who he is, but Aranor could be a good first step. Maybe when he realizes Aranor is not enough for him, his desires would go to the extreme and allow us to remind him of who he really is."

The sound of heavy armor approached us in the hallway, and Sir Petrus Ramsguard appeared before us, standing firm and resilient as always. "It is not just that he lost Aranor. He feels as though he's lost the pride of the people. He was leading the battle we lost Aranor, and it is my fault." Despite his admission of fault, his face did not change at all to represent it. "I was scared," he admitted further. "The moment Ubel himself appeared on the battlefield, I forced the king to retire from the battlefield."

Ubel's draconian helmet was intimidating, but I did not understand what was so terrifying about him. His only defining traits, other than the helmet, were his giant sword and dark red armor. "What is so dangerous about Ubel?"

Sir Petrus looked shocked for a moment, then he realized, at least from the story he was told, I had not met Ubel myself. Returning to his natural, emotionless state, he said, "He was the closest thing to a pureblood Arinthian at the time," his stoic face refused to change. "He fought with my grandfather as a grown man while my grandfather was still young. Ubel has to be over two-hundred years old at this point. His centuries of combat experience combined with that ancient weapon of his make him a most dangerous fighter. He had abandoned Aranor long before King Justain and left it to be defended by his army, but that day I guess he wanted it back." Terror crept into Sir Petrus Ramsguard's eyes for the first time since I met him as he remembered the battle, "Those dead eyes of his were focused solely on the king, and I knew I could not fight him. He was famous for killing Arinthians back in his prime, so I would not even stand a chance.

"I think the king just wants to be able to claim he defended Aranor once more," Sir Petrus finished. He looked at me, "And you should be more afraid of Ubel than any of us."

"Why?"

"That blade of his feeds off of magic and makes him stronger because of it," Sir Petrus explained. "He strengthens it as much as he can with his own magic. Even then, he is terrifying, but combine that with when he gets close to you, and he would be able to cut you into bits before you could blink. Your gous may be a useful tool for fighting other humans, but against that monster, it is your greatest weakness. He was notorious for being able to kill Arinthians with one swing, and you would be no exception."

I understood now why his blade was glowing so bright when near Drocan and me. We were a gold mine of power for that sword. Lady Erione spoke before I could even process how I would respond, "Thank you for scaring the new recruit. Come on, Horus, let's talk elsewhere."

"R-right," I stammered out, not fully realizing what I had just agreed to. She pulled me away from Sir Petrus without allowing me to say goodbye properly.

"What are you going to do about it?" she asked me suddenly.

"About Ubel?" I asked in reply. "The only thing I can do, find a way to beat him." To her, I may not have seemed fazed, but I was panicking on the inside.

"Calm down," Eyvindr offered, "he has to have some kind of weakness, we'll find it."

"Mother Arinth, he really did scare you, didn't he," Lady Erione said as if it was written on my face. Before I could even say a word, she said, "You are too easy to read. We'll figure something out, I promise."

"Promises are hard to keep for me," I said, half-joking, in an attempt to break the topic of the grave situation at hand.

"At least you were able to keep yours," she stated while looking relieved, then she continued with purpose. "Now I'll have to keep mine. I will protect you."

"I'm pretty sure I'm the one who is supposed to say that," I joked.

"We can protect each other," she clarified. Then she reverted back to how she was in Aranor and asked. "Can we promise that?"

"Promise," I agreed.

"Forever?"

"Forever," I confirmed. She embraced me harder than she had at Aranor, but this time I returned the favor and wrapped my arms comfortably around her and rested my head on hers. I could only hope for this peace to last.

D

"HE FOUGHT WELL," Princess Bellona began, then jokingly finished her statement with, "for how much he fought." The four of us were sitting around the grand dining table that was way too big for such a small group. Ubel was sitting, of course, in the king's seat facing the door. I was in the seat to his left, Princess Lyssandra was to his right, and Princess Bellona was next to her. It felt pyrrhic with so few to celebrate with.

"I did not even need to use the armor," I told Princess Lyssandra as I cut into a piece of meat on my plate, "but I was fully prepared to." I took a bite and enjoyed the rich meat from the cattle I shot on the way back to Dracadere.

"Against someone who is not my father or my sister? I highly doubt it," Princess Lyssandra said then continued to eat.

"Well," I started, "*he* was there."

"The other Arinthian?" Princess Lyssandra asked for clarification.

"Yes," I replied, "his name is Horus. I didn't need to phase once. Despite the help of his magic, he was still only so fast. His movements themselves are sluggish and predictable," I took another bite and, once I swallowed it, I continued. "Clearly, he has only trained with one person, and a human at that. He is not adjusted to fighting people who can match him in magic. The only time I had to use magic was when I flung him into the wall; he was just too heavy otherwise."

"Was he fat?" Princess Lyssandra asked, confused.

"No," I laughed a little bit. "But for some reason, instead of letting him capitalize on his speed, the Haven army has him in the heaviest armor I could imagine. He's untrained and ill-equipped; that is the only reason I think I was able to beat him. If he was in the armor you made me, he would have beaten me in an instant."

"I'm not sure about that," Ubel said. "He still would not know how to fight properly. Horus relies too much on his gous. As he is now, regardless of armor, he may as well have as much combat experience as Lyss."

Princess Lyssandra looked somewhat offended and also doubtful, "So you are saying I could beat him?"

"Probably," Ubel shrugged. "That Horus should have served under me, I could have helped him become stronger, then he wouldn't have to be held captive by that bastard of a king."

"Why does he want Aranor?" I asked. "Why are the two of you even fighting?"

"When I first seceded from his army, from my grandfather's house," Ubel began, "the king at the time took it upon himself to finish what had been started. They wanted me dead because I was an Arinthian that was against them. Over the years, I faced siege after siege from Aranor because they held it, but a few years ago, I took it from their grasp and reminded them of who they were dealing with. I'm sure Justain only recognized me from legends. He had never been beyond Aranor, so he did not know what exactly he was sending his army into, and I always just let my skeletons handle it. But the day one of his men finally made it into Dracadere, their first target was not even me..."

"It was our mother," Princess Lyssandra finished.

"Had it not been for that," Princess Bellona began, "we might have pursued peace with the current king."

"King Justain, as he is now," Ubel clarified, "is not who he was before I retook Aranor. Like I said before, he never went beyond Aranor. I suspect it was either because he was a coward or had lost the meaning of the war and wondered to himself why he was sending men to die in these wastelands. He might have been able to be reasoned with, but after her death, I decided that was the last straw. So, I took control of my army for once to take Aranor and stop the sieges into Dracadere. And ever since, they have been fighting to take it back."

"I'm sorry," I said. I could feel the sorrow and loss in this room as the others had all stopped eating and just stared into their distant memories of their lost mother and wife.

"There's nothing for you to be sorry for, Drocan," Princess Lyssandra responded.

"We could not do anything to save her either," Ubel said, holding back tears and replacing it with the fury that was underneath. "There's nothing you can do to save a woman without her head. I continue to live, but I can never get back what was taken from me."

Princess Bellona remembered in horror. "They killed her in the chaos of the raid and..." she decided to let a few tears slip through before she converted it into anger as her father had. "And they... they stuck her head on a pike and planted it in the dirt on their way out as if she was some kind of monster."

I looked over to Princess Lyssandra and noticed she looked nauseous. She held her hand to her mouth and held back tears as best she could, but instead of replacing them with rage, grief was replaced with disgust.

"I need to leave," she stated simply, her voice muffled. Everyone watched as she stood up and dismissed herself from the room, never removing her hand from her mouth. I had never seen any of them so broken like this, much less at the thought of a memory.

"I think I'll go make sure she's okay," Princess Bellona announced solemnly. Ubel just nodded.

"I'm sorry that happened," I attempted to comfort the king. "What was she like?"

"A perfect combination of both of her daughters," Ubel forced a smile, or maybe it was legitimate; it was hard to tell. "Kind and firm, she always knew what was on my mind without the need for magic. She was the one who reminded me I was capable of being me. She was the one who convinced me to meet with the king and make peace... but then they made that impossible. I was going to leave the next day with a white flag but ended up bringing my sword and my rage." He paused for a while and quietly recalled some of his happier memories with her before he, too, dismissed himself to his quarters. All of the plates still had about half of the food on them, but seeing as I was alone in the hall, I decided to take my leave as well.

This was the first opportunity I had to explore the vast and maze-like halls of this castle, all my other days had been training, eating, and sleeping. The stone was a dark igneous that glimmered with the torches along the walls, but there was nothing on display anywhere in the vast castle. I eventually came to a balcony that overlooked the nearby sea from high in the mountain on which the castle rested. The moon was not out, so all of the stars shone brilliantly and reflected off the relatively calm waters. There was no bench, but I sat down, closed my eyes, and waited in the breeze.

"Drocan?" I heard a voice murmur from behind me.

I did not turn to face the speaker but just kept my eyes closed in an attempt to relax. "That's me," I responded.

"How did you find this balcony?" the voice inquired.

This time I turned my head to face it and reopened a single eye briefly before returning to my previous state, "Honestly," I started, "I didn't. I just got lost, then stayed because it was calm up here." I heard Princess Lyssandra walk closer and settle herself down nearby. "Why do you ask?"

"Because this is where I come to sit as well," she said. "My mom used to tell me stories here of her home in the Northlands."

"The Northlands?"

"North of the mountains, there are scattered towns that stay out of the war. They are peaceful and protected by natural division; many Arinthians fled there during the first purge. I don't think my mother had any Arinthian blood in her; she was just a kind soul that had an encounter with my father," she told me.

"She sounds like she was wonderful," I said. "Your father shared the same sentiments. I would have loved to meet her."

"There's only one grave in this kingdom, and it's hers," she said while somehow remaining calm. With how she reacted during dinner, I had imagined she would be sobbing, but she just sat quietly.

I stood up and offered my hand to her, "Let's go see her then," she looked surprised for a moment, "shall we?" She took my hand, and I helped her up. "You'll have to lead the way because, at this point," I explained in an attempt at humor, "I don't even know my way back to the dining room."

She smirked and then said, "All right." She let go of my hand and led me through the convoluted castle halls and downstairs to what I guessed was a back gate. Through the gate was a relatively small plateau of a field that also overlooked the sea. In the middle of the field was a single large stone. No fences or walls protected the grave; it was just open-air and a great view. "There she is," Princess Lyssandra said before she looked back at the castle and above to the balcony where we just were.

"Wow," I said in awe of the entire area. I walked toward the grave, but no name was written on the stone. It was just a blank obelisk. It made sense why it would be blank, everyone who knew about the grave knew who she was, and they didn't intend to make any more. I looked back to her and said, "Thank you for showing this to me, Princess—" but she cut me off.

"Just call me Lyss from now on," she stated somewhat embarrassed. "You may as well be family. I don't know about Bell, but you mean a lot to... us."

"Well then," I began again, "thank you for showing this to me, Lyss."

"Thank you for coming back," she mumbled.

"I always will," I affirmed.

She walked up to me and hugged me. I was shocked for a moment before I returned the embrace. Then I heard her whisper through muffled tears, "Thank you."

PART II: CROSSING

DAY 54

H

AFTER A MONTH OF NOTHING but training with Ramsguard and Jerum, King Justain decided it was time for another expedition, but not to Aranor. "In the North, there is a lord that keeps a sword created to channel magic. He was an old friend of my grandfather, and he kept the last of the... hunting tools," the king said. "You are to go meet him and retrieve that sword in my name." He walked toward me and handed me a letter with a seal that contained the letter "H" as a symbol for the kingdom. "I've also sent a letter to the guards up north to let them know you will be coming."

"How many am I leading there?" I asked, while taking the letter and placing it in a pocket of my clothes.

"Much fewer than last time," he said. "I'm only allowing five representatives," he made his way back to his throne. "That includes you, so you get to choose the other four. Sir Petrus, however, is out of the question."

"Anyone at all?" I clarified.

"That is correct," he confirmed, "but I imagine you have a few in mind already. Sir Jerum? Lady Erione? Am I wrong?"

"What about Abaven?" I asked.

The king explained, "Abaven is acclimated to the forests, he's very reliable there and would not be much help in the northern wastelands." He shrugged, "But if you really need him, you may take him, I simply wouldn't recommend it."

"And the man from the Calidan household? I never got his first name, but the one who was with me at Aranor."

"Why him?" the king looked confused. "He was disowned by his family: a disgrace."

"I think he has potential," I explained. "I saw him doing some target practice," I lied, continuing the story he was told. "He fires quickly and accurately. He seemed reliable."

"He was disowned from his family for theft, failing as a knight on countless occasions, and abandoning his duties as a noble," the king said. He was beginning to raise his voice but realized there was no need to contest me on this. "But if you choose to have a disgrace like him alongside you, so be it. He has no right to the Calidan name anymore. I cannot believe he still identifies himself as such. His name is Arthur. He is in the general barracks if you need him." The king retrieved something from his pocket and tossed it onto the ground in front of me. "If you ever need any funding, just show the merchant that crest," he said. The crest was the same golden dragon that was displayed on my armor. It was cast into an obsidian disc, and the emblem also included three emerald gems in each of the cardinal directions and a crown beneath the dragon. I picked it up. "It's cold up there. Be ready."

"Yes, King Justain," I said with a bow, dismissing myself from the throne room. Once I was through the tall doorway, I, unsurprisingly, was met with Lady Erione once again.

"So," she began as we started our walk towards the barracks and away from the king, "when do we leave for Aranor?"

"We don't," I stated simply. "Aranor is not our mission right now."

"Then where are we going?"

"As much as I'd like to exclude you from the 'we' of this mission, I expect you would leave 'me' out of that decision."

"And you'd be right," she said with a terse nod, still waiting for clarification.

"We are going to the North. Our goal is to get the king's so-called 'hunting tool.' It is a sword marked with an 'H' and was left up there ages ago, it seems, with a friend of the king's grandfather."

"So, we are going to the Northlands to get the last Arinthian blade," she said, but I could not tell if she was amazed or horrified.

"What do you mean by that?"

She looked around to make sure no one important was listening, "Remember how Ubel's sword glowed brightly when he approached you and Drocan? That was the other Arinthian blade; only two of them were ever made. You know where Ubel's is, and the other has been kept locked in the Northlands, protected in the king's name, because no one from Haven has been able to make effective use of it."

"So now he wants it back," I said, "because he knows I can use it." We were finally out of the dark hallways of the castle and to the barracks' courtyard.

"Probably," she acknowledged. I could not help but notice the breeze today as it pushed through her hair and brushed my own skin. "Why are we walking this way anyway?"

I entered the barracks' dining hall and called out, "Arthur Calidan! You are requested in the name of King Justain." The entire hall went from bustling laughter and crude jokes to dead silent in an instant. The screech of a single chair being moved broke the silence. I looked to the source of the noise and saw Arthur standing up and holding his nearly empty plate. He looked me dead in the eyes, then turned away to discard the scraps leftover and wash his plate. "Arthur Calidan!" I called out again. "In the name of King Just—"

"I heard you the first time!" he called out in reply, not turning to face me at all. "What? It isn't an immediate request, is it?" I could hear his smile as he continued to rinse his plate. Then he finally turned to face me and leaned against the basin that held the food scraps. "Well, is it? If not tell him I'll see him tomorrow," he stretched and faked a yawn and closed his eyes. "After all, I am awfully tired."

"I said in his name," I started, "not that you would be meeting with him." He seemed somewhat intrigued now as he reopened one of his eyes. Seeing as he was no longer being requested by the king himself, the dining hall returned to its normal boisterous behaviors. I walked over to him, "You'll be meeting with me instead."

"Very well," he shrugged. "Need me to bring anything?"

"Just yourself for now," I replied. I filled Arthur in on the new mission and completed the explanation for Lady Erione out of convenience.

"Why do you want me?" Arthur asked, confused.

"You are the only one from that group of twenty men that demonstrated obedience and also a sense of independence. You displayed your skills, and I was impressed, nothing more."

"And you know why I was disowned right?"

"Yes," I said.

"And you still trust me?" he asked, leaning forward. He seemed to question my sanity.

"The fact that you are even questioning this just means you need another chance. You are aware you are 'untrustworthy' in many peoples' eyes, but all you have to do to prove that you are worthy of this chance is take it."

He leaned back and said, "Fair enough. When are we leaving?"

"I still have to track down Abaven and Sir Jerum. Assuming I find them soon, we will meet here to leave tomorrow morning. Pack quickly and as lightly as you can; be prepared for anything."

"Understood," he nodded and left to gather his things.

"Lady Erione," I started, "that goes for you too, assuming you are coming."

"Will you drop the 'Lady' already?" she said, standing up, then walking to the doorway. "And of course, I'm coming." She smiled, "You would literally be dead without me."

I smiled back, holding back my fears of her getting hurt. In the raid on Aranor, it was easy to keep her safe in the backlines, but with only five of us making the whole trek, it was much riskier to bring her along.

"Actually," Eyvindr muttered his thoughts to me, "without *me*, you would be dead."

Are you jealous? I thought back.

"No," Eyvindr said, "just right."

"Whatever," I said aloud as I walked to find Jerum. After some time wandering the halls, I finally spotted him and ran to him as fast as I could. "Jerum!"

"What? We aren't training today, are we?" he asked. "I could have sworn it was our day off."

"It is, don't worry; however, I need to ask you something." I filled him in on our new mission and gave him the same task I had given the other two thus far, then asked him, "Do you know where I can find Abaven?"

"Why him?" Jerum asked. "The Northlands would be far from his territory."

"I didn't ask for advice," I said. "I just expect that he will be useful."

Jerum still seemed confused, but he pointed me towards the front of the castle gates. "He should be arriving for his bi-weekly evening report in a few hours. You can catch him then."

"Thank you," I said. "We will meet tomorrow morning in front of the barracks. You are dismissed."

"It does not feel right that you give me orders now," Jerum said.

"I like it," I said with a smirk, shrugging my shoulders at him, then took my leave.

I made my way to the watchtower of the front gate and watched as the sky shifted colors from a cool blue of day to the warm reds and oranges of sunset and, lastly, the dark black of night. Finally, I heard Abaven call up to be let into the gates. I made my way down to the closed gate as they let him through.

"Abaven," I said, "you are coming with me."

"When and where?" he asked, somewhat startled but not stopping on his way to deliver the report to the barracks. While we walked, I told him how I expected to use his limited water magic and his survival skills. He needed to know why he was going. "You can teach me more than just map making?"

"Probably," I said. "According to Eyvindr, there should be a few more spells you can use. It is just a matter of 'expanding your vocabulary.' So will you come?"

"Absolutely," he replied, "but I'll need some supplies. I don't own much except this." He gestured to what he was currently wearing, a lightweight, dark cloak and simple shirt and pants, hardly enough to protect him from anything other than unfriendly eyes.

"No matter," I told him, then I pulled out the disc Justain gave me.

"That's the king's crest," he said in awe. "He just gave that to you?"

"I guess this is just that important to him," I shrugged. "Tomorrow morning, we leave for the Northlands."

D

LYSS AND I WERE SITTING TOGETHER, as we had started to do after my return from Aranor, looking over the cliffs into the vast sea by her mother's grave. We let ourselves just be as we rested in each other's presence. She was leaning against me and was resting her head on my shoulder. The two of us began to talk more ever since she first brought me here. She had recounted some of her mother's stories to me, and I had little to tell her since she had known me since I was four days old, so I just listened.

Now that we had time, we had become much closer, often enjoying each other's presence. The sea breeze was strong enough to make its presence known, but gentle enough to be nothing more than a soft touch on the skin. As the sun was setting and reflecting off the glimmering shore, we knew it would be time for the evening meal soon.

"We should get going," Lyss broke the silence. "I'm getting a little hungry anyway." She stayed sitting. I looked over and saw she was keeping her eyes closed as well. That is when I decided I would pull a small prank on her.

"All right," I said and stood straight up, allowing her to just fall to the grass below, but she caught herself and was visibly upset with me. "What?" I said jokingly. "Didn't you say we should get going?" She stayed silent as I offered my hand to help her up. She took my hand, and I helped her up off the ground. We stood holding hands for just a brief moment before she let go and motioned for me to lead the way to the grand dining hall.

The walk through the labyrinth that was Dracadere was awkwardly quiet, though I did not quite mind that. I enjoyed being around her. She definitely had a much better sense of humor than her sister. She finally broke the silence, "Do you think it is going to be another quiet meal?"

"From what I've heard about Haven from your father, they should be gearing up for another battle soon. So that might come to the table," I proposed, "but seeing as they don't have a bridge over to Aranor anymore, it may be another quiet evening."

"At least it is silence for a good reason," Lyss noted. Then she attempted a mildly morbid joke, "You don't need *another* chance to die."

I was somewhat amused and let out a faint chuckle. "I know," I started. "I already have plenty." As the hallways became brighter, I knew we were approaching our destination. Surprisingly enough, we were the last ones to arrive. Ubel sat in the king's seat facing the main massive double doors at the end of the needlessly long table, and Princess Bellona sat to his left. I had thought that because no one had come to get us, we were going to be the early ones, but the two of them seemed to be deep into a quiet discussion when they noticed us come in.

"About time you showed up, Arinthian," Princess Bellona said, exaggerating her annoyance. I still was not quite sure why Princess Bellona refused to use my name; it was strange but not strange enough to call her out on it.

"Good evening, Drocan," Ubel said. "Take a seat, we have much to discuss about what you are going to be doing next."

I was surprised, "Haven is attacking again? Even without the bridge?"

"No," he replied shortly.

"Then what is happening?"

"Nothing," he said, leaving me even more confused. "And that is the problem. Normally, they send about a hundred or so soldiers a month, and we normally just scare them off. It is unlike the king to give up like this. He would build a bridge if it meant taking Aranor back, but he has not even sent as much as a scout in our direction, or at least one of the normal ones. Not even a tree has been grazed by an ax to even attempt the bridge."

"I feel like you are worried over nothing. Is it not a good thing that nothing is happening?" Lyss chimed in.

"It is actually horrible that they are not visibly planning something, Lyss," Princess Bellona attempted to clarify, "because it means that they are doing something we do not know about. King Justain operates like clockwork; if he is not attacking Aranor, he's going somewhere else. No armies have been amassed. Or if they have, we can't see them, and then we don't know how, when, or where they will attack."

"And you want me to do something about that... how?" I asked.

"You are going to scout through the villages, and the capital if you can," Ubel answered. "See if you can find anything about what they are planning and, the moment you do, come back here. The undead can only make it so far, and we only know what our scouting birds have seen, not what they've heard. You are the only one who can reasonably make it there and back."

"But how will I get over there?"

"Isn't it obvious?" Ubel asked. "Back the way you came, through the Arcane Ruins of Arinthia. Seeing as you are an Arinthian, the forest will allow you easy passage through the woods."

"And I'm going alone?"

"You wouldn't be alone if you hadn't killed your gous," Princess Bellona muttered.

Ubel sighed at his daughter's comment, "Yes," he clarified, "you will be going alone. But while you are over there, do your best to blend in with the main population."

"You want me to interact with the same people that hate me?"

"But they won't know you are Arinthian. What it comes down to for them is fear, that's why they hate you. They don't know what you are capable of, but I don't want you to be the same."

"What do you mean by that?" I asked, somewhat offended by my comparison to the humans of Haven.

"I think the real reason you hate the humans, is because you are afraid they will kill you. You are just as afraid of them as they are of you. You fight them out of fear, that's not right, if you find a real reason to fight them, that's fine. But how you are now, you'll never be able to protect anyone." He looked over to Lyss. "The aggression you displayed against Horus and the rest of the humans was unfounded.

"I don't want you to go over there just to scout them out, I want you to live among them, as I had, and find out for yourself why you fight. This may come back to bite me in the ass, but if you choose to stay with them, then so be it."

"You are that confident I will change my mind?" I said, still in disbelief.

"It is one of those moments where I hope I will be wrong," he replied smiling. "You will always be welcome back here, never forget that."

"When do I leave?" I asked exasperated, daunted by the journey to follow.

"Tomorrow morning," Princess Bellona answered.

"What?" Lyss interjected and stood up. "That's too soon! Why?"

"We need the information as soon as possible, especially if they are changing how they plan to attack us," Princess Bellona explained.

"Father, let—" Lyss started.

"No," Ubel stated firmly. "You are going to stay here."

"But—" she tried again.

"No," he said even more firm, but there was a strain in his voice. "I'm not letting that happen again, not to either of you."

"He could die! Is he not already one of us?" Lyss objected. Ubel sat silently for a moment. "Father!"

"I have faith he will be able to survive so long as he is not faced with Horus *and* a mob, but that is just because he wouldn't be trying to protect anyone else," Ubel said dryly. "Do you not trust him to do the same?"

Lyss quietly took her seat again and admitted, "I do."

"I'll be fine as long as I have this," I pulled out the hilt of my flame sword.

"About that," Ubel said, "you'll be blending in with the humans, not hunting them. You are not to use any magic unless your life is directly threatened. Being able to use just a little bit of magic is enough to get you ostracized, then hounded into the king's army or killed."

"So, I guess that means I'm taking a regular sword?"

"Of course," Ubel said. "I will also teach you how to string your bow, so you don't have to use magic for it. I will give you arrows as well but keep in mind they are not as sharp or accurate as the ones you are used to, so use them sparingly. Not to mention, I won't be able to give you too much funding. We only get a few coins from looting the soldiers that raid Aranor, and I was not exactly entitled to my grandfather's fortune."

"So, you want me in enemy territory with weak weaponry and no funds so I can learn a lesson?"

"And get us some info, yes," Princess Bellona confirmed. "You can still use your Arinthian armor, but I would recommend using a cloak as well, it is more believable for a traveler to be in a cloak and light armor than just light armor." She was the only one who had touched her food during the entire conversation.

"I'll give you the wallet tomorrow," Ubel said. "As long as you don't get cheated for prices, I think we have enough to supply you for a month of food and lodging. You might not need funding for one of those if you hunt. Either way, that should be more than enough money as long as you don't get into any form of trouble."

"I am still not sure I fully agree with your plan, but it will be done," I said. "I hope to return soon with good news."

The rest of the meal was relatively quiet, and when we had all finished, we went our separate ways except for Lyss. She chose to wait for me and walk with me. "Please don't be long," she begged me as I escorted her back to her room. "Please come back."

"I promise I will," I replied. "Always." I knew I was going to miss spending time with her, but this was going to be a long journey, and I would just have to get used to that. Hopefully, neither of us would get used to it; hopefully, I'd be back before either of us knew it.

DAY 57

H

"WE'RE ALMOST THERE!" Abaven called from the front of our little pack. It had taken us three days on horseback to get here by midday, so rest once we got there would be well-earned. The king had loaned us some of his finest horses, but even they could only sprint for so long.

"Wow," said Lady Erione, awestruck with the beauty of the stone-faced mountain and the river that cascaded in a loud crashing roar from some distant point into the basin beneath. The river itself was shimmering in pure daylight and was as blinding as it was beautiful. The mountains around us varied in shades of gray and red as they stretched across the horizon as far as anyone could see. They loomed over the borders of the North, warding off any conquerors of the lands beyond them.

The air had gotten significantly colder as we moved north. Apparently, backing up the king's claim, an enchantment had been placed on the Northlands to make it forever frozen to deter armies from moving through it. At least, that is what Abaven had told me.

I had expected a grand fortress up here, but in the distance, there was only what seemed to be a small outpost with nothing but a shack and a couple guards lounging in some chairs set next to the shack. It was quite out of place, considering the majesty of the environment around it. One of the guards finally noticed us, shot straight up, and readied her bow. "Halt!" she shouted. We stopped our horses instantly and waited quite a distance away for her to continue. "What business do you have in the North?"

I dismounted my horse and began to approach the guards. The second guard stood up and readied his spear and echoed the first, "Halt! What business do you have in the North?" Suddenly, an arrow arrived at my feet, enforcing the order to stop where I stood.

"I am under orders of King Justain to retrieve an item from an acquaintance of his," I replied as I held my hands up. "I was under the impression you have a letter explaining our situation."

They looked at me with suspicion, "We never received one," the female guard said. She readied another arrow, "Do you have any other proof?"

"If you would allow me to get closer, I have a couple of things that could work," I stated.

"Drop your sword first," The guard with the spear ordered. "Then you can show us."

I removed my sword from its sheath and placed it on the ground. Then I began to approach them. I reached into my pocket and pulled out the crest and the letter I was to give to the king in the Northlands. "This is the king's crest, and this is the letter I am supposed to give to the acquaintance of the king." When I got to the outpost, they took the crest and letter from my hand and inspected it with awe.

"This really is the king's crest. Just what is your relationship to the king?" the male guard asked.

"Jerum!" I called back to the rest of the group. Immediately, Jerum dismounted his own horse and came marching toward us with perfect posture and composure. The guards tensed up as he approached, and the female archer dropped her bow, knelt, and bowed her head just before the male guard followed suit. Jerum finally removed his helmet.

"Sir Jerum," the female guard, "my lord. It really is you."

"Of course, it is," Jerum said, irritated at the delay. "And believe it or not this man is my superior for this mission."

They turned toward me and apologized, "I'm sorry, I didn't know you outranked one of the Crown Guard."

"Not many do," I replied with understanding. "It is a fairly recent development."

"One I'm still not too happy with," Jerum continued. "And please stand up already, this is no way to converse." They obeyed his order instantly and rose to their feet.

I gestured for the rest of the group to come over. "We got it sorted out," I shouted to them. Lady Erione led Abaven, Arthur, and the dismounted horses to the shack. "Ah, I almost forgot. *Icerepin tebucomi icecurom islucia*," I said aloud, the sword rose from the ground and flew into my hands. I placed it back in its sheath.

"Just who are you?" the male guard asked. "Are you an Arinthian?"

"What kind of question is that?" Abaven asked, vexed with how my spell was not enough evidence for my Arinthian status.

"Relax, Abaven," I said, putting a hand out. I turned back to the guards and introduced myself and the others, "I am Horus, a new member of the Crown Guard. You, of course, know Sir Jerum and the rude man would be Abaven," then I pointed to Lady Erione. "This is the king's healer, Lady Erione," then to Arthur, "and Arthur Calidan," the guards picked up on that name and seemed disgusted.

"What is he doing here?" the female guard asked.

"What does it matter to you?" Arthur asked in reply. This was the most agitated I had ever seen him. He was hot-headed, I knew that, but this was a new level of indignation.

"Why are you still using that name?" she asked again. "You were removed from our family. You have no right to go by that name."

"You are a Calidan?" I asked her.

"More than he is," she spat. "I am Lucile, the third heir to the Calidan household." She stared murderously at Arthur as she spoke, "He was removed for a reason, why is he with you?"

"Because I trust him," I replied. "And that should be all that matters. Now if you could stop trying to kill him with your gaze, that would be appreciated. We are going to rest here for the day, and I will need him for my expedition in the Northlands, the more alive he is the better."

"Very well," Lucile agreed, "I suppose if you trust filth like him that is not my business. The barracks are inside the shack, and if I were you, I would leave your horses here on this side of the mountain."

I gave a short nod of understanding, then turned to the others. "Abaven, Arthur, Lady Erione, and Jerum," I started, "unpack our horses, we will leave them here. After that, get some rest." They all agreed and turned to do as they were told, the male guard went to assist them in my stead. "Lady Calidan—" I was attempting to be extra polite to earn her trust as well, but she cut me off.

"Dame." She stated simply.

"Excuse me?"

"I earned and *kept* my knighthood," she looked disdainfully at Arthur. "I'm a 'dame,' not a 'lady' and you should refer to me as such, I don't care what rank you are," she said, folding her arms, "because unlike Arthur, I actually am proud to uphold my name."

"Fair enough, Dame Calidan," I began again. "What would it take for Arthur to be redeemed and welcomed back into his own family?"

"At this point," she said, "the only honor he could bring us now would be his own death. If he wants to be a Calidan, he has to die for the king. It is the only price that could match the disgrace he brought on the name."

"That's... unfortunate," I sighed. I walked to rejoin the rest of my group. Seeing as we were about to enter the Northlands, I decided that moment was the best time to start teaching Abaven those extra words he would need for our survival. I saw everyone was consolidating as much food and water in our bags as they possibly could. Abaven was unsurprisingly already done with his own bags and was helping Jerum with his own, seeing as he packed an egregious amount of unnecessary baggage.

"I don't even understand how you managed to not kill your horse with all this weight," Abaven noted.

"She's a strong horse," Jerum smirked.

"Leave him be, Abaven," I said, stifling a chuckle. "I think it is time for you to learn a few more tricks than just map making, follow me."

"Understood, sir," Abaven obeyed. I led Abaven to the nearby pool at the base of the mountain and sat down near the water. "Well?"

"That's not what I would call it," I motioned to the nearby water. He did not laugh. So, I continued, "Sit down first, we have some other things to go over before I start teaching you the words. Eyvindr tells me that you have the potential to use more magic, you just need to refresh a little bit more frequently. Relax for a moment and take in the air around us."

He obeyed my orders and sat even closer to the water than I did. "I think this is the first time I have been able to rest without sleeping," Abaven noticed.

"Good," I said. "You've earned it, that's for sure. Take a deep breath in. Let it fill your chest and extend through to your entire body before letting it all out. Eyvindr tells me that being near your element helps you recharge even faster. I guess that makes it easy for me."

"So that is why you chose the river pool," Abaven guessed while continuing his deep breathing.

"That, and I have something I want to test," I said.

"He is already as well-rested as he can be, his body won't accept any more magic, it is entering as fast as it is leaving him, he can try it now," Eyvindr said.

"Perfect," I acknowledged Eyvindr, then I turned my attention back to Abaven. "Repeat these words and focus on the pool behind you: '*Icerepin nauga tubaal igocla iveeno.*'"

Abaven echoed my words perfectly. A massive chunk of ice about the size of a horse appeared in the center of the pond and began to float down the river before getting stuck from its size. It was nearly the size of a tree. "I did that?" Abaven remarked, his lips remaining parted after he spoke. "I did that!"

"Try not to make it as big next time," I said. "We'll be using those small chunks of snow and freezing them into bricks to build ourselves a few shelters in the Northlands. We could help you out, but this will be much more efficient. Now rest again, I think you spent your entire pool of magic, but you'll need to do that quite frequently once we are beyond these mountains. We will need to go over how to control your output, but that's it."

D

"REMEMBER, DON'T USE YOUR NAME while you are in Haven," Lyss reminded me for what felt like the hundredth time. "The less people know about you, the better." She accompanied me throughout the entirety of the barren wastes of what used to be Arinthia. There were a few scattered pillars among the wastes, but the land was otherwise completely empty with nothing but dust for as far as the eye could see. The forest stood in stark contrast as a border of life.

"So, you are finally ready for me to leave and go to Haven, huh," I joked. We had already been at the border of the forest of the Arcane Ruins for a whole day, but we decided to stay here in order to just have a few more moments together before the long road ahead. Ubel was concerned she would follow me into Haven and originally would not allow her to come with me at all, but then he allowed it, or at the very least hadn't sent a search party yet. "He's gonna be furious," I said, "at both of us probably. Either that or just me."

"I'll tell him you begged me to sneak out and follow you," she taunted.

"And you are comfortable living with that lie while I'm gone?" I asked.

"Of course!" Lyss smiled, then she hugged my arm even tighter. "It will be so much funnier once you get back, but of course father is going to believe me no matter what."

"I wouldn't be so sure about that." I turned to hug her fully, then I whispered in her ear, "After all, I did see him watch you leave Dracadere after me."

"No, you didn't!" she objected while pushing me away.

"Maybe. Maybe not," I said with a shrug. I did see him on the eastern balcony as Lyss rode up to me a couple of days ago, "But you'll find out once you get back."

"So, you are finally ready for me to go home as well?" she baited.

"Not at all, but I am more scared of what your father would do to me if you died under my watch." I stood up and held out my hand to help her up from underneath the tree we were leaning against. Her horse was not too far away, grazing on the grass at the edge of the forest a little further south than us. My own horse was near hers, but it would not be cutting through the forest with me. I whistled our horses over to us and helped her mount the giant, at least compared to her, black steed she was gifted by her father and handed her the reigns to my own dark brown horse. "Ride fast, Lyss," I told her, "I'll see you soon enough." I urged her and the horses back to Dracadere and felt my heart sink into my chest as she rode away, staring back as often as I did.

Once I could no longer see her face in the blinding whirling winds of the desert sand, I turned toward the remains of the Arinthian forest and checked what I had with me. I had my personal bow, a steel sword, a knife, and about 20 arrows, but if it came down to a desperate situation, I could remove the string from my bow and use my magic. Hopefully, it would not come to that. I had a few days of rations and a bag of gold in terms of other equipment but not much else.

The only things I got to keep for this mission that used my own damn blood were the bow and the armor. Now that I was going on a longer journey, I really appreciated the lightweight nature of the armor and the cloak I was given to hide from the weather and dangerous, peering eyes.

The forest was more daunting than I remember it being when I was born there. The trees were wide and tall, casting shadows far beyond the border; the interior of the forest was almost pitch black from the leaves blocking any form of light from entering.

"How in the name of Arinthia does Ubel get through here? With that caravan of his no less," I thought aloud. I took my first step into the forest, and the trees seemed to move out of my way. Underneath, where one of the trees used to be, was the half-decayed body and face of someone I had seen in that caravan. "So, Ubel was right," I said in awe and some disgust. "The forest only lets those with Arinthian blood through." I continued walking as the forest opened a path deeper back toward the Arcane Ruins, as Ubel called them. The trees behind me began to consolidate again, and my path out was blocked off. It was now completely dark where I stood despite it being midday.

"*Icerepin*," I said aloud while finishing the spell in my mind to generate a small flame in my hand so I could see where I was stepping. The trees may move, but the rocks and ground did not.

The flickering flame in my palm only shook when a strong wind broke through the canopy of the trees and illuminated the area around me with a soft, warm glow. Without any other light, the forest was somewhat haunting, with all the creatures I could hear moving around. The beasts' steps were heavy and followed by hisses or clicking growls, and soon the sound indicated I was surrounded. However, they would not stand a chance if they did anything, and they were about to find out.

The first one leapt to attack from behind me, so I grabbed the dagger Ubel had given me and stabbed it mid-jump. "*Itumo taarruce itomrec*," I ordered my magic. And it completely incinerated the beast, leaving nothing but ashes and a few burning leaves behind. I never knew exactly what kind of creature it was. After a moment, those leaves were also burned to nothing, and I started my flame again. "*Icerepin*," I said aloud again and resumed walking. The sounds of those creatures that were following me through the forest grew distant as they retreated back to wherever they came from.

"That worked brilliantly," I said to myself. I was uncomfortable with the complete silence and darkness of these ancient woods, so I looked around for any trees with relatively low branches so I could climb above the canopy. I found a half-fallen tree leaning into another tree that stood firm and strong. None of the branches were low, but some were definitely within reach of the top of that fallen tree. "Perfect," I said, "that will work."

I carefully maneuvered my way to the tree and cautiously began to walk up the slope it gave me as it shifted beneath me on occasion. Once I arrived at the top of the trunk, I readied myself to jump to the branches above. *Here goes nothing*, I thought. I pushed off the fallen tree with all of my might, jumped, and successfully grabbed the branch of the large tree. After a moment of me dangling from the branch, I heard the tree I was previously standing on croak, crack, then fall into the dirt. "Up it is," I agreed with the forest. I wove myself through the dense branches of the tree into the upper canopy to peer above it all.

The view above the canopy was breathtakingly serene. Before me was a sea of deep green leaves graced by the touch of the setting sun behind me. Ahead of me, I could see a break in the forest and what appeared to be the top of the tower of the Arcane Ruins, where I was born. "I am almost there," I muttered. I took a few breaths of fresher air before ducking back beneath the canopy and making my way toward the clearing of the Arcane Ruins. I decided to stick to moving among the branches instead of the ground just in case there was ever another creature wanting to attack me. I just wanted to avoid combat with anything and it would not hurt to get used to trees.

It was tricky at first to get used to the new arboreal environment around me, but it certainly served an advantage. I was able to move safely, quietly, and quickly among the branches instead of stumbling among the rocks and roots of the trees and the beasts below me. As I drew closer to the Arcane Ruins the breaks between the trees got wider and larger, and more light broke through the canopy allowing me to extinguish my familiar flame. The light of the night stars illuminated more than my flame could for the first time in a while. The next branch was further than any of the others I had jumped to before, but it still seemed doable, so I readied myself and leapt, but I missed the branch I was aiming for.

"*Savu*," I swore the moment before my gut hit the branch below and I fell flat on my back on the roots of the tree below.

My body was aching, but I knew I only had a little more distance to cover so I pushed myself up much to the disdain of my entire physical existence.

"Good job," I sarcastically told myself while gritting my teeth, "that could not have gone better." I was wincing with every step, so I paused for a moment and stood straight up to stretch my back in an attempt to relieve some pain somewhere, but it only made it worse. "I will not let myself die doing something so stupid," I said aloud, there was something comforting in speaking as such. "Only take jumps you know you can make," I commanded myself. I spent the rest of the time walking to the Arcane Ruins rubbing my back and rolling my neck whenever I could.

Soon enough, the clearing of the Arcane Ruins was before me. The tower that signified the border of Arinthia was looming over me, the moon casting the tower's shadow over me. "Finally," I said. I wandered around the base of the tower for a moment, looking for where I had entered before and found those first robes. "There you are," I exclaimed when I found it. I placed my hand on the wall and uttered, "*Icerepin ipare,*" and once more, the bricks fell into the room, and I fell in with them. I crawled a little deeper into the tower so my legs would not be crushed by the bricks as they replaced themselves to seal the tower off again. The bricks reformed the hole, and I was left in the dark again.

Then I suddenly felt something I had not felt in a while. "Oh no," I uttered. I turned onto my side and vomited flames again. "What the——," I started, but they came out again. I had been using magic almost the entire day; why was this happening now? Then it clicked with me: it was the ruins. They were feeding me so much magical energy, and without a gous to empty it out, I was left with no other option but to keep using magic. After vomiting one last time I started a spell, "*Icerepin ingnis icounten.*" I figured I would have to sustain this even as I slept.

I thought back to when I was here last time and wondered to myself if Horus had left anything above. I forced myself up again and looked for a way through the ceiling above me. Seeing as I could not find one, I decided I would make one. I focused my attention on the wooden ceiling and chanted, "*Itumo tebucomi itomrec iveeno.*" The flame I was using for light moved to the wood above me and burned a decently sized hole through the ceiling; a couple of books fell through the hole.

I climbed up through the hole to see what else was up there. I winced as my hands touched the recently burned wood. I checked my palms, and though they now carried ash in their creases, they were otherwise fine. In this room were cabinets filled with clothes and a couple of bookshelves. I opened one up and found it written in Acelin script. It was simple enough to read and was a simple history as recorded by the Arinthians. I opened it and read for some time before drifting into sleep, my mind still full of the legends of the ancient Arinthians.

DAY 58

H

THE TUNNEL LUCILE LED US to was cold and dark. A strong wind howled through it and pushed us back into the land of Haven as if the tunnel itself refused to allow us passage. The chilling aura of the passage made it feel like it was already the middle of winter. The tunnel was marked with man-made carvings of flowers and Arinthian runes.

"No one has been able to pass through in ages; the wind just pushes them back out. No one from the other side has come either," Dame Calidan explained. "Even if you have the king's permission, that does not mean you have the permission of the mountain." She stared up to the peak and said, "Some say they are alive. That the mountains themselves guard the border, I say they are cursed. That damned Ubel probably has something to do with this."

"I wouldn't be so sure," I muttered under my breath as I approached the markings on the wall. I ran my hand over the carvings of flowers and felt the deep cuts into the stone. Then I turned my eyes toward the Arinthian runes.

"Actually, those are more ancient," Eyvindr told me. "It is possible someone cursed this passage. It reads '*Tesvun icemmenntur icounten.*' it is a spell to constantly increase the wind in the tunnel!" he exclaimed. "And quite a simple one to break at that. Just say '*Iveeno*' and the spell should stop."

"*Iveeno*," I echoed. I began to walk back into the tunnel, despite the continual howl, but was immediately blasted back again. "Any other ideas, Eyvindr?"

"Who's that?" Dame Calidan asked.

"I've learned to ignore that," Lady Erione answered. "It's never important to anyone but him." I nodded to confirm the somewhat painful accuracy of her statement.

"I see," Dame Calidan said, straightening her back. "I told you, no one can get through, the mountain refuses to allow anyone through."

"Let me borrow something to mark the walls with: a knife, a chisel, anything really," I requested. "I have an idea."

"I think I would like to see you knocked off your feet again," she hopefully jested.

"Please," I begged. "Just obey your orders."

"Yes, sir," she said, rolling her eyes. Then she handed me a dagger marked with a large "C." Dame Calidan refused to let go for a moment before she let me know with the deadliest intent, "Be careful with it; it was my grandfather's, and I'll be damned if it breaks with you."

"I understand," I comforted her, she immediately let go of the knife.

Eyvindr, despite being the all-knowing being surrounding me, was not always the quickest wit, as he only just now realized what I was doing. "I see," he began. "It is the mountain's spell, not ours. Our words mean nothing."

"Exactly," I said aloud. "Now how do I write it?"

"I'll show you," Eyvindr said, then suddenly everything went blank for a moment. When I reopened my eyes, I was presented with a world empty of the physical but filled with everything in terms of knowledge, "It is about time I imbued you with the knowledge of how to read and write your own native language, it might take a while, but it is much faster here in this realm than in the physical. This arcane dimension is accelerated in terms of time," he explained, "and it will allow me to directly input knowledge into your mind." Suddenly, I felt a rush of wind, one I had not felt since I was born, the memory of which faded the moment it was revealed. The knowledge of Arinthians' runes, of Acelin, rushed through me with the wind. I gasped for air and woke back up in the real world on the ground.

"What just happened?" Lady Erione asked. "Are you okay? You fainted for a moment."

"Yes," I said, "I am fine. Eyvindr just had something to show me."

I stood back up and began to carve, or rather scratch, onto the stone. The line drawn above the runes ended with a small circle drawn on it. I extended the line, then drew a perpendicular one at its end, representing the word "*Iveeno*" in a simple single stroke. The moment I had finished writing it, the wind from the tunnel ceased and remained still before natural winds started to move through it.

"At last," I said as I relaxed my shoulders from writing above my head. I turned to Dame Calidan, "Your job might start to get tougher. I don't know what might start coming through here. We should be back soon enough. But don't wait up." She remained stone-cold, disinterested in my attempt at humor.

"I don't intend to," she said, her eyes feeling like they were penetrating my very soul. It was rather haunting. I handed her her dagger back before her eyes could finish contemplating my death.

"So, we can pass through now?" Lady Erione asked for clarification.

"It seems so," I confirmed. Then I called out to the rest of the group, "We are going! Get over here!"

"Finally," Dame Calidan said, letting out a forceful breath, "maybe now Arthur can walk to his death." I did not like her at all. I did not like any of what I was seeing with his family. I had to wonder if his entire family shared her opinion of him, if any of them thought that he had a chance to restore his inheritance.

"The sooner I'm away from you the better," Arthur agreed.

I sighed with exhaustion at the sound of their near-constant bickering. "We are leaving. Everyone, follow me. We don't know what could be in there right now." I led the group to the opening in the mountain and realized at last how dark the inside of the mountain was. A few steps in and we would already be blind. We needed a source of light. "Abaven!" I called back. "Get me a torch."

"Right away, Sir!" he replied immediately.

Within a moment, I was holding a lit torch, and we continued on our way through the dark, cold, and dry tunnels. We shared stories as we walked to stay awake. The cold we had felt back at the outpost was nothing compared to how we felt after passing the halfway point. The chilling air that flowed into the tunnels was relentlessly cold. It was somehow colder than the winter air I felt outside, and it nearly extinguished our fire on multiple occasions. The air felt thinner as well, as the tunnel was long and definitely sloped steeply upward on a few occasions. Then, out of seemingly nowhere, the wall of a small cliff stood before us.

Lady Erione stopped dead in her tracks with a realization, "I... can't..." she attempted to say, but she was out of breath and fell to the ground before she could finish.

"Lady... Erione..." Jerum exclaimed as he attempted to lessen the burden of her fall, but he spoke just as breathlessly and broken as Lady Erione, and he collapsed as well.

Abaven and Arthur were the only two still standing, and they refused to speak. They were the only two that were used to being quiet. Abaven pulled out his rope from his pack and pointed to me, then to the rope, then to the top of the cliff.

I nodded in understanding. I walked over to him, and he traded the rope for the torch. I returned to the base of the wall and said, "*Icerepin,*" I began, my breath felt heavy, and I began to feel dizzy, but I needed to complete the flight spell.

"Don't speak another word," Eyvindr told me. "The moment the second word is spoken, whatever is here will drain your very breath. It must be some kind of curse to deter those that just pushed through the winds. Finish the spell with your mind."

I almost spoke aloud as I was accustomed to but caught myself before my mouth opened again. I thought my questions to him instead. *How? And will the others be alright?*

"Finish the spell by thinking of the words instead of saying them aloud. '*Icerepin*' is the only one that needs to be spoken and lucky you, you already said it," Eyvindr clarified. "As for the others, they might need to rest for the rest of the day once we get out of here, then they will hopefully be fine."

I began to think through the rest of the words. *Ilatteve icounten*, I finished, and I began to levitate through the air and made my way up the wall. Once I was above the wall, I thought, *iveeno*, and the spell stopped and set me down on top of the wall. I turned to look at Abaven and Arthur, they had seen me use spells before, but flight was new to them, as they were completely shocked. I think Abaven just assumed I would climb. Despite going up even more, the air felt thicker, as if I was back at the outpost.

"This must be where the curse breaks," Eyvindr explained, "but let's not risk it."

I agree, I thought back to him. I would not be able to use a spell again if the curse was still active up here. Then I let the rope down and motioned for Abaven to come first. He followed and made quick work scaling the wall with the rope. Arthur soon followed. He was not quite as graceful as Abaven was with his ascent, but he made it up anyway. I motioned that I was going back down to get Lady Erione and Jerum and that they would need to pull me back up, they nodded in understanding. I was able to make quick work of it with their help. Now that we were all up the wall, I motioned that I would carry Jerum, Abaven would guide us with the torch, and Arthur would carry Lady Erione. Jerum and Lady Erione's breaths were irregular, as if they were fighting off being drowned in their own air.

We spent the rest of the walk in silence and were lucky enough that the remainder was a flat path making it easier to walk through. I saw the white light of the Northlands as the chilling wind combined with fresh snow burned my face with piercing cold. Once we were out of the tunnel, I decided it was safe to speak.

"Abaven, quickly make us a shelter against the wall of this mountain, and Arthur, help him out. We will rest here for the day." They nodded, then I continued, "And good job to both of you recognizing the pattern and keeping quiet. There was some kind of curse drawing breath after spoken words. They'll be fine with rest; we just have to give them time."

"Actually, Sir," Arthur said. I could hear the smile creep into his voice, his definite features hidden behind a scarf, "I just had nothing to say, other than I was glad everyone shut up for once." His smile was incredibly smug, "I just figured that could wait."

Abaven quickly formed many ice bricks for us to use, and Arthur patted the bricks together with the thick wet snow of the Northlands. The shelter was built before the sun set below the distant horizon, just in time.

D

I WOKE UP WITH THE sun directly above me, the sunlight seeping its way through the cracks in the wooden ceiling. I pushed the books off of me and stood up to stretch my back and neck. I groaned to myself as I tried to pop my neck, knowing I would regret sleeping on the ground without a cushion. Looking back up through the ceiling, I noticed I desperately needed to get moving if I was to make use of the daylight.

Getting out of the tower was a little more difficult than it was getting in, mostly because I had to drop a decent distance before I could even try to leave. I repeated the words from before to open the magic opening at the base of the tower and immediately started to make my way toward Haven. I was still sore from yesterday, so progress was slow. Soon enough, I found another tree with thick enough branches to not worry about falling off in my sleep and took a short break in the branches before continuing through the dense forest.

Just before sundown, a small village came into view, or rather the smoke from their fires and huts. "Finally," I sighed. I followed the smoke and picked up my pace in hopes of a well-earned rest. I had been keeping a flame lit and following me for the sake of draining my magic constantly so that I would not vomit from any excess. The village drew closer, and a thought occurred. I needed to go to the other side of the village; they would not expect strangers from the forest to be human. I groaned at how right I knew I was. It was going to be an even longer journey than my body anticipated. I sat in the leaves of a tree near the village and observed for a moment to see if I could come up with any information about them or why I would be arriving so late to their meager establishment.

During my survey, I spotted the hazy image of what I could only assume to be a lord's castle some distance to the south. They seemed like a quiet people leading quiet lives, they seemed to grow wheat and potatoes, but I could not find out much else. I had to get into the walled-off village soon while guards were still watching. They grew the wheat in the fields just outside the pointed logs that fortified the village all around, only allowing one way in and one way out. I suppose I did not have a choice in my entry point either way. My rations were going to run out soon, so I needed to restock, and being within guarded walls again would be nice.

I descended the tree and ordered my flame, "*Iveeno,*" and it was extinguished immediately. I ducked low and made my way carefully through the fields of wheat so that I would not make too much noise or draw any attention to myself. The gates were still open. *Lucky me*, I thought, but I still had to go further down the road before I could turn back and look like a traveler from the kingdom.

I made sure guards were not watching and leapt from the wheat grain and ran as far as I could before stopping to gather my breath. I did not want to look like I was just sprinting when I approached the gate. The sun was almost finished setting beneath the distant horizon, so I approached the gate with confidence.

I walked like I belonged in the village, but without even looking, I could feel the suspicious glares of the guards. "Stop him!" a guard from above called out. Instantly the guards at the base of the gate's open doors crossed their halberds to block my path. Their faces were unchanged. They firmly blocked my path but looked forward instead of at each other or even me. "What business do you have here?" the same guard asked.

"I am a simple traveler seeking refuge here for the night that is all. My business is elsewhere," I replied. It was not a lie, but my business was the entirety of the Kingdom of Haven.

The guard was still suspicious of me, "And where is your destination?"

This was a tougher lie. If I said the Arcane ruins or even the forest surrounding it, they would have viewed me as mad and expected me to continue in that direction tomorrow morning. If I said Haven, they would have wondered why I was coming from the east and why I would stop here.

"I'm going north," I said with as much confidence as I could muster. "Just before nightfall, I saw the smoke of this village and decided I would like to rest here for the night. I am running low on rations as well and need to restock."

It seemed he believed my lie, but he still wanted to pry more, "And what business do you have in the North?"

"My business is my concern, not yours," I said bluntly. I would make other humans like me, but I did not care about this one. He was too intrusive.

He stared intently, ever more suspicious of me, but at the same time, unable to refute my claim. "Fair enough, but we will be watching you," he sneered. "Let him through."

"Thank you," I said. "I promise I won't cause any trouble."

"You are wise not to," he agreed. The guards removed the halberds from my path and resumed their position as vigilant guards of the village.

"What is this village called anyway?" I asked the pair of guards. They were both young.

"Rascur," one of them replied in a tired and dry voice. "Now move along. We are closing the gates."

"I was just in time," I mumbled to myself. The atmosphere inside the walls was drastically different than what it seemed from the outside. At least near the gates, there was an incredible amount of light coming from most of the huts as they were trying to sell food or their crafted weapons or baskets. I assumed what I saw before must have been the more residential area compared to this place.

In the backs of some of the shops, I saw beds, but I think the farmers were deeper in the village, so they were easiest to protect. It was not even a real gradual change from the bustling city-like atmosphere to the calm and quiet homes of a rural town. After about six stores on either side, the rest of the village was pitch black, all of the lights were extinguished, and the entire area was silent. I approached one of the shopkeepers and asked, "Is there a place I could stay tonight?"

"The street," he spat, then suddenly changed his attitude. "Or if you buy something and have some coin left over..." he suggested eyeing my coin pouch. This vendor was selling fletching supplies, including a few knives designed to saw and refine branches and sticks for arrow shafts. I was not particularly interested in learning any fletching skills. I had not even been required to fire my bow yet.

"I'll check somewhere else," I said and began to walk away, but he grabbed my arm and did not let go.

"Wait," he pleaded. "You can sleep here tonight for five copper pieces, but

I can't go any lower." He looked at my full quiver. "I'll even throw in enough to make one arrow, just in case you ever need it," he offered. "I don't get a lot of business. I just need something," he explained.

I remained silent for a moment before I said, "Let go of my arm." He did instantly, and I brushed my arm off. His hands were sweaty from being near the torches, and his large size did not help either. "How much food do you have?" I asked.

"Plenty for myself," he admitted, "but not much more."

I sighed and reached into my coin pouch, pulling out a single gold coin. I had not expected it to be this cheap. I held the coin up, and his jaw dropped. The coin was from Haven, just not earned. I made an offer to him.

"You can have this if you keep your current offer and go get me enough rations for a few more days, bread, water, nuts, I need it all, salted meat if you can. Also, you feed me tonight and tomorrow morning before I leave. This will be enough, right?"

"Of course!" he exclaimed. "Go make yourself at home!"

He gestured for me to go into the shop and directed me up a ladder to a shallow bedroom that I had to bend over to walk around. As I rested my eyes in the dark room that was really more of a loft than a bedroom, the shopkeeper returned with a completely filled sack with salted meats, bread, and filled water skins. "I'll be closing the shop for the night, then I can make you dinner," he said, "but here are the rations you asked for." He set the rations by the opening to the ladder.

"Thank you," I said. Ubel was right, they were nice, so long as you were not Arinthian; however, that did not make them any smarter or less greedy. Based on the weight of the sack, he must have pocketed some of the change from the gold coin. I estimated about twenty silver was unaccounted for. Not to mention he abandoned his shop entirely while he went out to get me supplies. He really was not the most thoughtful shopkeeper. Good news was I think he liked me, or at the very least the money, and I knew I would be able to come back to him in an emergency.

I sat up as much as I could, got out of the bed, passed the rations as I went down to the first floor, and found the remaining silver. He used it to buy some expensive-looking cuts of meat and some vegetables to go with it. It was almost as luxurious food as I ate at Ubel's castle, and he bought enough for both of us. I imagined he was planning a similar meal for the morning.

"Why do you have that bed up there?" I asked, simply curious about who would be able to live in the attic regularly.

"My son used to live up there until he joined the king's army," he answered, but I could not tell if he was proud of his son or concerned. "You'd be welcome to sleep up there any time," he added. "He followed in his grandfather's footsteps, not mine. I have not seen him in so long, but he is still writing me letters every now and then."

I thought he would make for a convenient supply of information and thus a much simpler solution than going all the way to Haven.

"So, what is the army up to anyway?" I asked, as casually as I could.

"He does not really write about that too much," the shopkeeper said, boiling water and adding ingredients. He was wasting valuable cuts of meat in that stew. "He did say there was an Arinthian in the army now, though, full-blown one at that. None of the half- or sixteenth-blood ones that are already there, but a full Arinthian! Can you believe that? I thought they went extinct, for good reason, too. With all that magic, they can only be dangerous."

"I don't know if I can believe that," I lied. "An Arinthian? Are there any more?"

"My son only mentioned the one," he replied. "So, I don't think so, but apparently, the king sent that Arinthian on a suicide mission. Then when the Arinthian came back, he was sent away again."

"Do you know where?"

"He didn't say, but he said that the king has requested more troops and builders oddly enough, but that isn't really news now, is it? They'll probably all be sent to their deaths at Aranor."

"What is your son's name?"

"Petrus, he's in the Crown Guard. Earned the title himself and his own name. Ramsguard, they call him now. He doesn't give any orders except to the rest of the Crown Guard. The last battle he was in was the battle they lost Aranor," his face drew grim. "I'm just glad he survived."

DAY 60

H

I SAW IT. A gargantuan tower surrounded by equally large stone walls. Between the flash flurries that blinded our entire group, I was able to catch a glimpse of our destination, the North King's Castle. I was leading the group through the frosted tundra that was the Northlands, following a map that poorly described the layout of the land or the location of the castle; I was glad I finally saw the landmark. It seemed to just appear out of nowhere, and we were nearly there.

"Everyone pause for a moment," I ordered the group in the frigid cold. I had to make sure everyone was still with us, seeing as it was easy to get lost in the constant blizzard. I did a quiet roll call, making a quick count of all the visible figures contrasting the white snow in their dark cloaks. I was still in my heavy armor and helmet, but I could feel the weight of the snow beginning to pile up while I was standing still here.

"Alright, everyone, we are almost there, just a little while longer, and we can rest within the North King's gates. Stay close and stay awake," I announced, raising my voice over the howling winds.

"Let's hurry then," Lady Erione called out. "I don't know if I can endure this cold any longer."

She was shivering underneath a silvery hood and kept an arm against her chest. The cloak she had on was joined by leather strings and the emblem of the king. It suited her dark hair nicely. Her face was red from the biting cold, and she was using her other hand to pull the hood down over her face whenever the wind tried to pull it off her head. Her black hair, out of a braid for the first time in likely ages, was flowing out the front of her hood and shuffled with any movement of the wind. When she woke up yesterday from the curse, she was still out of breath but recovered quickly.

"I may find it difficult as well!" Jerum called out. His armor was just as heavy as mine, but he did not have the benefit of a gous helping him carry it. I admired his strength. He woke up before Lady Erione and recovered even faster, but if he was exhausted now, there was a high chance of anyone collapsing at any moment.

"Abaven!" I called out. "Tie us all together with the rope. That way, we can keep track if anyone falls. Now would be the worst time for anyone to fall behind." He obeyed my orders without saying a word; he did not like to spend his breath when he knew he did not need to. Once he finished, I motioned for the group to continue moving forward with me.

We arrived outside the gates in what seemed like no time, with me dragging the entire group along. The gates were huge, daunting, black iron, and suspiciously unguarded. Not even the watchtowers were manned. From the outside of the mountainous gates, the city seemed deserted, just like the rest of the area around it.

"Hello?" I called out to see if anyone was merely hiding from the storm, but I got no reply. I turned to the group behind me. "Jerum," I said, and he drew near from somewhere beyond my short-range vision. "Help me with the gate; we are going to pull it open."

"But Horus!" he attempted to dispute. "Shouldn't we wait for—"

"We don't have time! Now get up here!"

The two of us latched onto the end of one of the doors and pulled with all of our might. The snow was completely detrimental to our efforts. I started to kick as much snow as I could from the door's path and asked that Jerum do the same. We finally got the door to budge, but the door was heavy and refused to move much more. I screamed with all my might as I tried to pull even more, but the door would not move.

"Damnit!" I exclaimed. I untied myself from the rest of the group. With a frustrated breath, I forced the spell between my teeth and freezing jaw, "*Icerepin ilatteve icounten.*" I brought myself up and over the gate. The inside streets of the town were completely deserted. There were no guards anywhere along the wall, not even lying down beneath the ramparts. I dropped behind the gate, the archway behind the gate was pure stone and the ground was relatively clear of snow.

"Jerum, I'm going to push this door open, and you are going to pull. On three." I counted off, then pushed my entire weight on the door and shoved with my feet. After a few moments, with our combined might, the doorway fell open. I was relieved that my idea worked, but I had to get everyone inside and shut the gates before who knows what came through. I ushered the rest of them through the gates and pulled the gates shut using handles, which was much easier than pulling on scraps of the gate from the outside. Though it was still covered in snow within the walls, most of the wind was kept out.

Once everyone was inside, the gates were closed. It was pretty obvious where I needed to go next. We followed the empty winding streets past many silent houses and walked up to the castle gates themselves.

"It's too quiet here," Lady Erione commented. "It's terrifying."

"I agree," Arthur noted. "Let's get this over and done with as soon as we can." I had not expected him to speak up, considering how quiet he was for most of the journey. His attitude had tamed on this expedition, but I was not sure if I liked that.

When I got to the gate, which in this case were over-glorified wooden doors, I knocked and announced, "We are representatives of the Kingdom of Haven here to retrieve something for King Justain." The doors creaked open and two thin and seemingly starved guards in light fur armor, if it could even be called that, appeared behind them.

"The North King welcomes you," one of them croaked. They ushered us in, shut the doors, then guided us to the king's hall. It was designed similar to King Justain's hall, with columns standing firm and holding a high ceiling with a long carpet running between the sets of columns, followed by a set of steps leading to the tall throne that held the North King. The walls and columns were beginning to crack, and it was clear the entire castle had not been properly maintained for a time.

An adviser in a black ceramic mask, covering only the top of the face, stood near him. She was fair-skinned and had thick blonde hair that ran to her lower back. She was thin but still appeared healthier than anyone else present. The moment she noticed me, she seemed surprised and whispered something into the North King's ear and placed her hand behind the throne as she spoke. The North King was lounging on his throne, mouth agape, looking almost dead with his graying, unkempt hair and disheveled appearance. However, when the adviser finished speaking, he roused himself and sat up on his tall throne. The guard that welcomed us presented us, "Representatives from the Kingdom of Haven."

"I see," the North King said. His voice echoed deep throughout the entire hall, and his eyes were full of suspicion. "What business do you have here?" his booming voice did not match the frail body it lived in.

I knelt down, and the rest of the group followed my example. Then I handed one of the guards the letter from my pocket and replied, "We are on business from the Kingdom of Haven on behalf of King Justain and have come to retrieve something that once belonged to him that was left here years ago."

The guard took the letter to the North King and bowed before and after handing it to him, all before returning to his post by our side. The king's breaths were deep and slow, and he seemed to be straining himself to do so. His body was aged beyond any other that I had seen, and I had to wonder just how old he was. After breaking the wax seal on the letter and reading it in the cold silence of the hall while the adviser looked over his shoulder, he took the largest breath he had taken the entire time we were there and with a loud booming voice demanded, "What forgery is this? I know that King Justain would never trust an Arinthian! This is a trick! You will not take it with you, now leave!"

"But, my lord!" I pleaded. "Is that not the king's seal? Is that not his signature?" I produced the crest King Justain had given me to show to any merchant to cover any costs. "Is this not the king's crest?" I hoped he would recognize any of these things to know that I was to be believed.

"But these must all be fake! You do not deny that you are Arinthian?"

"I do not deny this, but I serve King Justain as a member of his Crown Guard, as does Sir Jerum here. Look at this armor," I pointed to the emblem on the shoulder of my armor. "This is the symbol of the Guard, and he bears it, too."

"Imposters!" the North King proclaimed. "Imposters! All of you! You must have taken that armor when you killed the real Crown Guard!" I looked over to the adviser; she was smiling mischievously.

"What have you done to him?" I asked while rising from my knees to stand up. She did not reply. I began to walk toward her, "What have you done to him?" I repeated, but I was stopped by the polearms the guards carried with them. They pushed against me and despite their frail appearance, the two of them overpowered me and pushed me to my knees again. Their polearms held me to the ground, pushed my shoulders down, and crossed my neck; even I was struggling to breathe.

The North King rose from his throne, and from behind it, he pulled out a blue, guardless greatsword, similar to Ubel's in size, that was glowing faintly. It was a wide blade, definitely meant for being wielded with two hands, but he held it in one. Its cobalt-steel color and gold border announced the blade's dignity as a royal weapon. The edges of the blade were curved inward for most of its length, and near the hilt, it produced flared points. In the center was an inscription that I could not quite make out.

The North King's face progressively transformed into an even more maddening expression.

"Arinthians are meant to die by Nor, this blade has already killed countless of your kind. It was a tool meant to destroy you!" he boomed, referring to the blade he now held in his hands. "You want to take it from us! To kill us all!" Then he seemed absolutely disgusted and revolted, "To kill the king!"

His wild accusations against me and my intentions caused the rest of the group to speak up in my favor, but like me, none of them had anything to prove that was not my goal that could not be twisted against each of them.

"You are all traitors to the king!" the North King accused us. "Leave! Die in the tundra!"

"We came here on orders of the king!" Lady Erione echoed my plea from before.

"If you persist in that lie, then I shall kill you all myself."

D

I LEFT RASCUR AS SOON as I woke up yesterday. I followed the path out of the village east until I ended up at the capital. Haven was huge, and its labyrinthian streets carved a narrow path to the castle itself. I had to find out what the king was planning. Recruitment posters were everywhere, as the man from Rascur said, meaning Justain was building an army. But why was he waiting this long to start?

I kept my hood up to limit the number of people who could see my face; if even one of the soldiers Horus was working with ran into me, I would be dead in a matter of minutes. With all the guards around here, I would not have enough energy to defend myself if they pursued me beyond the first attempt. The bad news was I was already being followed. I did not know by whom, and they certainly did not try and make a secret of it.

"Sir," I heard from behind me as a hand fell on my shoulder. I turned around to see a guard about my height with his sword at his side, and he was not even ready to draw it. I had not even made it very far in the city, and I was being noticed already. Then he continued, "You have to declare your business here. Also, any weapons you have must be left at the gate; only soldiers are allowed to keep theirs. And if your business is trade, then you also have to pay a fee to the trader's guild, as I'm sure you would know, but," he scanned me up and down, "you don't seem to be a trader."

"I understand," I said calmly as he led me back to the gates.

At the gates, there was a little hole in one of the walls that served as a post for the guards to take the information of anyone arriving in the city. "What is your business in Haven today?" the guard inside the post asked without looking up from his parchment.

"I am here to finally explore this massive city. I have been stuck in my small town for so long, I figured it was worth it to finally come," I lied, but it was also partially true.

"Any weapons?" he asked again carelessly.

"I have my sword, a quiver, and my bow," I said, "but if at all possible, I would like to keep my bow with me; it is very precious to me. I will leave the quiver and bowstring with you, but the bow stays with me."

"Fair enough," he agreed. I offered him my sword and quiver, and as I began to unstring the bow, he stopped me. "Don't worry about that. If you don't have any arrows, you can't fire the damn thing, so I'm not concerned. Just don't do anything stupid here, and you'll be fine, farm boy."

I was a little insulted by that last comment, but I pushed it off and said as realistically as I could, "Thank you, sir."

He replied dismissively, using only his hand to send me on my way. The guards here were so lazy; I wondered if anyone could be safe with them on the watch. I am pretty sure I could have lied and said I had nothing but my bow, and they still would have let me keep it. "Now off you go," he ordered when he noticed I was still standing there. It was the first time he spoke with any ownership of authority.

I started walking back into the city I was almost removed from and was instantly reminded of how crowded it was. The flow of people was dense and made it difficult to pass through the streets. I still had room to move my arms, but not much beyond that. I wove as quickly as I could through the crowds checking the nearby signs and their doors for a tavern with plenty of flow.

One particular tavern I noticed actually had guards posted outside. That was either a really good sign for what I needed, or a terrible one. The sign above it read "The Dragon's Fire." A bit of a strange name for a tavern, but it seemed to match with all the other dragons thematically placed throughout the city. Even on the shoulders of every guard was an emblem with a golden dragon; I assumed it was the king's favorite creature. I ducked through a few more haggling and wandering citizens and nodded to the guards standing at the tavern, but they stopped me by crossing their spears at the door.

"Sorry, soldiers of the king's army only."

"What?" I said. "Don't you recognize me? Never mind. It's fine if you don't; I'm one of the king's rangers." I worried I may have spoken too quickly for my lie to be believable, but it seemed to be working. They needed just one more tip over the edge. They looked at me with suspicion and confusion, so I gestured to the bow on my back, "Only soldiers can have weapons in these walls, right?" They were still unsure, so I finished with a sigh, "They cleared me at the gate."

They looked at each other, nodded, then removed their crossing spears and let me through. That was much better result than getting thrown out of the city, as I half-expected. The tavern was full of soldiers I could talk to. It seems the guards were there for privacy, not because the tavern was filled with irresponsible drunks. But after a few moments in the tavern, I entertained the possibility that it was for both.

Inside the tavern, everyone was loud and incredibly drunk. I went up to the bar, asked for an ale, and placed a pair of copper coins per the bartender's request. I was amazed by how full the tavern was this early in the day. The bartender handed me a tall, wooden mug filled to the brim with ale. I took one large gulp to clear the top and walked over to a nearby table with an empty seat. I sat near the end of the table and set my bow against the table's edge as I joined the company of soldiers enjoying their day off.

"Who are you?" one of them asked, slurring their words.

"A ranger," I replied, taking down even more of my ale.

"Oooh," one of them mocked, waving their hands around, "a ranger! So..." he looked almost shocked; if it wasn't for his clear drunken state, he might have been believable. "Mysterious!"

"Where are you posted?" another asked, but he sounded still relatively sober. His mug was still almost full.

"I've been scouting around Aranor," I answered, it wasn't a total lie.

"I can't wait to go back there!" one of the drunks exclaimed sarcastically, probably not a good move on their part, but still good for me.

"Oh really?" I asked the drunk, equally as sarcastic, then in a very purposeful, condescending voice. "When do you head back?"

"In a week," he slurred and slammed his mug on the table angrily and thirstily. This was going to be easier than I expected; these drunk soldiers would spill out any information I asked for.

"It really depends on if that Arinthian comes back," another drunk corrected, his words just as slurred as the others. Then, in a not very quiet whisper, he said, "I heard he went into the Northlands. Serves him right, he'll just die up there. We don't need an Arinthian fighting our battles for us!" he was clearly getting angrier by the moment. "He's a traitor, is what he is. I watched him walk right into Aranor and then come marching back in defeat. Then, next thing you know, our bridge is gone! I bet he destroyed it!" I was not so happy that Horus was receiving the glory for my accomplishment, nor was I excited to know this soldier was among those who marched to Aranor last. At least he did not realize the destructive force came from the gates and not from Horus.

"Nah," another denied, "Ubel did that." I remembered that everybody here thought Ubel was some all-powerful, invincible demon of a man. It was good they were clear of the idea of another Arinthian. That kept me at least relatively safe. I still had to keep my guard up, though, because who knew what kind of rumors may spread throughout an entire kingdom in a day if even people in Rascur knew about Horus? I figured it would take far less time for word about me to spread. I didn't need their king hearing about me.

"Ubel, huh," I acknowledged. "They say no one has fought him and lived. What if that Arinthian was the first survivor?"

"That just makes him worse," a drunk soldier replied. "If he lived, then he must have struck a deal with Ubel to let him live." Well, he wasn't totally wrong, but Horus still left as an enemy, not as an ally.

"Did he go in alone?" I asked a question I already knew the answer to, but I had my reasons.

"Nah, I was with him," the sober one answered. "I was one of the archers in the back, so I didn't see much." I was amazed he didn't recognize me at all. "Wait," he began, "I don't recall seeing you among any of the ranger corps."

"I like to work alone. I just do my job and report back. This is the first time I've actually stopped in here," I said.

"And that's what bothers me," he replied. "We all work alone, but we still belong to a corps." Then he pointed to a unique patch on his own cloak of a yellow silhouette of a fox, "I'm a Fearless Fox. And you?"

"Like I said, I'm not a part of one."

"Then prove you are a ranger with your skills. Let's have a competition, right, men?"

All of the drunk soldiers at our table cheered in agreement. The other tables must have heard the cheer and echoed in near unison, likely not even knowing what it was they just cheered for.

"Fair enough, but I left my arrows at the gate," I agreed with a shrug. If I could make this sober soldier believe me, I might be able to report back with even more than just they leave in a week or whenever Horus gets back. Besides, what's wrong with a little bit of competition?

"You can use one of mine. Come, there's an indoor range over there." He guided me to what felt like the edge of the tavern. The range was not terribly long; a child could hit the target wooden dummies at the end of it. "A lot of people like to practice. Some people swing their swords at the dummies, and others, like us, are stupid enough to shoot in this crowded building, but any ranger can hit their target through trees, right? So, they should be no problem, right?"

"Sure," I lied. I was good enough when I was using magic, but through these crowds, someone was bound to get hurt. He handed me an arrow, walked me back about thirty yards from the dummies, and motioned for me to fire. I took a deep breath in and focused on the right dummy. I pulled the bow as far back as I could. The tension felt a lot higher with a real string and bow, but I still managed to hold it steady. I let my breath out when I saw an opening between the many heads of the hall and let loose the arrow. Much to my own surprise, it landed right in the head of the target dummy after whistling through the crowds.

"Impressive," my opponent nodded. He mirrored my exact movements but much faster, smoother, and significantly less effort. He had hit the head of the left dummy. "Shoot again." I did not notice he was handing me another arrow before I made a mistake.

Without even thinking, I said, "*Icerepin*," as I pulled the bow back, and the bowstring burnt away, replaced by the flaming bowstring and arrow. "*Savu*," I said aloud to myself. "I'm smarter than this."

H

THE NORTH KING WAS CROOKED and clearly angry. He held Nor in his right hand and slowly approached me, dragging the blade against the stone floor. I was still being held against the ground by the scrawny yet somehow oppressive guards.

"Arthur, Jerum!" I ordered. "Take these guards down now!"

Arthur instantly shot two arrows, landing firmly in the skulls of both guards, but neither of them faltered. Jerum tackled the guard on my right, giving me an opportunity to throw the one to my left to the side. Both of them got up relatively quickly, even the one under the weight of Jerum. The knight grappled with the guard, refusing to let him near me, but the other one was still charging at me. I was not going to be able to defend myself against that guard and the North King's assault.

The North King raised the blade, his left arm remaining slack, and brought it down with all of his might as the guard prepared to pin me down. Without orders, Abaven took advantage of the guard's charge and tackled him, allowing me to defend against the North King's blow. I pulled out my own sword and held it at an angle relative to the floor while I was still on my knees. Nor came crashing down into my steel sword and stayed in the center. I had hoped that my block would force his blade to the side, but the pressure from the attack just kept getting stronger and the blade brighter as if it was draining me.

"Because that is what it is doing," Eyvindr read my mind. "That blade is just like Ubel's, remember? It will only get stronger the more magic it is around, and it will drain me soon enough."

"Arthur, shoot the adviser!" I ordered.

"What?" he asked, unclear of the near traitorous order I just gave.

"Just do it!" I commanded as the pressure from the North King's blade only increased. Calidan fired an arrow straight at the adviser's head, and just as I expected, the North King released the pressure on me and chopped the arrow down mid-air giving me a chance to move back and collect myself. I watched as the king's blade gradually dimmed. Eyvindr was right; the more I fought the North King, the worse it would get for me. I coughed hard and felt like I was suffocating.

"Eyvindr? What's happening?" I got no response. Eyvindr had been drained out; my breaths now felt cold and dry. I was no longer breathing the air Eyvindr supplied me but the real air of the Northlands. Everyone else was able to breathe it, but I had yet to acclimate.

"Horus?" I heard Lady Erione ask over the winds and the wrestling of Jerum, Abaven, and the guards. "Are you okay?" she rushed over to my side and put her hand on my back.

Hunched over and kneeling, I forced out a reply, "I think I'll be fine, but Eyvindr is gone." I strained myself to stand and resumed my commanding position. "Arthur, keep pressure on the adviser! Jerum, how many guards do you think you can handle?"

He grunted out, "Just this one!" before unleashing a punch right into the guard's face.

"Abaven?"

"I might need some help." He was struggling to keep the guard down.

"Lady Erione."

"On it," she said, leaving my side with her staff in hand, and she rushed to help Abaven.

The North King, meanwhile, was still distracted by the constant fire from Arthur's bow, but he was going to run out of arrows soon. The king wasn't using his sword to block the arrows unless he was too far away; he was choosing to block them with his own body. He forced his way to Arthur with every arrow that hit him, staggering him for a moment. "Uh, Sir Horus? He's not stopping!" He reached back for another arrow but found only air. "And I'm out!"

"Noted!" I rushed to Arthur just as the North King was going to attack and once again blocked his blade with my own. Nothing changed. I was still unable to move, but now I did not have the bonus of having Arthur being able to distract him. If Arthur or I moved, we could die. I was too close to Arthur to make a move, and if Arthur tried to run, the North King would surely change his focus. I had to decide quickly what I was going to do.

For the first time, I looked into the North King's dead eyes and noticed they were glowing blue. He did not even have whites in his eyes, and he was staring directly at Arthur. I looked past the king and saw the adviser was moving behind the throne for her own safety, but her lips moved on occasion when she peered at the skirmish.

"Arthur," I grunted between my teeth, "get as far back as you can as fast as you can. When I tell you, rush the adviser and get her to shut up." I was right. The moment Arthur took a step back, the North King's eyes grew even more furious, and he lightened the pressure on me ever so slightly, but it was enough. "Now!" I shouted out as I ran into the North King and brought my blade to the top of his thigh, and cut deep into his leg. He did not bleed or shift focus from Arthur, but I pushed that as an advantage and forced my way all the way through his leg, severing it.

"On it!" Arthur shouted as he dodged his way around the now legless North King and ran to the back of the throne to tackle the adviser.

His attack was surprisingly quick, much faster than I expected, and successful. Arthur pinned her down and shoved a knife into her wrist, forcing a scream. When she screamed, both the guards and North King stopped moving momentarily, then they became more violent and started thrashing, making it difficult to even control the single-legged king and keep him down. He was swinging his sword violently, and it became necessary to disarm him. I waited for the right moment and cut the North King's hand off; he did not even scream. He was only grunting, a vastly different character than moments before. His rage was still murderous, but he was significantly less pronounced in vocabulary and humanity. Nor fell to the ground in the grip of a lifeless hand, and I kicked both the hand and the sword to the side. Abaven and Erione were suppressing the guard easily, and Jerum was now just sitting on top of the other guard. I walked over the North King and made my way to where the adviser was writhing in pain beneath Arthur.

"Abaven, Jerum," I ordered, "cut off the limbs of the guards, none of them are alive anyway."

"What?" Jerum asked.

"Just do it," I finalized. When they had finished, I told Arthur to remove his hand from her jaw and the knife from her wrist, then asked the adviser, "Who are you, and what did you do to the North King?"

"I am an adviser to the North King, that is all," she spat while holding her bleeding wrist.

"Well, at least you are still alive, which is more than I can say about the North King," I said, looking at the blood pouring out of her, "Arthur," I turned my attention to him. "Leg."

"But, Sir," Arthur tried to refute.

"Do it."

"Wait!" the adviser pleaded, panting in fear. I put my hand up to stop Arthur. "I'll tell you."

"Go on," I said.

"Everyone here died years ago. I was banished to the Northlands, sent to die in the cold by King Justain. When I got here and found corpses and that sword," her voice switched from fear to awe. "It was just filled with magical energy and up for the taking. I've been using the magic from that sword to animate these corpses, bring them back to life momentarily. I don't have nearly enough on my own. I'm no adviser; I'm a quarter-blood Death Arinthian. My grandmother was the same as Ubel's, though he does not even know I exist. Unlike my cousin, however, I chose to stay here. I don't even think he knows who I am anyway. I should have joined him ages ago."

"Wait," Jerum stopped her. "How old are you?"

"That's rude, but at least one hundred years. I stopped paying attention after that. Now please just kill me; I think I've lived long enough."

"Why did Justain banish you?" I asked.

"Ever wonder why there isn't a queen? Or a prince? That was me."

"You are Arien, aren't you?" Jerum asked. He walked over and ripped the mask off her face, revealing dark eyes and fear. "It is you." He was shocked and removed his helmet.

"So, it really was *the* Sir Jerum," Arien said, her attitude returning. "The Crown Guard of the royal family, the screw-up. Where does the king have you working now? Oh, right, running errands with an Arinthian. You are lucky you weren't banished alongside me. It's funny how even though we are both equally to blame, it's the Arinthian that receives the death sentence and the other a job."

"It was not my fault," Jerum had clearly tried to forget about whatever happened, but it was getting to him. He backed up a few steps and continued, "It can't be! I had nothing to do with it."

"And that was exactly the problem," Arien taunted. Lady Erione went to comfort Jerum, and Abaven approached us now as well.

"You should stop moving your snake tongue before I cut it out," Abaven threatened.

"I've already made my request," she stared directly at me, knowing that I ordered everything. "Kill me. Call it a blessing or a curse, but Death Arinthians are granted a long life, so long as we are willing to expend others."

"You are terrible, no wonder everyone hates our kind," I said, disgusted.

"Then *kill me*." I looked at Jerum and Lady Erione, but they were too distracted to give me a consensus on it. Arthur was purely focused on keeping her from escaping, and Abaven nodded in agreement with Arien's request. I walked away and pried Nor from the king's severed hand. It was even more draining now that I was holding it, but I felt more power recursing through me, even more than when Eyvindr was around. The power itself was almost overwhelming, and I felt the magic flowing in and out of my veins as I coughed harder than I had ever before.

I brought myself over to Arien, and she rose to her knees and lifted her neck, making it ready for a clean cut. "Thank you," she whispered through tears of what seemed like joy. "Thank you." I motioned for the others to stand back. The moment they were clear, I brought the sword smoothly through her neck. It toppled to the ground with the face still carrying a peaceful expression.

"I'm sorry," I forced myself to say. I don't know why I said it or why I felt myself on the verge of tears.

D

THERE IS NOTHING QUITE LIKE revealing you are an unknown Arinthian in a tavern full of soldiers in Haven. I let go of the flame arrow I was holding and split my last arrow in half. The flames dissipated back into thin air, leaving nothing but scorch marks between the halves of the arrow. "You are an Arinthian," my opponent said, dumbfounded.

"Well, now that I've made that clear, I really should be going," I said nervously. "Nice meeting everyone." I backed up slowly toward the exit, but I was still a long way from the door.

"Where d'ya think you're goin'?" I heard someone from a table slur as they grabbed my wrist. I jerked myself free. It was dead silent as everyone in the tavern was watching me. I needed to get out; too many had seen my face. I would need to leave the entire kingdom and likely never come back. More of the guards were standing up, and many of them were preparing to draw their short swords. If I wanted to, I am pretty sure I could have wiped them all out, especially if I had *my* sword, but it would have drawn too much suspicion coming in. Unfortunately, that sword would have been my only exit.

"Don't bother trying to run. We have you surrounded," someone a little more sober said. He was right about me being surrounded, but I thought I still had a chance if I could take advantage of their fear and drunkenness.

"Alright," I said, putting on a facade of confidence. "I did not want to do this or to state the obvious, but you are dealing with a Flame Arinthian in the middle of a wooden tavern. If there was ever a recipe for disaster, this would be it. I suggest you let me walk out of here before I burn everyone here to the ground."

Much to my surprise, that worked better than expected. The guards cleared a path to the exit, likely the most organized they had been since they last formed ranks for an invasion or a march. I made my way to the exit slowly and steadily, keeping up the confident appearance. When I arrived at the exit, there was a single guard blocking it.

I sighed in annoyance, held my hand out in front of me and said, "*Icerepin*," then finishing in my mind, *ingnis icounten*. The flame appeared in my hand and even the guard blocking my way ducked away for cover. "*Iveeno,*" I ordered the flames and they dissipated from my hand.

The guards at the door had no idea what was happening when I walked out, other than they seemed suspicious of me for leaving a now quiet tavern. I walked for a while until I was sure I was clear of the peering eyes of the guards that had seen me before I picked up the pace, maneuvering through the crowds. I flowed against the herds of people flocking to the Dragon's Fire to see what the commotion was about as the guards were frantically searching the area for me.

I remained underneath my cloak and kept my head and face low, but it was clear I was against the current. I could not leave the city quite yet; it would be too suspicious to the guards. Then again, they probably wouldn't even care, but I was not willing to risk it.

"Sir," someone asked from over my shoulder, "have you seen an Arinthian? He was last seen around this area."

"No," I lied. "Should I be worried?"

"No, sir, and thank you. You may go about your day," the idiot said. He continued to ask others. No one other than the guards knew I was an Arinthian, but it doesn't seem that they all had a clear grasp on what I looked like.

"There he is!" a different voice cried out. "There's the Flame Wielder!"

"Oh, now that's a boring name," I sighed, exasperated.

"The Ranger! Right over there," the same voice proclaimed.

"That's a little better, but not by much," I shrugged to myself.

"Get him!" they cried out again. "That's definitely his bow!"

"Really? That's what gave me away?" I asked myself aloud. The guards were rushing toward me, and the people were making it easy. "Right then," I said to myself. I looked for a way onto the roofs of the buildings and found a nice scalable wall that had a few wood beams higher up if I leapt. I climbed up the protruding elements of the wall and got on top of the roof. "So why are you chasing me?" I called down to the guards that began to surround the building I was standing on. It would be easy enough for me to move, so I don't know why they were even bothering to try, but I figured I would ask them. "What did I do?"

"Why would an innocent run?" one of them sneered.

"Because..." I paused to think for a moment, then realized I didn't have an answer. "Good point. But do you not have a better reason than that?"

With this many guards around the building, there's no way I would be able to use the front gate. That meant I wouldn't be able to get the rest of my equipment.

"You are an Arinthian! You threatened to kill us all!"

"That's a little better of a reason, but you started it." That was a little childish of me, but it was fun, nonetheless. "I don't believe I made any real threats. Did I?"

"You said you were going to burn the tavern to the ground!" They were finally getting annoyed.

"I merely implied that if you did not let me leave, I would burn it to the ground," I clarified. "It worked, you let me go, but now that doesn't seem so true."

"Just get down from there and you will have your trial," one of them beckoned angrily.

"What trial? The same trial you gave the queen of Dracadere? Ubel's wife? Lyssandra's mother? All of the Arinthians before me?" I replied furiously.

"They killed our queen and our prince!" one of them replied.

"That's impossible! They never crossed the border of Aranor!" I objected.

"They sent an assassin! And with your defense of them, how do we know you aren't one either?"

"Who did they send?"

"A relative of Ubel's named Arien! She was sent to die in the North years ago, but that wasn't enough. Justice had yet to be paid," one of them explained. "One life is not enough when two were taken!"

"I promise you; they did not send Arien. We don't even know who that is. They've never brought her up. How do you even know they were related?"

"They are both Death Arinthians," one of them said. "She even claimed it."

"So, she forced both countries into full-out war?" I conjectured under my breath. "It was all a ploy?"

"Now get down here before we have to tell you again!" a guard demanded.

"Right," I said to myself, "I'm still on the same roof." Then I leapt to a different rooftop and called out to the guards still within earshot, "I'll come down eventually, and please come up with a better nickname for me. I'm thinking, 'Firelord.' I quite like the idea of being a 'lord' to you people!" It really was fun to taunt the guards, and my mobility on the rooftops made it even more fun to taunt them then get away. However, I knew would have to throw them eventually somehow.

Then, I saw my chance. From a ground-level visibility point, they wouldn't know, but there was a set of houses with a bit of a courtyard in the middle. So, I ran to the other side of the set of houses to where they would see me running presumably on the rooftops, then I turned back just before going to the next roof and crawled to the inner border of the houses and dropped into the courtyard and snuck out what could only be the back entrance.

I was hooded and my bow was under my cloak. I hunched my back to make my stature less clear and kept my hood low on my face and walked calmly to the front gates. It was nearly nightfall so a lot of people from outside the city were making their way back to their homes in nearby villages. They seemed to be checking any man that left the gate to see if it was me, I quickly found a covered wagon, not unlike the one I was initially captured in, and ducked inside.

My escape plan seemed to work; they didn't check the wagon, and I was soon enough outside the gates. I made sure to look out the back of the wagon to know where I was. I needed to be able to get back to Dracadere as soon as I could. I did not have nearly enough information as Ubel would have wanted, but it gave us a time frame, and I did not have a lot of time to get back and warn them. If they left in a week, I would have thirteen days from today before they arrived at Aranor. Hopefully, I would get there before Horus did. If he got delayed, I might be able to make it back in time to fight him.

Once it was dark enough that I could leave under the veil of night, I looked again out the back of the wagon to see if the coast was clear for me to slip out. I would have to start moving a lot farther north, but I had a different problem. Wolves were trailing the wagon. I opened the cover and looked at the wagon driver, a human, though I am not sure that was an improvement, and called out to him, "Excuse me, you seem to have a problem."

"What in the king's name!?" it was a bald, old man who was quite reasonably startled by my sudden appearance. "Other than you?" he asked.

"Yes," I said, "I'm going to get out of your hair." That was kind of insensitive, considering he had none, but what was wrong with a little fun? "As soon as one of us takes care of these wolves."

"What wolves?" he asked before turning around to see the large wolves and their glowing red eyes prowling just behind the cart. "Oh, those dire wolves," he said, as if he was just accepting his doomed fate. "I don't suppose you can do anything about them, can you? Oh, I knew I shouldn't have stayed so long in the city."

"Relax, will you?" I said. "I'll handle them. Just don't tell anyone you saw me."

"Why would I—" he started, but I interrupted him.

"*Icerepin*," my bow lit aflame once more, and the old man began to shout but decided to remain calm.

"Oh," he said, collecting himself, trying not to panic, "as... as long as they are taken care of."

"They will be," I assured him. I breathed in and fired right at the center of each separate set of glowing red eyes in the dark. They were all direct hits, but they kept moving. For the moments my arrows were embedded in their heads, I saw their thick black fur, and their faces only snarled. "Well, that didn't quite work as expected."

"What?"

"Nothing," I lied. I shot again, multiple times. Each dire wolf took three more arrows to take down, but even then, they still only seemed wounded. "How much farther until you are within walls again?"

"Not much more; it is right there," he replied.

"Right, then," I said. "I think you are safe now. Keep it that way. And next time, stay in the city if it gets that late, but thank you for the ride." I hopped off the back of the wagon, tumbling into my fall.

"Wait!" he called back, reminding me of the unfortunate events from earlier today. "Who are you?"

"Nothing more than an outcast. Call me whatever you like!" I replied. My name in this kingdom would never matter, especially since I was not going to give them my real name. Then, I started running north through the plains of Haven.

DAY 66

H

WE ARRIVED BACK IN HAVEN late at night, and I saw something I never hoped to see. Plastered all around the city walls and on every single door and post was a poster with a charcoal sketch of Drocan. It seems that they did not have his name, though. They were calling him various names, but "Firelord," "Flame Wielder," "The Outcast," and "The Ranger" were most common in their respective orders.

"He was here?" I asked no one in particular.

Lady Erione was just as stunned as I was, "It seems like it."

"This won't be good," Jerum's voice trailed off, clearly disturbed by the knowledge that Drocan had been anywhere near here. "If King Justain knows about this..."

"Then our story about why we couldn't take Aranor is no longer going to hold true, and we've lost the king's trust," I finished for him. "Let's get moving; the sooner we know what the king wants us to do, or if he even knows, the better."

We picked up our horses a few days ago from the outpost by the North Mountains, and there was no doubt they were tired from carrying our weight, especially the added weight of Nor, for so long. But we pushed them to take us deeper into the city as fast as they could. We stopped at the inner gate and called up the guards working the gate so we could enter. Once we arrived at the entrance near the throne room, I ordered everyone but Abaven and Arthur to dismount.

"You two take our horses over to the stables, Lady Erione, Jerum, come with me. We are going to see the king."

"Wouldn't he be in his chambers by now?" Lady Erione asked.

"I hope not," I said. "We are going to check the throne first, nonetheless." And somewhat to my own surprise, the king was pacing around the throne room that was otherwise devoid of life.

"You made it back," he was definitely stressed, and his voice was obsessive. "You brought it didn't you? The sword?"

I removed the sword from the sheath that used to be on the throne of the North King and presented it to the king. On the sword was a faded inscription, "*Acemagi itomum Rimepimu Icounten.*" I dropped my knee to the ground to explain.

"Your Majesty, it was not easy," I knelt before him and held the sword laterally with both hands above my bowing head so that he would be able to take it at any moment. The sword was glowing a brilliant blue as it radiated from the magic energy it was taking from me. "And unfortunately, there are no more allies in the Northlands. Arien got to them first. She is slain, but..."

"The North King was dead," the king finished the obvious statement. "Curse that Arien! At least she's finally dead."

He had still yet to remove the sword from my hands, so I asked him, "King Justain, do you not want this sword?"

"What gave you the impression it was for me, Horus?" he asked in reply. "This sword will surely turn the tide in your next confrontation with Ubel, he has one just like it. Not to mention you are now going to also hunt down this 'Firelord' who suddenly appeared in my kingdom."

"I'm sorry, sir?"

"My builders have been working on a new expansion to the bridge, to make it wider for more troops to cross and to fill that gap they blew in it. After all of this time, it is finally ready. You'll be taking a larger force with you just to carry the damn thing. You leave tomorrow morning; you got back just in time for us to keep schedule. My survey team went out after you informed me of the bridge's demise and have been developing essentially a cover for the bridge. It should be able to slide right on top of the old bridge without any issues. You have two 'troops' of soldiers ready to go, one for the invasion, one for the bridge. The second one won't be armed, as their sole purpose is to carry it."

"And what about the other Arinthian?" I said trying to keep as much of what I knew to myself.

"Try and recruit him if you can. Otherwise kill him," he responded uncaringly. I wasn't sure if I could do that after the mercy Ubel gave me after the last time we met. Apparently, my discomfort with the idea was painted all over my face because the king asked, "Do you have a problem with that?"

The king was just as intimidating as he normally was, but this was somewhat more threatening.

"No, Your Majesty. No problem at all," I lied.

"Good," the king said. "Lady Erione, Sir Jerum, I expect you will hold him to this duty? Not to mention, Sir Petrus will be coming with you all this time to ensure there are no..." he paused momentarily. Looking at me disparagingly, he finished, "mishaps." It was plain that he knew I was lying about the last attempt for Aranor.

"Y-yes, Your Majesty," Jerum stammered out. Lady Erione answered with a small nod.

"Very good. Now you may all leave. Get some rest," he encouraged, his tone returned to benevolence. "You have a long journey ahead of you tomorrow."

I stood up, finally accepting the sword as my own, and Jerum and Lady Erione followed me out. Only after I left the throne room did I realize I had been limiting my breathing. I released all the air I had been keeping in my lungs.

"I don't know if I can do it. Ubel offered me mercy, and even if I could beat them, killing them is extreme."

"I agree with you. What does Eyvindr say?" Lady Erione suggested.

"That's the thing," I said looking at the sword. "Ever since I picked this thing up, I haven't even felt Eyvindr's presence, much less been able to talk to him. This sword replaced Eyvindr for absorbing the excess magic."

"So, you don't have that safety net anymore?" Jerum asked.

"Not at all," I said.

"Can you even fight without him?" Jerum taunted.

"I'm not sure," I said. Jerum instantly swung his sword right at my face. I instinctively reacted with Nor and blocked it faster than I would have before. The blades met with a metallic ring and forced Jerum back in recoil as if he had just struck a stone wall.

"Well, that's certainly an improvement," Jerum said, "though it doesn't say much as it was just a block. But your speed is new." He looked for a moment at his hand, testing it. "Stronger, too. I don't think you have ever parried me that hard before."

"I would have appreciated it if you two waited to test that until after I was gone," Lady Erione said, holding her hands over her ears, writhing from the ringing we caused. She removed her hands and then reminded us of the real problem at hand, "Regardless, what are we going to do about Drocan? He would never join the kingdom."

"We have to hope he has changed his mind," I said. "It's all we can do."

"The king also never has to find out," Lady Erione suggested, "if we let him go, that is. But this time, we have to take Aranor, or all of us will be dead."

"But if Drocan ever shows his face again—"

"We are also dead, yes," Lady Erione said flatly.

"There's no point worrying about this now. I'm going to my quarters," Jerum's voice was exhausted. He dragged himself away from our conversation down the hallway toward the Crown Guard's quarters. Which left just Lady Erione and I to be alone for the first time in over a week. We walked out to the courtyard illuminated by the full moon and the stars scattered about the midnight sky.

"Lady Erione," I began, "I... I don't know what I would do without you. Would you please consider—"

"That's not happening," she argued, interrupting me quite rudely. "Especially now that Eyvindr is gone, I'm not staying behind. Without me, there would be no one who can heal your injuries, and I get the feeling you'll need it. Last time you fought Drocan, you were nothing more than what an injured mouse is to a cat for him. No offense, but even if you are fast, you still can't fight."

I chuckled a little bit at the truth of her statement. "None taken," I said. "But that wasn't what I was going to ask you. Like I was saying," I took her hand in mine and looked her straight into her eyes. "I don't know what I would do without you. Would you please consider accepting my hand in marriage?"

She was stunned for a moment, but her lovely dark hair shone beautifully in the light, and the eyes I gazed into began to shine with the beginnings of tears.

"What? Horus? But," she stammered out, "I... Of course!" She let go of my hands, leapt into me, and wrapped her arms around me, throwing me off balance for a second before I fully embraced her and gently set her back on the ground.

"I take it this means I can drop the 'Lady' part now?" I toyed with her.

"You could have done that ages ago, and you know it," she replied, wiping away the remainder of her tears. She was smiling and looking into my own eyes, "Horus, it's about time you asked."

"I love you, Erione," I said. "I'm sorry it took this long." I leaned in and kissed her briefly.

Erione blushed and led me through the area surrounding us underneath the cloister. It shaded us from the potential gaze of patrolling guards, even though there seemed to be none. She insisted, "You can do better than that," as she leaned in and kissed me, holding onto it as if it was her last breath. When her lips left mine, she ended our interaction with nothing more than, "Goodnight, Horus."

"Goodnight, Erione," I said in response.

After she was out of sight, I wove my way back through the castle and into the Crown Guard's quarters where Jerum was waiting to hear the news. Our room was at the midpoint between the throne room and the king's chambers in case anything happened. I had shared my plan with him, and he played his part perfectly. I walked into the room with the elation of a successful proposal still sitting on my face, and he asked likely the dumbest question he ever asked.

"Did it work?"

"She said yes," I let out. I was expecting Ramsguard to be around. He was, but he was fast asleep with his set of armor set to the side of his bed.

"Congratulations," Jerum said, a soft smile on his face. "You two always seemed happier together."

"Thank you," I said. After that brief exchange, I took my own armor off and got in my bed, falling asleep the moment my head hit my pillow.

D

"UBEL," I said, "we only have one more day before they begin their march." I had been running for what felt like months in the past few days as I rushed to get back. The journey south had made it harder to navigate my way back, costing me almost a full day.

"We are always well prepared for that but thank you for the precise day. Any other news on why it was taking them this long to attack?" he responded.

"Yes, they've been waiting for Horus to get back," I answered. "From the Northlands. They could actually be delayed depending on when he gets back, but—"

Ubel cut me off and asked for clarification, "Did you say the Northlands?"

"Yes," I said, curious of the detail now myself.

"Did they say why?" I could sense the rage and concern rising in his question. He was leaning forward, and his frustration was growing.

"No reason that any of the guards knew," I said. "Why?"

"Up in the Northlands lies the only sword that can rival my own," Ubel explained. Now he seemed somewhat impressed as he regained his cool, tempered attitude. "So, he's finally gone for it. This could actually be a problem. Are you still confident in your ability to best Horus in combat?"

"Absolutely," I said firmly. "He's only fast; he can't fight. Just like you."

"That is honestly insulting," Ubel said, "but you may be right. Do keep in mind that if Horus is the one wielding the sword, he will be much faster than he was before and faster than me."

"I won't even break a sweat," I assured him. "He is weak."

"Don't underestimate your opponents," he reminded me stubbornly. "That's exactly what almost got you killed on multiple occasions when you sparred with me. If you keep this up, I might never let you marry Lyss."

"I'm sorry, what?" I felt as though I was beginning to sweat. I was not sure how much he knew of our relationship.

"It's obvious," he said. "It has been for a while. The way you two always sneak off together, look into each other's eyes; I've just been waiting for either one of you to bring it up. It reminds me of when I met her mother. But I'm not going to let you make the same mistake."

"What do you mean by that?" I asked and walked closer to him. We were meeting in the dining room, and instead of waiting at the doorway, I finally took a seat next to him.

Ubel sighed and waited for a moment to begin talking again, "You will have my blessing when you survive this battle. Once you are clear of danger, you can marry her. That way neither of you will have to lose each other like my queen and I did. You won't make the same mistake."

"I see," I said, disappointed that I would need to wait.

"Now stop wasting time on me. We will be leaving tomorrow to set up camp in Aranor so we can be ready for them. If they are coming, they probably have a way in, so we have to be ready. Go see Lyss," he smiled. "She's been anxious for your return."

"Thank you," I said, standing back up from my chair. I started out but turned back as I recalled my conversation with the guards in Haven. "Though I have one more question. I heard of an Arien while I was in Haven that apparently assassinated their queen. She claimed relation to you."

"Is that why they..." Ubel wondered. "I don't know who she is or was. I had nothing to do with her, of that I am certain."

"I see."

"Now go," he encouraged again, then I left for Lyss' chambers. I rushed through the labyrinthian halls and knocked on her door.

"Who is it?" Lyss sang from behind the door, and I could hear her approaching.

I decided to impersonate one of the skeletons as best as I could and snarled, "Only checking on you, Princess Lyssandra." I could hear her eyes roll as she opened the door

"Again, I'm still fine. You can tell my father that-," she stopped when she finally saw it was me. I could see she was extremely excited to see me as her eyes bulged, and she leapt onto me. "You're back! Oh, thank Arinth." She let herself down and patted my arms, shoulders, and face, verifying that I was still there.

"I'm fine," I assured her. "I'm still very much alive."

"Good," she said. "You kept your promise." We walked over to her bed and sat on the edge as I filled her in on my story of Haven. I talked about the idiocy and laziness of the Haven city guards, but she stopped me once I started telling her about the tavern. "You call them idiots, but you nearly got yourself killed?" she asked, raising her voice. "What's wrong with you?"

"It worked out, didn't it?" I tried to shrug my mistake off. "I'm alive."

"You need to be more careful!" she demanded, placing her hand on top of mine. "Promise me you will be more careful."

"I will, I will," I promised. Then I continued with the rest of my story, including the long, boring journey back. "You want to go to see your mom? It feels like it has been ages since I last was able to be there."

"Maybe soon. First," she said, pulling my left arm over her shoulder and leaning into me, "you are going to just sit with me for a while."

I was about to protest, saying that we could just do that outside, but I also found comfort in the torchlit room. "Fair enough," I agreed. I rested my head on hers, closed my eyes and took a breath, listening to her own breaths and her heartbeat. I felt her cold body leaning against mine, I guess I was nothing more than a campfire to her, but I appreciated it. I reopened my eyes and saw her long hair was falling over her resting face. I lifted my right arm and brushed the hair back over her ear. She looked incredibly beautiful and peaceful.

She must have been waiting for me to move her hair because after I did, she smiled and said, "Thank you, I wish we could stay like this forever."

"You know we can't," I said, mischief creeping into my voice. "We're going to have to eat at some point." I chuckled a little bit at my own joke, ultimately destroying her ability to rest on my chest. She shot me daggers with her eyes, opening them for the first time since she set her head on my shoulder. I calmed down immediately and collected myself for the sake of her own comfort.

"Well, aren't you two adorable," a voice from the hall teased. Princess Bellona was standing in the doorway that we were too stupid to close and she, as usual, was fully equipped in her armor. However, in her defense, the only thing I had removed from my person since getting back was my cloak and my bow.

"Thanks, Bell," Lyss said, annoyed. "Thank you for ruining our moment."

"It's only fair," she shrugged.

"How so?"

"Door's open," she shrugged again. "I figured I would stop by to see how you were doing. But now I see you were doing just fine. I'll leave you be."

"Thank you, Bell," I said, knowing she still did not like it when I called her that.

"Whatever," she said.

"I think she finally understands I'm not complete refuse anymore," I said, impressed with myself.

"She really is only being polite. She'll get to you later," she said.

"Please just let me have this," I begged.

"Never," she denied, while finally letting go and removing my arm from around her. She interlaced her fingers with mine, then stood up and invited me to join her, "I think I'm ready to go see mom now."

"Let's go then," I said. We never let go of each other the whole way to the grave overlooking the ocean. We laid ourselves down on the grass by her mother's grave and looked up at the stars above us.

"You look beautiful, Lyss," I said, staring at her bright, black-streaked white hair as it contrasted her dark dress.

"Thank you," she blushed lightly. "You are not the worst, Drocan."

I accepted her compliment and smirked that my personality was rubbing off on her, or maybe her personality was becoming mine. "I'm leaving tomorrow to go back to Aranor," I said, regretting it the moment the words left my lips.

"I figured you wouldn't be staying long," she said, turning her eyes to meet mine. "My father is probably just keeping you busy so that I don't get too attached, but little—"

"He actually knows about us. He has for a while," I interrupted.

"What?"

"He's not against this at all, he just wants us to wait," I clarified. "He wants us to wait until after I win the next battle, then I have his blessing to come back and make you mine."

"You mean," she sat up excitedly and gripped my hand even tighter.

"You'll be getting married before your older sister, yes," I said, smiling.

"You're mean," Lyss said, shoving her elbow into my side. Then she taunted me again, "I'm beginning to see why she doesn't like you."

"Wait, Lyss," I stammered out because I was not sure if she was being serious, but she just smiled again and rolled on top of me. "What are you—"

"Just shut up," her eyes were endearing until the moment they were gone behind her eyelids as she leaned down to kiss me with her entire being. When she pulled away, she said smoothly, "But just know, that means I like you more."

"I love you," I said, completely stricken.

"I'll tell you what I feel when you come back," Lyss said, smirking. "Promise you won't make me regret waiting?"

"Absolutely," I said. "I will await your answer." She removed herself from my chest and snuggled against me.

"You're warm," she said, her voice soaking in the peace.

"I am part fire," I said, half-joking.

"Shut up," she said, but I could hear the smile in her voice. We drifted off to sleep that night outside in the clear night and ocean breeze.

DAY 73

H

I REALLY HOPED THIS WOULD WORK. I had to trust the rest of them. I left Erione, Petrus, and Jerum in charge of the main battalion for the invasion; I had a different mission for myself. By now, the others should already have the bridge replacement set up and ready to cross. They would take a similar formation as I suggested last time, but this time they would stand three wide and the front guard would not have any protection other than their shields.

I had left the main force a few days ago, snuck my way through the Arcane Ruins of Arinthia, and now I was deep in enemy territory. I had stuck to the trees for as long as I could, but the western edge of the forest opened into vast wastelands that stretched as far as the eye could see. I made my way south from the forest while following the edge of the chasm surrounding Arinthia and found the bridge Ubel's army crossed. I could not destroy it, nor would that be wise for me; I was going to use it myself. I was standing on the wasteland's side of the bridge watching the backline of Ubel's troops waiting for them to move forward so I would know the battle started.

I did not have Eyvindr to guide me, nor anyone else to protect me. The whole plan depended on my success. Then I saw my cue. Their backline finally moved up to start their volleys, and I could start moving. I was getting nervous from the lack of movement, but now I knew things were well on their way. I felt more trapped in the wide-open wastelands than I ever did by the castle walls in Haven.

"Come on, Jerum, you got this," I cheered, knowing he wouldn't be able to hear me. I was sure that by this point, the lack of my appearance on the front lines of Haven's troops would draw suspicion from Drocan, at the very least. I didn't know what he learned while he was in Haven, but I guessed it wasn't nothing if he was there. "He has to be here," I said to myself while I was trying to walk as quietly as I could across the bridge.

Once I finished making my way across, I found the back gate wide open, as I expected. This was the deepest I had ever been in Aranor, but this side of it was not any more impressive than the other side. It was certainly much less defensive back here. Their force was as large, if not slightly larger, than last time. There were no guards posted back here, and the entire force was facing toward Haven, completely unaware of my presence. There were also some new foes I had not seen before that were very concerning. Six skeletal goliaths, at least twice my size, were equipped with blades that were as large as me.

I could hear the faint orders of the female general that led the forces last time.

"Volley!" she ordered. I seemed to recall some of them referring to her as "Princess Bellona," but she was always supposed to be here defending the city, so the plan had not changed.

Why would she order a volley if Jerum is leading them through the same plan I had? I thought to myself. *Does she really not have any other answer to that formation?*

My question was answered when she ordered another volley. However, after that one, I heard Ubel's voice projected across the whole city.

"Cease fire! Don't waste any more arrows! Move our archers back! Prepare for close combat!"

Ubel's orders could completely ruin me if I did not act fast. I started looking for any form of cover and found it, ducking behind the remains of some destroyed buildings. This far in the city, it seemed like there were quite a few sets of ruins; old piles of bricks that indicated houses with separate rooms. There were no standing shelters left in the city, but these remainders of stone walls would definitely work.

I set my helmet aside because I supposed it would attract attention, with the midday sun reflecting right into the skeletons' eye sockets. The giant skeletons moved forward through the ranks up to the front alongside the rest of Ubel's high-ranking officers. The skeletons moved much further back than I expected, and I had to move slowly to the area between the outer wall and the buildings. The experience was nerve-racking.

Focus, focus, I reminded myself, *focus!* The rattling and general clamor of the armor of the skeletons haunted my very presence as the army of archers marched uniformly to the back of Aranor.

"Just because we are back here doesn't mean any of you can slack off!" one of the skeletons ordered. It was dressed in somewhat fancier armor than the others, making it likely that it was a captain. "Keep ranks and stand by to fire. We are the last line of defense before they get to Dracadere. Make sure that no matter what, you hold the line. No. Matter. What."

"I'll make my own orders. Ubel put me in charge of the backline. You all do what you must, but know you won't have to."

I knew that voice. Drocan was standing there with his black cloak on but the hood down. His black hair was ashen and somewhat greasy, and from what I could see, his eyes looked dreadfully tired but watchful. Something had changed. Normally, or rather based on what I saw last time, despite his tired expression, he was sarcastic and confident, but this time he seemed worried and careful. I could only look for so long before I ducked back underneath the protective shade of the stone-brick walls.

The captain of the archers snarled at Drocan's comment and said, "Just whatever you do, don't force a break anywhere in my formation."

"You aren't the last line of defense," Drocan dismissed. "I am. The moment Horus breaks through those frontlines, wherever he is, I will be the only one with a chance of taking him down."

He knew I was coming, but he did not know where. I still held the advantage. He kept moving his eyes, looking for any sign of me, and I was surprised he had not seen me yet. At the very least, he was not going to make a move, not yet at least. I kept my new sword low so that it was hidden beneath the rubble with me. I left the sheath for my blade on the other side of the bridge so that I could be ready to fight if I needed to. Keeping my grip tight on the sword, I moved away from my current position when I saw Drocan look the other way.

I found more rubble to hide behind that was in a better position for flanking Ubel. I would have to save my fight with Drocan for last. Drocan's arms were still crossed as he waited impatiently for the fight to come to him. So, I looked to the front gates as I wondered why it was taking them so long to break through. Ubel had even recalled the archers above the wall and had them wait with the rest of the archers. They closed the gates and braced it with some of the skeletons pressing against it. I remembered breaking down that gate last time and was glad they got it repaired. However, I knew Jerum's strength was much greater than my own. Those gates were really just large doors, and sure enough, Jerum was able to break through even the reinforced gates without much help. The resulting crash of the gate caused a large boom to echo within the city walls. I could feel the smile underneath Jerum's helmet.

"Hello!" he greeted Ubel and his army as if they were old friends. "Remember me?"

"It's been a few years since you and I last fought, hasn't it?" Ubel returned the formality. "You've gotten older."

"I would imagine you have too, but it's kind of hard to tell under that mask of yours," Jerum commented.

Ubel removed his helmet, revealing his short ruffled dark hair. His face and skin made him seem as young as Jerum if not much younger.

"Does this help?" Ubel asked rhetorically, then he put his helmet back on and reassumed his position as a king of his army. He drew his glowing blade in front of him. The faint, dark red glow told me that although it had some magic, it was certainly not going to be as strong as mine. His blade may as well have been nothing more than its metal in comparison.

"Not sure. I don't think I saw your face last time, but thank you for giving me time," Jerum said as our troops funneled into the city and spread out for a wide frontline, just as we had planned. Petrus brought up the rearguard and was the last to arrive in the city. Arthur stood in the front, armed with his bow and a dagger. I'm surprised Jerum let him stay there. Abaven was to the right of Jerum, opposite of Arthur, wielding two short swords and was already ready to fight, the perfect actor for our scheme.

The main force was still under the impression they would be fighting Ubel without me, and they were all ready. The only ones who knew I was in the city were Jerum, Petrus, and Erione. Erione was on standby on the Haven side of Aranor.

"You can fight me once you get through them," Ubel said, then he ordered, "Dracadere, charge!" He saw no need to be wary if I was not among the frontlines. The skeletal army charged forward and the skeletal goliaths as tall as the walls themselves marched slowly forward.

"Hold!" Jerum ordered the troops. "Hold!" The army was just steps away from them now. "Volley!" Then from outside Aranor, on the bridge, a thin volley shot over the walls, some through the opening where the gate used to be, and knocked down a decent amount. "Forward formation!"

Arthur dipped behind Jerum, and they all formed a triangle to break the line with Jerum in the center. Other soldiers next to him were standing further back to brace themselves to spread out the enemy's forces even more. The problem was the goliaths. I couldn't do anything about them, and we had no plans to meet any. I saw Jerum signal for Petrus to take his position as the point as he went out and targeted each of the giant soldiers, and within moments, he brought the first one down with swift, crushing blows. Arthur was firing at the other giants focusing on their weaker joints to disassemble them as fast as he could.

"Good job, everyone," I told them underneath my breath. They were holding their own against the largest army freeing up my target: Ubel. I inhaled deeply and prepared myself to end him in one swift motion. I felt Nor's power channeling through me as I began my spell aloud with a quiet, "*Icerepin,*" then I finished the rest of my spell in my head, *ricopros tesvun isorapen icemmenntur icounten!* The sword would grant me speed and strength by absorbing my excess magic, but then needed to combine that with what it could not absorb. I felt like I was about to expend all of my magic to ensure that it got done fast.

I let my breath fall out of me as I launched myself forward, moving faster than even I could comprehend. Ubel was on guard, watching for Jerum, just as I had planned, and before I knew it, I slashed my blade through the back of Ubel's neck to the front and severed his head instantly without him even knowing I was coming. The world felt slow as I watched his head slide off his neck and onto the ground with nothing more than a final grunt.

"No!" I heard someone shout, but it was not the princess, she had only just noticed the head as it rolled to her feet. Drocan had wandered up to the front moments too late it seemed.

The princess dropped to her knees and picked up her father's head. The emotion of loss escaped her. Her sorrow was replaced by anger as it fueled her cry, "Horus!"

I was on the opposite wall from where I started my spell and ordered my winds, which were still howling around me, "*Iveeno.*" I was confident Drocan could see me.

D

"THERE THEY ARE!" I called back to Ubel. "They've brought twice as many as last time, but it seems only half of them are armed. The other half is carrying... something."

"It's probably how they intend to cross the gap," Princess Bellona noted. "It's huge."

The device they brought with them was the entire length of the bridge and had two protruding boards that were wide enough to fit the current bridge. It had diagonal beams that would support the outer edges of their new bridge. It was made of incredibly dark wood that contrasted with the light tan stone of the original bridge.

They lined up the protruding boards with the remains of the bridge and let one end fall on the end furthest from them. Then using all the strength they had and backing up, they pushed it as it slid into place. Then, some of them attached rope to the replacement and anchored it on their side. Finally, they got into formation. It was not unlike when Horus led them, but he was nowhere to be found among their ranks.

"Something's not quite right," I muttered to myself, deeming my suspicions as unimportant.

Horus would show up. Either that, or he died in the Northlands. But I doubted they would come this quickly without him. I saw somewhat familiar faces that I had not seen in ages; the same knight that Lady Erione and Horus talked to after our last confrontation was now leading the troops. Lady Erione herself was among their ranks on a beautiful white horse. Rather than the robes she wore last time, she was wearing clerical armor, which really just added a few plates to her shoulders and chest.

I could not shake the feeling that Horus had something planned, that their king had something up his sleeve.

"Where is he?" I asked Princess Bellona. We were watching over the ramparts as Ubel and Commander Treynar managed our melee soldiers in the city walls.

"Who?"

"Horus!" I responded. She thought about it and started scanning the enemy forces for a hint of the specialized armor that Horus wore, but it was nowhere to be found. "Do you think he could be disguising himself, so we don't target him?" I suggested.

"It's possible. That would be a reasonable plan," she agreed. Then she directed her attention behind her and shouted out her command, "Prepare the archers. They will start moving at any moment. They will crack under the pressure of our volley." She was very sure of herself.

The archers that had been standing in the back of the city marched forward through the ranks as our giant skeletons moved back to make room for them. She then turned back to me and said, "Drocan, you focus on accurate fire once they get close, assuming they can."

"Understood," I obeyed. It felt good to have my full equipment again; my bow was in my hand, and my sword was attached to my belt. The weights on my body were much lighter without all the unnecessary metal from the daggers and arrows I was carried before. "*Icerepin*," I ordered my bow, and it lit aflame ready for me to draw and fire at a moment's notice.

"Ready!" Princess Bellona shouted loud enough that I'm sure even our enemy could hear it. "Long-range! Volley!" I raised my own bow and shot as part of the volley.

All of the arrows that were sent flying up, arching over the city's walls, once again blotted out the sun with how concentrated they were. But the enemy was not even fazed by the darkness of the sky and kept marching forward in their tight, protective formation, moving much faster than Horus had directed them before. Princess Bellona snarled at the inefficiency of volley fire against those shields.

"Mid-range!" She ordered, then waited for a moment. "Volley!"

Then I heard Ubel take control, "Cease fire! Don't waste any more arrows! Move our archers back! Prepare for close combat!" His voice shook the city.

I descended from the ramparts after the princess and went to stand by Ubel, putting my bow in the holder on my back underneath my cloak. I pulled my hood down, not only to make it easier to put away the bow, but also to make sure I was going to be able to see whoever barged through those gates.

"Why did you stop me?" Princess Bellona contested. "It was going to work."

"No," Ubel said sharply, addressing his child, "it was not going to work. They were moving too quickly from long-range to mid-range. You did not even slow them down."

"But father!" she tried to contest again. "Once they got close enough, I was going to focus on accurate fire to melt them down. Horus was not leading them this time, but some other knight."

"And how do we know it is not Horus?"

I joined in the conversation, "Because none of the arrows were curving off course this time. Eyvindr would never allow an arrow to even approach Horus."

"What if his gous has been absorbed by the sword?" Ubel argued, but he was still commanding our troops. "Brace the gates! We aren't going to just let them in this time." About twenty skeletons went to reinforce the gates with the remains of their bodies.

"There was nothing glowing among them," I stated.

"It could be hidden. Either that or Horus has something planned that we would not expect," Ubel conjectured. He thought for a moment and then turned to me. "I think he is going to sneak through the Arcane Ruins and come in through our end. Drocan, go join our archers in the back and make sure nothing is out of place. With Nor in his hands and his wind magic, he could easily make an effective assassin."

"Would it not be better if we were all here? Protecting each other?" I refuted as politely as I could. I did not like the idea, but if Horus did come through our end of Aranor, it would be left completely unguarded. He would have no trouble killing anyone but me. I was the only one that could challenge him. We both knew that.

"It would be best if you could stop him before he even gets to the rest of us," he reminded me. "Now go," he ordered. "You are in charge of our rear. Bell and I will manage the front."

"Very well," I obeyed and regrouped with the marching archery company as they made their way through the rest of the army. We made our way to the western side of Aranor. Nothing seemed out of place quite yet, just the same old broken buildings.

"Just because we are back here doesn't mean any of you can slack off!" the captain of the archery company ordered. "Keep ranks and stand by to fire. We are the last line of defense before they get to Dracadere. Make sure that no matter what, you hold the line. No. Matter. What."

"I'll make my own orders, Ubel put me in charge of the backline. You all do what you must, but know you won't have to," I said. I knew that if any of them got this far, I should order the archers to retreat. They were already near useless skeletons, but these ones would not even be able to handle themselves in close combat.

The captain of the archers snarled at my comment, annoyed with my very presence back here, "Just whatever you do, don't force a break anywhere in my formation."

"You aren't the last line of defense," I said dismissively. "I am. The moment Horus breaks through those frontlines, wherever he is, I will be the only one with a chance of taking him down." This company really should have always been under my command, and Ubel did put me in charge. So, I turned to the captain, and in a stern, hushed tone, I told him, "You will obey my commands. I am in charge of you. Remember that."

The skeleton officer was frightened of me; I could tell. "Y-yes, sir," it stammered out, fully aware of its place and likely haunted by my tired eyes. I had not gotten a good night's rest since sleeping outside with Lyss. Losing this battle was too real of a possibility. I stood watching for a while, keeping my head moving to scan the maximum area I could.

"Captain Kaillin, keep a lookout behind the gate. I'm going to go take a look around," I told it. Something still did not feel quite right. It was a little too quiet.

"Yes, sir!" Captain Kaillin obeyed, then he barked some orders to a pair of archers that were thought to be the best in our company.

I wandered through the southern side of the city, through the rubble, looking for something, anything. There was the unshakable feeling I was being watched as I browsed. I heard Ubel in the distance order our men to charge. So, Haven made it through. But we still had not seen Horus. I checked the skies to see if maybe Horus had decided to fly, but the skies only held a few scattered clouds. Scanning my eye level again, I then looked at the ground for any tracks but found none.

The sunlight broke through some of the clouds, and something reflected into the corner of my eye. I followed the source of the reflection and saw the worst thing I possibly could. In the corner of one of the ruins was Horus' iconic helmet.

"No," I said quietly, before I ran over to it. I picked it up and started to furiously turn my head, looking for a more recent sign of him. "No, no, no, no!"

I felt my heart beating through my chest. He had to be in the city, and I had no clue where he was. He must have snuck in while we were moving our archers forward for the volleys, and now Ubel's biggest fear was coming true.

I ran as fast as I could back to the front lines to warn Ubel about the potential danger, to tell him to keep watch, but I could only move so quickly through the rubble. I had gone too deep into the ruins of the city. Ubel was standing ready to fight, with his sword glowing only very faintly, which was good news. It meant he was already on guard. But then, something else caught my eye.

I was still a short sprint away from Ubel and saw Horus standing, still muttering something under his breath. Then he nearly disappeared from sight, moving faster than I could follow with my eye, releasing a large boom from where he stood.

I looked back to Ubel and saw his limbs go numb, he dropped his sword and his arms sagged at his side. His head slid forward and then toppled to the ground. The head rolled to Princess Bellona's feet as his body collapsed. Princess Bellona fell to her knees and picked up Ubel's head.

"No!" I exclaimed as I felt my heart sink in my chest.

Ubel, my friend and my king, was dead. I scanned the line from where I saw Horus to the other side of the city and saw him. Horus was leaning against a wall; his sword was glowing a bright blue that was getting dimmer by the moment. I felt myself get angrier by the moment. Now that he was in my sights, I knew what I had to do.

H

I was struggling to move. My legs felt weak, I could barely stand, and Drocan was looking at me with nothing but hatred. The tired, watchful eyes I saw before were filled with rage and sorrow.

"How could you?" he asked through his clenched teeth.

"I did what I had to, Drocan. I'm sorry," I responded sincerely.

I felt my heart tighten at my deed. Ubel was hardly a direct danger to anyone in Haven, but under the watchful eyes of the king's right hand, Sir Petrus Ramsguard, I had no choice. I pushed myself up against the wall and tried to regain any and all strength that I could.

I had hoped that by killing Ubel, the entire chain of command would get disrupted, but the princess was taking firm control of the troops. She quickly reorganized the troops into a more defensible position, walked over to Ubel's sword and lifted it from the ground.

"Horus," she said with her head hung low. I was amazed at how well she was holding herself together, especially given the reaction Drocan had. "Just know, I believed Drocan was right. My father may have had misgivings about killing another Arinthian in his day, but I have none."

"Bell," Drocan called over, "don't fight him. Make sure you get back to Lyss, make sure she hears it from you. Order a retreat."

"Only after his head is on a pike," she said as her eyes flared. It was clear she did not know how to use the sword, as she was only charging at me with a normal speed as she roared with anger. Drocan was soon in front of her with his hand to stop her. "Get out of my way!" she commanded him. Princess Bellona tried her best to push past him, but Drocan managed to restrain her.

"No," Drocan said solemnly. "Ubel sent me to the rear to watch for him, and I failed. I will make up for my mistake, and end all of them, here and now. I won't make the same mistake we did last time." The princess was breathing heavily as she tried to calm herself back down.

"Fine," the princess finally agreed, wrenching herself free from his grasp. "Treynar! Help me bring my father back!" A taller skeleton in pitch-black armor assisted the princess, retrieved Ubel's body and head, then ran to the rear of the city. He placed the body on a horse and carried the head in his arms with the princess not far behind him.

I looked back to my own forces for a moment and saw that many more were falling than I expected. Our line was breaking. Drocan noticed my losses were increasing as well. "So, Horus," he said, "same terms as last time? I can call off our troops if you call off yours, and we can have a nice, friendly duel to the death."

"Interference punishable by death?" I confirmed.

"Yes," he responded while stripping his cloak from his shoulders and setting his bow aside.

"Winner takes Aranor?"

"Absolutely." He drew his sword and ignited it with a simple "*Icerepin.*"

"No one else gets hurt right?" I was just stalling to catch my breath. That last move was incredibly draining in every sense of the expression.

"As long as they don't interfere," he said, swinging the flames a couple of times.

"Everyone!" I called out from my position. "Stand down!" Some of them looked confused, but they understood as soon as Drocan spoke.

"Army of Ubel, fall back." An unusual calm seemed to sweep over him as his tone now seemed absent of any pain. "We are going to settle this."

D

I still had a majority of my soldiers, including four giant skeletal goliaths, all obeying my orders. Armies from both sides retreated to their respective end of the city but made sure they were still able to watch the duel that was about to determine the fate of Aranor, if not the fate of the continent.

The dead and mostly dead of the Haven army were removed from the city by a select, unlucky few and likely sent to Lady Erione if they had a chance of living. They needed more than just the one healer with the number of casualties they faced. Horus and I were left with an open space without any distracting noise to throw us off.

"What are you doing, Horus?" a stranger in heavy armor similar to Sir Jerum's demanded.

"Saving the rest of you, Petrus," he replied, finally removing himself from the wall. "Don't interfere, this is the only way to prevent a massacre."

"This was not the plan!" Petrus tried to contest. "With Ubel gone, we should be able to win this."

"You realize I was the only one to beat Ubel in a duel, right? And I am the one who is still standing?" I reminded the entire city. "I could wipe all of you out in a moment, but this duel will suffice."

"You are impossible," Petrus sounded horrified, but I kept my eyes on Horus so that he would not be able to try anything to assassinate me like he did Ubel.

"Trust me, Petrus," Horus agreed with me. "Drocan is as formidable if not more formidable than Ubel was. Ready for our rematch?" The entire time he spoke, he kept his eyes on me.

"I should be the one asking you," I replied. "You look like you could use some extra bones to help you stand."

"Rematch?" Petrus interjected. I was getting really annoyed with him.

"One more word out of you, and I will consider it interference. Yes, we've fought before, and no, it was not even remotely close," I threatened.

"Stay quiet, Petrus," Horus commanded. "I don't want you to get killed."

I got into my ready stance, the same one I used last time that would allow for as much defense as offense. Without his helmet on, Horus seemed younger. He still kept his hair short, and his gray eyes were filled with determination. It took him longer to prepare himself, the armor seemed heavier on him than it did before, and his motion seemed more restricted, which I hoped would make this an easy fight. I could feel the heat radiating from my own blade as I held it parallel to the ground and in line with myself so that any attack I could see would be blockable.

"Ready?" he asked me again, lowering himself into a simple stance not too different from my own. He must have been practicing because he seemed ready to fight without discussing anything with Eyvindr. He seemed confident, for once, but exhausted.

"As ready as I have ever been." Then my curiosity got the best of me, and I had to ask, "Where is Eyvindr?"

"He's gone," he coughed strenuously, yet he remained firmly in his stance.

"About time," I said. Then, I muttered under my breath to prepare for the worst-case scenario; the trump card that let me beat Ubel on countless occasions, "*Icerepin.*"

H

I was used to being on the defending end, thanks to all my training with Jerum. However, the flurry of accurate, narrow, and precise attacks that Drocan sent flying at me was a little difficult to handle. His attacks were unending. At the very least, Jerum left a few openings before his demanding attacks due to his immense amount of strength behind them, but Drocan's attacks left no room for error while I was blocking. He would feign an attack from the right and then drive his fist into me.

I hoped that after enough of those punches, his fist would start to bleed or at least bruise against my armor's metal, but his deliverance of the punches seemed to only hurt me. I was only able to keep up with his pace because of the speed granted to me by the sword. There was no time to push aside his attacks or to even block properly. The heat of his sword was equally overwhelming, and I was quick to start sweating from the heat and exertion of all forms of energy trying to defend myself. He had not fully landed a hit on me quite yet, but there were scorch marks littered all over my armor.

"*Icerepin,*" I pushed through my teeth, trying not to get distracted by the flaming sword threatening to cut my head off. "*Drocan tesvun,*" I had one word left to say, but he attacked from above. When I went to block it with my sword, he kicked me to the ground, not only putting distance between us but also breaking my concentration. Normally, when I cast any kind of magic, I could feel the power being sapped away from me as the spell continued. I knew the spell had failed when I felt it all rush back into me. The sword escaped my grasp, and I could feel my energy increasing again incredibly rapidly, but the sword still retained much of the energy I had already lost to it as it glowed. I was somehow still standing, and the sword was in front of me with Drocan on the other side of it.

"Even though you have so much more power, you have no idea how to use it, do you?" Drocan asked rhetorically. "You killed the only person who was fighting for *us*!" He walked over the sword, threatened my neck with his sword, and continued to walk forward, forcing me into a wall.

"I never wanted to fight you," I said, "and our king is willing to offer you a place in his army. We don't have to fight."

"What's wrong with you?!" he asked angrily, forcing me down to the ground. "Join him? Join you? After what he's done? What you've done?"

"I did what I had to!" I protested.

"Enough with that!" Drocan demanded, he placed his foot on my chest, and we were in the same position as last time we fought. "You really just don't know what've you done, do you?" He was fighting back tears that seemed to boil as they began to fall. He roared as he brought his sword from my neck and started to plunge it down. I braced myself for the end of my life, but the weight on my chest was removed. I looked to my right and saw Petrus pinning Drocan down against the ground with the sword, still flaming in his grip.

"Petrus!" I cried out. "No!"

"Leave now, Horus!" he ordered.

"I can't!" I refused. "I can't leave you!"

"Damn this beast!" Petrus cursed, struggling to keep Drocan pinned down. Drocan's blade was beginning to turn to the knight and forced Petrus to turn his head away.

"He's no beast!" I shouted back. "Let him go! You should not have interfered."

D

I could not quite reach him with my blade. He was holding my wrists and locking them into a position that made it impossible for me to turn my blade anymore. The weight on my legs and chest made blood flow difficult and painful, but I did my best to not let it show.

"He's right," I began, "you should not have interfered!" I finished the spell for my trump card in any battle in my head, but for the reason I originally intended, "*ricopros revisnuus itomum ingnis icounten.*"

I hated doing this, but it was the only way for me to get through Petrus. I felt myself die again. All of my entire existence was converted to flame, and I could only hold it for a moment. Petrus fell through the flames that used to be my body, face planted onto the ground, and was lying on his stomach as I rose through him. He could feel the flames of my existence burning through him as they boiled him alive in his armor.

"*Iveeno*," I commanded the magical energy around him, and I reformed into my normal, physical self. I took a deep breath, though I felt the need to gasp for air, and turned to face the writhing Petrus as he was trying to roll away the boiling of his flesh.

"And now, you will get what you deserve." My flaming sword was still lit as I shoved the tip of it through his heart. All of the air in Petrus' lungs left him, and he stopped his screaming. "You made your choice," I reminded him as I watched the light slowly begin to leave his eyes. Then I turned to Horus, who was now standing defiantly where I left him, then to his entire army as they stared in shock at what I had just accomplished, "We said not to interfere!" I reminded the spectators. I tried to hide my exhaustion from using that spell. I would not be able to do a full-body flame for at least another day.

Horus walked over to Petrus and cradled his head and back in his arms, trying to keep him upright as Petrus coughed up blood in desperate attempts for air.

"Petrus, I won't let you die like this. Erione will heal you. Just hold on a little bit longer," Horus insisted, then he called back to the army, "Get Lady Erione! Please! Someone!" But his entire army remained standing in shock and fear, unwilling to move even an inch.

Petrus used the last ounce of his strength and weakly placed his hand on Horus' shoulder and whispered strenuously, "Horus, don't." He had blood dripping out of his mouth. "Just win." And with that, Petrus drew his final breath, and his entire body went, limp and his eyes were devoid of life.

"I will give you a moment to move his corpse," I said with little remorse. Horus was still just staring at the body of the fallen knight and would not move. So I signaled to one of Horus' other men to come and retrieve their dead. Sir Jerum stepped forward cautiously. "We are not dueling right now," I reminded him. "I won't hurt you. Just get this one out of the way," I gestured lazily to

Petrus' body and then to the exit of Aranor. Sir Jerum signaled to a few other men. One of which I recognized as Calidan, but the other that I did not know was dual-wielding blades. They came over and assisted with prying Petrus from Horus' hands, carried him back across the bridge and out of Aranor. I turned back to Horus, who just seemed weak and completely defeated now. The confidence that inspired him to stand was completely gone. "I met his father," I told Horus, guilt suddenly seeping into my veins. "He lives in a town called Rascur. It is not too far from here," I explained. "I did not want to kill him. His father was kind to me. I would not want to receive a letter from the king. Find his father if you win. I will tell him if I win."

"Isn't this enough?" Horus asked with his head hung low. "Isn't this already enough blood for Aranor?"

"Were the two of you really that close? Didn't he tell you to win? And you're giving up now?" I prodded.

"That man was the right hand to the king and a good soldier. A good man," Horus said. "And I'm not giving up. You're right, I can't, but you still can."

"This again?" I asked vexedly. "I said I won't join you."

"Then run. Let us take Aranor and never come back," his breaths were becoming heavier as he cycled more air through his body.

"One of us has to die, you know this, and I have no intention of it being me," I told him. I could feel that he was about to try something, so I readied myself for a punch or kick or some kind of physical attack. He could not reach his sword; it was too far away, at least twenty feet.

H

"Neither do I," I said, then I turned my attention to my sword that was still lying on the ground where I dropped it. "*Icerepin*," I had to finish the spell quickly, "*tebucomi tesvun icecurom islucia*!" Nor was wrapped in wind and drawn to my hand as it soared through the air. I took advantage of the surprise and my speed and attempted an upward slash into Drocan, but he backed away just in time with a look of surprise. He seemed impressed by that spell, and I was surprised it worked on the magic absorbing Nor, but I had to remain focused.

"That's new," Drocan stated.

"I won't let Petrus die in vain," I said, preparing to launch myself at him and lowering my sword and body to a more ready position. "I will kill you, Drocan," I focused myself and took a deep breath. I almost forgot how taxing Nor was when it drained my energy once again and gave me the speed I needed to attack without Drocan being able to defend. The sword was glowing brighter, about as bright as the day I first picked it up, and I used just the speed it gave me to start my attack.

My entire body felt weightless; my legs were barely touching the ground as I nearly flew into Drocan and started my slash. I could not move as fast as I moved against Ubel, but it was still fast enough for me to somewhat lose track of myself. The blade was at my side, and I brought it through and carried the slash and all of the weight through the area in front of me where Drocan stood. But it clashed with nothing, not his blade or his body.

I tried to redirect my attack by allowing the blade to pull me into a short spin as I kept my momentum and aimed for his neck, but I must have missed again. I knew he was right there, but nothing I was throwing at him seemed to connect. The blade just kept getting brighter, and I felt myself getting faster. I started to pay extra attention to Drocan's body.

Every single time that I swung my blade at him, part of his body would turn to flame for a moment and let my sword just pass through where his body would be. He started to turn the fight back to his advantage by using the few moments I would be off-balance to make a swing at me with his ridiculously hot sword. With the speed I gained from the sword, I was able to parry his attacks but not much more.

"How are you doing that?" I asked after backing away for a moment to catch my breath after our blades had clashed. My wrists hurt from the shock of our combat and the constant weight of the sword, and my arms were beginning to ache.

"By practicing with a fighter much better than you," he responded. "I had no choice but to figure it out." I looked carefully at my opponent.

Currently, the tip of his index finger was replaced with flame. He must have been keeping the spell constant, then just changing which part of his body was pure flame. I decided to test my theory. I would go in for a single attack against his neck and keep an eye on his finger to watch if the flame disappeared.

I made my move, launching with as much speed as I could right for his neck. I tried to make my attack as clear as possible and hoped that he would not parry it. Luckily, he took the bait, and I was right. The flaming finger returned to flesh, and his neck was replaced with flame. Once my blade had passed through his neck, it returned to flesh, and the flame returned to the tip of his index finger.

"So, I'm right," I said, pulling away from the fight again. We began to pace in a circular path.

"You think you have it figured out?" Drocan taunted.

"I'm pretty confident."

"Well, even after I explained it to Ubel, he still couldn't beat me. So good luck with that."

"Thank you," I nodded.

I had two options: speeding up to be faster than he could think, which at that point did not seem likely, or completely stopping mid-swing, which would be near impossible with all of the momentum from the speed I needed to use. My only option was to fake out my speed and trap my blade in him. I had to do both.

I continued to increase my speed of attacks, and kept my blade slashing at a continuous pace, not giving him much room to do anything other than let me slice through him. Hoping I could wear him down by forcing him to expend enough magical energy as he protected his vitals, I pressed my assault. He never seemed to grow tired of turning fragments of his body into flame.

"*Icerepin*," I muttered under my breath, then cast the next part in my head, *tebucomi tesvun*. I had to wait until my sword was in his flames to finish the last words, but I also could not lose my concentration while I waited for a wide enough window. My sword was glowing as the wind magic I summoned surrounded it.

I would not have long before the sword drained the spell of the magic I had already pushed into it, so I made a bold swing for his chest. He could not parry it in time, so he let it pass through. Once it was in the middle of his body, I shouted at the top of my lungs, forgetting my own secrecy, the final words of the spell, "*istongfar icounten!*"

D

What? I thought. I looked down at Horus' blade protruding from my chest. It stung. The glowing blade was not moving, but I could feel it sapping the life away from my body. I wanted to fall, but the blade could not move with me, so I remained standing, suspended by a sword.

"*Iveeno,*" Horus whispered, then he drew the blade painfully from my chest. For the first time, he looked genuinely sorry. It was becoming difficult to keep track of anything. I placed my hand over the center of my chest and observed the dark blood that matched my armor stain my hand. I fell to my knees in shock, still staring at my hand. "I'm sorry," Horus said. "You did not give me a choice." My vision was darkening, and my ears were becoming deaf to the noise of cheers from Horus' troops. He beat me, and I was dying.

"*Iveeno,*" I coughed out, and blood followed my air. My sword stopped burning, as did my flames.

"You didn't deserve to die, Drocan," Horus said remorsefully. "I really am sorry." In my limited vision, I saw him throw his sword to the side and rush to catch me as I fell backward. I tried to put my arm over the wound in my chest to stop the bleeding. It was no use. I felt my entire arm coated in a slippery layer of my own blood.

I had to stop the bleeding, so I gritted my teeth and forced out the simplest spell I knew, "*Icerepin,*" then with the rest in my head, *ingnis icounten*. A flame lit in my hand, and I dragged the flame over where I felt the wound, only searing myself. I had no idea how effective it was. I put my hand behind me and tried to do the same thing and sear my flesh shut. All of the light in the world was fading from my eyes. I was losing consciousness from the loss of blood and the pain of searing flesh. It was hard to think straight, but there was one thing I knew I wanted.

"Horus," I turned my eyes to where I thought he was, as the gray skies were the only thing I could see. "Please, use that speed of yours, and take me back to Dracadere."

"What?" he asked.

"You'll know it when you see it. Please," I begged through the pain. "I have to see Lyss one last time," I was running out of air in my lungs, and it was hard to take in anymore. "To apologize." Then everything faded to black.

H

I turned to look at Jerum. He must have seen everything I felt because he just nodded in understanding. I picked Drocan up in my arms as his weakly cauterized wounds still continued to leak blood, and said as fast as I could with a combination of speech and thought, "*Icerepin*" *ricopros tesvun isorapentropic icemmenntur icounten*.

I started running faster and faster through the forgotten streets of Aranor and back through the gate I walked through earlier this day. I ran as fast as I could. "Faster, faster!" I urged myself and sure enough, I kept getting faster, but I could also feel myself getting weaker. I was already drained from the sword and the fight. I pushed through and sent magic coursing through my body. Suddenly, all of the wind went quiet. It was no longer flooding my ears with noise and when I spoke, I could barely hear my own voice. It sounded like it was coming from behind me instead of my own mouth. I saw Princess Bellona and Ubel on their horses galloping as fast as they could, but I passed them with ease. Up ahead, I saw what I assumed to be Dracadere in the distance. I could not hear my coughs as I strained to continue this incredible speed. A young woman with mostly white hair with black streaks was waiting anxiously at the gate. "*Iveeno*," I ordered my magic. I must have timed it perfectly because by the time I was able to slow down, I slid in the dirt right next to the woman while on my back, making sure Drocan was safe above me.

I stood up with Drocan still in my arms, and the woman was on the verge of tears and asked one simple question.

"Why?"

She collected herself, and determination filled her. Then she signaled for me to follow her to a room with a large table, and the room was filled with various cloths. I set Drocan down on the table, and he moved his head toward the woman as she rummaged through supplies in the room.

"Only one left?" she asked, holding a small vial with a red liquid. "This won't be enough." She was short of breath but rushed over to Drocan and forced it down his throat.

Drocan reopened his eyes for a moment and stared vacantly at the woman. "Lyss," he whimpered out, "I'm sorry." Then the fiery glow that normally filled his eyes faded, and his eyes closed.

"I'm sorry," I echoed. I had no idea he was trying to protect someone as well.

"Leave," she ordered.

I walked to the doorway and apologized again, "I'm sorry."

"Go!" she demanded.

The path back to Aranor was dark. Our battle had taken nearly the whole amount of daylight, and the frigid cold of the season was creeping into my armor as I slowly made my way back to my army.

DAY 74

THE YOUNG WOMAN HAD SPENT her entire life surrounded by death. Skeletons, corpses, the loss of her own mother, and she hoped that would be the end of it. Unfortunately for her, however, it was not. She loved her family. Then came a young man who, through the time they spent together bonding over their own loneliness, fears and memories, captured her heart as well.

The night before, she was brought a body by a stranger. A body she had hoped she would never see without any animation, the body of the young man. And what seemed like only shortly after the young man arrived, barely able to voice his last whispers, her sister returned with the head and body of their father. With the severance of her father's head from his body, he would never be able to come back. But the young man, she hoped, still may have a chance. Lyssandra, daughter of Ubel, made her choice.

L

"Lyss," Bell said. She seemed lost, confused, and angry. "I can't believe this happened. First mom, and now this? It's my fault. It has to be." She was pacing around the room as she racked her brain for where she went wrong. "Father is dead, and I left Drocan alone to fight Horus even though I knew he was stronger than before." She was speaking fast. She was normally able to retain herself and her emotions, but in the twenty years I have known her, this was the most I had ever seen her doubt herself.

"Bell," I tried to calm her down while I was repressing tears myself, "it isn't your fault. You couldn't have done anything. If you had stayed, I may have lost you today as well, and I think I've lost enough. And Drocan isn't dead yet, at least."

I had been thinking for the last few hours about how I could use my limited magic to preserve the life of someone who was quickly running out of it. I had given him the last of our healing potions, but it was only enough to stop the bleeding from areas he failed to cauterize. He was losing blood internally, and as an Arinthian without a gous, there was nothing he could do about it. He would die of blood loss before his body would be able to heal even one of the many cuts in his organs. Drocan's short black hair was covered in dirt, as was the rest of his face. His face and arms were also covered with his blood, and the dirt mixed with it to form a horrid mud on his face.

"But he will die, won't he?" she asked. I was still amazed at how much she cared about Drocan, or maybe it was just the shock of having lost the one who cared for us the longest. I loved my father, and I loved Drocan, but she still seemed out of control.

"Help me get his chest plate off, clean the wound and his face. It's hard to see him like this, and I will need to be able to access the wound. We can't do anything about father, but we can still save Drocan." I was not sure how quite yet, but I knew what my magic could do. It could move magical energy from one person to another and prolong someone's life. Most Death Arinthians drained life from others to keep for themselves, but it was useless against major wounds like limb or head loss.

I could sense the diminishing life of Drocan, or rather his diminishing magical energy. He was normally overflowing with it, but I could sense it being erased. He wasn't just losing blood; he was losing the very essence of his life. Bell rolled Drocan onto his side, undid the back straps, and removed both the chest plate and shirt Drocan was wearing for the battle. Then she set him back on his back and crudely poured water over the entire upper half of his body, using his shirt to wipe away the excess water, dirt, mud, and blood.

Even after all of that, Drocan still did not wake up, and his breaths continued to struggle with any form of rhythm. Father never taught me many words in Arinthian, but he had brought me enough books from the ruins that I think I knew the spell to make this work. First, I would have to drain all of the magic Drocan had left, and he may truly die during that. Then I would have to transfer all the magic I had plus his own back to him and then focus that energy to heal his own wounds. The spell would be all or nothing; there was no such thing as a partial drain of someone's life essence for a Death Arinthian. Nor in the past has there ever been a time a Death Arinthian, at the very least, wrote down how to partially give life to someone else. But I knew it had to be possible because that was how my father had extended my mother's life, at least while it lasted.

"Bell, I will need to you make another potion while I do this. I know you never got your magic quite under control, but I will walk you through this."

"Just tell me what to do."

"Do you have a knife on hand?"

"Why would I need—"

"Yes, or no?" I interrupted. She did not give me an answer, she just stood shocked for a moment. "Yes, or no?" I asked again.

"O-Of course," she said.

"Okay, fill that vial over there with some of the grass from mom's grave, then fill the other vial over there with your blood."

"What?" For a general, she was horrible at taking orders, but I've known that for a while.

"Just do it, Bell! We really don't have much time."

"Fine," she finally obeyed, and disappeared into our halls. Now I had the space cleared for what I needed to do.

Drocan's body was resting on the table, and his chest was moving irregularly as it struggled with the bleeding throughout most of his central body. I began the spell the same way I heard my father and Drocan begin any spell.

"*Icerepin.*" Then I searched my memory for the next words and said them as they came to me, "*aiman... itratslavan... Drocan... usi icounten.*" All that remained of his life was pulled from him and dragged into me. I felt myself fill with life. Then his chest stopped moving entirely, and his weakly beating heart halted. I said, "*Iveeno,*" to tell the magic that enough had been drained.

I took a few deep breaths because I realized what I was about to do could very well kill me if I did not do it properly. I focused on myself and had to convert my own magic into life energy as I struggled to generate the words for the spell in my head again.

"*Icerepin... acemagi... itomum... aiman... revisnuus,*" I felt all of the magical energy in me completely deplete, and I felt light-headed. I rested my hands on Drocan's chest as I waited for the dizziness to disappear. When the headache persisted, I decided to just push through the pain; one more spell should finally do the trick. I knew there was some magical energy loss in each of these stages, but it was the only way I could think of to maximize the healing I would give him. "*Icerepin.*" I was struggling to think and even breathe at this point, but I pushed the words through. I just had to reverse the spell from before, "*aiman.... itratslavan... usi... Drocan icounten.*" I could feel my life force being sucked away, my knees collapsed underneath me, and I fell to the ground in a fit of coughing but kept my hands on the table for support. My vision was turning black, so I forced the last word out, probably earlier than I should have, "*Iveeno.*"

Slowly, the human parts of me began to regenerate what life I had lost. I had to stay awake to help Bell make the potion too. I listened as carefully as I could in this quiet room for the sound of another heartbeat besides my own or the sound of air flowing in and out of lungs, but I heard nothing. Had I just given my own life to a corpse and gotten nothing in return?

"No," I said weakly. "No," I finally let some tears through my eyes. I had just killed Drocan; I knew it was risky. I could have given him more of my own life, but I was selfish. I did not know what else to do. Then I felt a hand on top of my own, "Bell, I killed him," I said, distraught. "I can't believe I killed him." But I got no response. I looked behind me, expecting to see my sister looming over me with the ingredients I asked for, but no one was there.

I pushed myself up using the table and looked at my hand. Drocan's own hand was lying on top of it. His breaths were slow and quiet, and his heartbeat was slow but steady; however, he was still asleep. His life force was not increasing back to its normal level, nor decreasing anymore as it was when he was dying. It remained stagnant, which was the best I could hope for. Bell returned with the vial of grass but still had yet to fill the other with her blood.

"I got the grass," Bell said, but I was having trouble hearing her or really anything. It all sounded slightly muffled. She looked hesitantly at the other vial and took a knife out, "You really need my blood?"

"Yes," I confirmed tiredly.

"Here it goes," I watched her cut horizontally into her palm and let her blood drip into the vial until it was full.

"Bandage that up," I ordered, and she obeyed without speaking.

I poured the two ingredients into a larger bowl; the grass swirled in the shallow pool of blood. I stirred the mixture. We grew the grass from grass found in the Arcane Ruins and the blood of an Arinthian, or at the very least, a partial Arinthian. Due to the nature of that particular grass, it dissolved in the dark red blood and changed its color to a brighter red. I gave Bell a small sip so that she could heal her wounds. I swallowed a gulp, poured the rest into Drocan's mouth, and sat him up so that it would drain to where it needed to go.

"Thank you," I told my sister.

"Will he recover?"

"Yes. But he will only live about as long as you," I told her, leaving out the fact I had used much of my own magic and life to restore him to that point and that I may have stopped myself too late. Placing my hand on my chest, deeply aware of the life within me, I felt I had little time left. It had taken me many years to store up that much life, and it took only a few minutes to give it away. Drocan's heartbeat was finally restoring itself to a normal pace, and his breaths began to quicken. I couldn't risk taking back what I had given of myself. Then his eyes opened as he sat up suddenly, winced, and lay back down.

"Welcome back to the land of the living," I said, trying to imitate him as best as I could, despite my current tired state. "How was dying?"

DAY 83

H

WHEN MY ACHING BODY DRAGGED itself from Dracadere ten days ago, then proceeded on the rest of the long journey back to Haven without any rest, I expected I would finally be able to rest at ease. But soon the events at Aranor caught up to me. When we returned to the city with fewer men and with one of the Crown Guards lying dead on horseback and my state as being, well, alive, it drew plenty of suspicion from the townspeople watching us as well as the attention of the king.

We returned to the kingdom from our rather pyrrhic victory to a path made by the people through the city to the castle. I could feel the wishes of death that everyone seemed to have for me. Once more, I had Abaven and Arthur take our horses to the stables with the rest of the men returning to the barracks. Jerum carried Petrus Ramsguard in his arms as I led the way to the throne room, but this time I had Erione stay back to continue to help the injured we still had not gotten around to healing.

"Your Majesty," I said, entering the throne room, cautious of what my news may bring out of him. Justain was sitting impatiently on his throne, and the room seemed empty without Petrus waiting for us.

"Yes, Arinthian?" he asked rudely. "Come in." I entered the throne room first and signaled for Jerum to wait outside. "What news do you have for me?"

"I have good news, Your Majesty, and bad news," I explained. I made the mistake of hesitating, and the king took notice.

"Well?" his impatience was growing, and with it, his typical rage. "What is it?"

"We captured Aranor," I said solemnly, "but—"

He cut me off and asked quickly, "You did not lose it again, did you?" I shook my head. "Then what is the bad news?"

I was struggling to muster the courage to tell him. "Sir Jerum," I called to the doors behind me, "could you bring him in?" Jerum pushed the doors to the throne room open with his back and carried the dead knight through with him. He walked with a heavy heart to lay the corpse at the king's feet. We had done our best to wrap him up and preserve him with what we had on our journey. The knight's face was entirely hidden by bandages, but it was still clear it was the former captain of the Crown Guard and former right hand to the king. The king rose from his throne and stared in awe of what was in front of him. The strongest knight he knew slain in battle.

"What happened?" the king asked with only a slight hint of loss and pain in his voice. "How did he die?"

"He died saving my life," I told him. "He was killed by the Flame Wielder."

"And the Flame Wielder?"

"I avenged Sir Petrus Ramsguard without hesitation. The Flame Wielder is dead," though I hoped I was wrong about that. That young woman seemed to have something in mind. After Ubel, I would not know what to do with myself if I had truly killed Drocan, but I couldn't think about that.

"Good, then he did not die in vain," the king said coldly. "Bury him with the royal family; it is where he belongs."

"Very well, Your Majesty," I said.

"Sir Jerum, take Sir Petrus Ramsguard to the morgue and spread the word for his burial as fast as you can. We shall observe a day of mourning for him," the king commanded.

Jerum picked up the fallen knight and passed me on his way out. As he was passing, I told him, "Send a messenger to Rascur, wherever that is, as fast as you can and bring his father here." I thought of Drocan's command. "I want to be the one to tell him." He nodded in understanding and continued on his way out.

"Where will you need me next, Your Majesty?" I asked, placing my fist over my heart, and dropping down to kneel.

"Is it not obvious?" he asked with a clear sense of superiority in his voice. He was questioning my intelligence and patronizing me as a fool. "Defend Aranor. You are to establish, at the very least, an outpost there and hold the city for the rest of your life. Eventually, I hope to establish it as a city of Haven once more. It is time to reunite these lands back under my rule."

"How much time do I have?"

"I suppose it can wait until after Sir Petrus' burial," he said dryly. "As promised, Lady Erione will continue to serve under you, and it is up to you to determine how many you need to defend the city. I will send troops through periodically to retake the western lands under Ubel's rule. Which reminds me, did you encounter him?"

"Yes, Your Majesty, and he is dead. I beheaded him myself," I told him; the words felt like poison as they left my mouth. The king seemed elated for the first time in ages, and he let out a short chuckle.

"Amazing, he really was no match for an Arinthian with Nor." He walked down the steps of his dais and placed his hand on my shoulder. "If that's the case, I will go with you to Aranor and help you reestablish the city. We have nothing to fear anymore. Our conquest will be swift," he seemed to have forgotten completely about the loss of Petrus. "Rise," he commanded proudly, "Sir Horus, Liberator of Aranor." That title did not seem right to me. I did not feel like I was really liberating it by placing it under Justain's control. "You will be granted the highest honor for defeating the oldest enemy of mine. You will be remembered as a great hero in our history. Congratulations."

"Thank you, Your Majesty," I could not look him in the eye. Petrus was his most loyal knight, and he treated his death with such an absence of care. I couldn't say this was the beginning of my doubts about serving him, but my mind was beginning to clear. I could understand wanting to reclaim Aranor for the people but claiming it as an outpost for an invasion was wrong.

"Go, Sir Horus," the king said, "get some rest. I will send someone for you when it is time for the burial."

"As you wish, Your Majesty," I said, remembering the great loss for such a pale victory.

"Please, Sir Horus, address me as Justain," he said. "You've earned my respect."

"Thank you, Justain," I said.

"You are dismissed," he reminded me. I nodded and left the throne room.

Navigating the halls of the castle as tired as I was proved difficult. I was holding myself together while I was in the throne room, but the moment I left, I was using the wall to support myself as I walked through the halls. On quite a few occasions, I had to push myself to the other side of the hall to get through the maze of the castle. As I approached my room, I saw Erione waiting by the door for me. I had not shown any of my weakness around her the whole journey home, and when she saw me struggling to stand, she rushed over to support me as best as she could.

"You really shouldn't push yourself this hard," she said as she guided me through the door and to my bed. After setting me down on my bed, I sat upright as she crawled onto the mattress behind me and helped take my bloody and bulky armor off. She took the components of my armor off, one by one, starting with my arms as I struggled to hide the pain and soreness from keeping the armor on for so long.

"Thank you, Erione," I said, thinking of my new role at Aranor and what it would mean.

"Something is bothering you," she noted. "And I don't mean your armor. What is wrong?" She was unbelievably good at reading me, or maybe I was just worse at hiding it than I thought.

"How do you do that?" I asked.

"Stop. Don't avoid the question; what is bothering you?" she said sternly as she continued to remove my armor as delicately as possible to not agitate any wounds.

"The king—" I started before correcting myself, "Justain wants me to go back to Aranor and defend it."

"What's wrong with that?"

"He does not just want me to defend it to defend the people, the kingdom, which is what I agreed to do. He wants me to defend Aranor so he can use it to invade and conquer Ubel's kingdom as his own. I don't want to help him hurt others anymore." I said somberly. "I've done enough of that for him."

"What are you thinking you are going to do?"

"Shut the door."

"Why?"

"I don't want anyone else to hear this," I explained. She got off the bed, walked to the doorway and looked around before closing the door quietly.

"So, what is your plan then? Because clearly, you aren't agreeing with him outright," she asked as she walked back to me. She stood in front of me and waited for my answer.

"I will defend Aranor," I said. I hesitated, unsure if any keen ears could hear through the walls. "But I won't do it in the service of the king. I will defend Aranor as its own independent city. I want to secede from Haven and defend it from both kingdoms. These lands need rest from the war that should not have even started in the first place. Arien made it worse during a time when there was a chance for peace. I'm going to force that peace out of the king."

"I don't know if he will see eye to eye on that," she reminded me.

"I'm well aware. I'll just have to convince him that it is the right thing to do."

"You could be branded as a traitor, you know that, right?"

"I know."

"Do you have any other plans?"

"No. This is what I have to do. For the sake of Haven, for the sake of the king, and for the sake of Arinthia," I said. "I just have to hope he'll see it the same way. He will have my allegiance, not my loyalty."

"You might as well tell him then," Jerum said from behind the door. He opened the door and let himself in. I sat upright slowly, gaging his opinion from his mannerisms. "I agree with you," he clarified, casting my concerns away. "Aranor cannot belong to anyone. I'm sure the more of us that side with you, the more likely he will be to accept it."

"Thank you, Jerum," I said.

"Let's go now," he suggested. "Better to get this over with." I finished stripping my armor off, then the two of us went to the king's chambers. I still struggled to stand, so Jerum helped me through the halls.

I knocked on his chamber doors and called inside, "Your Majesty, I have something I need to tell you."

"Please, come in. Remember, Justain is fine." He was pouring himself a glass of some of his finest wine, then he poured another, and another after that. "Your victory at Aranor is something to celebrate, and Sir Petrus' death is one to commemorate with honor. With Aranor in my hands..." he failed to finish the thought, grasping at the air with his fist.

"Justain," I said after a moment. I took a breath. "I will be taking Aranor as my own."

His mood changed as I would have expected, but he still offered me and Jerum the glasses of wine he had poured for us. "What do you mean by that?"

"I—"

"We—" Jerum corrected.

"We believe that Aranor is too critical of a city. Haven needs rest from the war, as does Dracadere."

"Rest? They have to pay for what they have done! They destroyed my pride and killed my family!" He threw his glass to the ground, spilling wine all over the floor. A frightened attendant opened the door, but he held up his hand to dismiss them. "And what of Sir Petrus? Will he have died in vain!?"

"King—" Jerum tried to interject.

"Yes! I am your *king*. This is treason of the highest order; Sir Jerum, take him to the dungeon. Perhaps you can suffer as that cursed Arien did."

"King Justain," Jerum said with conviction I had never heard before, "I am on Horus' side."

"So, then you have turned against me as well?!" He backed away, staring cautiously at Jerum's sword.

"No, we will defend Aranor and both kingdoms from each other. This is about finally bringing an end to this war. Think of your people! The city will still belong to Haven, but only as a vassal city."

"I swear the city's allegiance will never betray you," I said.

"Yet you betray me now."

"No, I am still at your service. There is but one command I will not obey: the invasion of Dracadere. I will not stand for the continuation of this war. If you want the city, it is yours to claim publicly, but I will not allow passage for the sake of war. Your family is avenged. Arien is dead. Ubel is dead. Sir Petrus is avenged. The Flame Wielder is dead. Aranor is reclaimed. What more could you ask for?"

He seemed to ponder it all for a moment. My words struck him in some way, but then a smile crept across his face as he chuckled once to himself.

"I suppose you may be right," he agreed. I thought I saw a tinge of fear, malevolence, or perhaps even mischief in his eyes. "I'll let you keep Aranor. I suppose without Ubel or the Flame Wielder, as he called himself, there's no reason for me to attack. There's nothing over there anyway. It all burned to the ground ages ago. As long as you defend this kingdom, that will be enough for the people." I felt sure we finally reminded him of why he wanted Aranor in the first place, for the pride of the people. Either that or, as something in his eyes told me, he feared in the back of his mind that if I managed to kill the unkillable king of Dracadere, what is a lone mortal king of Haven?

"Thank you for understanding, Your Majesty," I said, bowing and walking out to begin my new mission.

D

I WOKE UP GASPING FOR AIR, Lyss sleeping softly next to me. She had refused to leave my side ever since I woke up. We used her bed, seeing as mine was significantly less comfortable and roomy. I was still amazed by her beauty, but I was sweating in fear of my nightmare. Lyss died in my dream, giving birth to our daughter. I brushed the dream off as nothing more than what it seemed to be: a dream. I removed Lyss' arm that was wrapped around me, sat up, and put my feet on the floor while still sitting in the bed.

"That won't happen," I assured myself quietly.

I got up completely and turned to make sure I had not disturbed the sleeping wonder in my life. She was still quietly and peacefully breathing without a care in the world. I had been having that nightmare every night since I first woke up days ago, and it was the same every time. I still had not told Lyss what I had seen, and I had no intention to.

"It can't happen," I assured myself again before I walked out of the room, leaving for the nearby balcony. It overlooked the two graves that were surrounded by grass on top of a small hill next to the vast ocean. We buried Ubel shortly after I was revived last week. The still-fresh mound of dirt that signified where he was buried contrasted with the lush greens around it, and the obelisk that stood as the sole reminder for Lyss' mother now bore two names on it, those of her parents.

I struggled to believe Ubel was dead. Even when I was fighting him, he always seemed invincible, but somehow, he was bested by an Arinthian that wasn't me, then I was bested by the same Arinthian. I should not be alive. I knew that much, so I would have to stay dead to the rest of the world. The castle halls of Dracadere seemed empty compared to how they were before, despite only missing Ubel. "I can't let anyone else die because of me," I said resolvedly. There was only one reason Ubel was dead, and it was because I did not notice the danger earlier. I saw Horus, but I could not warn Ubel in time. I was too afraid, too shocked.

There was light in the sky already, but it was dim, and the shadow of Dracadere darkened the area around us even more. A shallow fog on the ocean made the area seem gloomier than it already was. I had not woken up to see the dawn in a long time. Most of my other nightmares happened when it was still pitch-black outside, after which I would go back to sleep until the light coming in through the balcony made sleep impossible.

"How many times do I have to tell you; it wasn't your fault," Lyss said from behind me. She must have been faking her sleeping state earlier. She seemed to have a talent for such a task.

"Then whose fault is it?" I asked.

"Horus is-," she started.

"But I could have stopped him," I interrupted to remind her. We had this discussion many times over the past week already, but I was still not convinced that I could not have done anything.

"No matter what you think you could have done..." she started, encouraging me to finish what she started saying.

"There is nothing I can do about it now," I said, followed by a few deep breaths to calm myself down. Lyss approached me and hugged me tightly from behind briefly before walking to stand next to me and overlook the dark waters beneath us. She never wanted me to feel like I was at fault. She was trying to keep me from living in the past and had told me as much. "Thank you," I said.

"You're welcome," she said. "I like it when you have a cool head."

She was terrible at jokes, but it was cute, nonetheless. "Very funny," I commented dryly, trying to hide my smile.

"Oh, you love it, and you know it," she said coyly.

"Nope," I denied and forced a frown. She stared at me, then shoved me with her shoulder to break my concentration. I couldn't help but smile. "Fine," I said with a slight laugh in my voice, "I do. I do." I was never able to force myself to be angry or even upset with her.

We could not see the sun, as it was on the other side of the castle this early in the morning, but the sky was brightening regardless. Unfazed by the massive mountains or castle around us, the sky turned a warm orange color.

"Come on," she said, grabbing my hand and walking back toward the rest of the castle. "We should get something to eat."

She dragged me through the halls to the dining room, where I had met with Ubel on many occasions for our own morning meals before he and I would train together. When we arrived in the dining room, even this early in the morning, the table was covered with a decently sized spread of food for us to choose from, and our plates were placed in our normal spots. The seat at the head of the table had no plate in front of it; the emptiness felt ominous and lonely.

It was then that Lyss saw the bare tablecloth in front of her father's old seat. She stopped and stared at it, her grip loosened from my hand, so I tightened mine. She was good at pulling me from the past, but I could never seem to do the same for her. Every time she saw that empty seat, she would lose her appetite, and it was no different this time.

"Sorry," she said quietly as she left the room.

I went into the dining room, grabbed what would be her plate, and filled it with some of the foods I knew she liked. The plate was difficult to manage with the amount of food I put on there, but I needed to make sure she ate.

"Lyss?" I called out after leaving the dining room, but I got no response again. I did a quick survey of the area around me and found her simply sitting on the ground just outside the door in plain sight. "Lyss," I said, offering the food. "You have to eat something at the very least. I get that it is hard to see that seat without your father, but you'll have to face it eventually." Then I tried for a little bit of half-joke, "I won't be around forever."

"Don't," she said very seriously. I could feel the pain in her voice, "Just don't even joke about that."

"I am staying by you until the end of time, Lyss. Sorry I said that." I sat down next to her and put my arm around her and let her rest her head on my shoulder. She was a Death Arinthian, so I knew she would live longer than I would for sure, especially considering how long Ubel survived. Technically he was dead for most of it, but he held on for a long time. Even then, his death was still premature. "I love you, all right?" I assured her. "I'm not going to let anything happen to you, to me, or to your sister. We won't lose anyone else." She mumbled something quietly that was very unclear and hard to understand. "What was that?" I asked for clarification.

"What if..." her voice fell, and she struggled to force herself to voice the concern she held behind her lips. "What if it isn't something you can control?"

"I'll stop it anyw—"

"No!" she interrupted again. "I mean it. What if nothing *you* do could ever stop it?" She was beginning to cry, though she seemed neither to notice, nor care. I knew for sure that something was bothering her, that she was hiding something. I just did not want it to be related to my own concerns of my nightmares.

"Why do you want to know?"

"Just tell me."

"What do you need to hear?"

"I need you to promise me that no matter what happens to me, that you won't blame yourself. Ever," her voice was strained.

"But—"

"No!" she commanded, pushing herself off of me and standing up. "No exceptions. Just promise me that you won't blame yourself."

I stood up and my height dwarfed her. "You say that like something is going to happen. I won't let—"

"You don't get it, do you?" she asked, trying her best now to stifle her tears. "I'm asking you to promise me you won't blame yourself if something does happen, something you can't control. It doesn't matter whether or not you 'let' it happen. Because if it does happen, you won't be able to do anything about it."

"I promise, all right?" I started to walk to her with open arms for a hug, but she took a single step back.

"Promise what?"

"I promise that if something ever happens to you, or to anyone, that I can't control, I won't blame myself," I said, reaching my arms around her and holding her close. "That is what I promise, right here, right now."

"Thank you," she said, reciprocating the hug I gave her.

"Cute," Bell said from behind me while Lyss was buried in my chest. "Drocan, I need to talk to you," I turned to look at her as I let go of Lyss, and Bell seemed serious. "Alone. Don't worry, Lyss, I'll bring him back to you once I'm done with him."

"Fine," Lyss agreed, letting go of me entirely, then wandering back through the halls I assumed to her room or to her parent's grave.

Once Lyss was out of sight, Bell guided me into the dining room and gestured for me to sit. She took the seat at the head of the table after I had sat down. She was the new queen of Dracadere, and I assumed that because I was up and about, she was going to send me on a mission somewhere.

"What is this about?"

"You failed," she said outright. "You didn't kill Horus, and it almost cost you your life. Now that he has Aranor, there is no telling what he may do next."

"So, you want me to go kill him then?" I rolled my shoulder while I asked the question. "I'm not sure if I can."

"Not quite that," she said. "I want to know if you would be willing to form an alliance with him."

"What?!" I stood up from the table, and my legs pushed the chair back a decent distance.

"Hear me out," she said. "I've been thinking about this. He did not want to fight you. He did not want to kill my father. He brought you here instead of leaving you to die, and if he didn't, you would be dead. I don't think he wants a war; I think he was just obeying orders. We will see what his next move is, then you and I will confront him, just the three of us, to see if we can settle this. Continuing this war does nothing for us. We've lost enough."

"When are we leaving?"

"Again, not quite yet," she said. "We are going to wait for him to come to us. We are far more defensible here than we would be launching an attack on Aranor. This is our safest option. I just want you to be aware of it."

"I'll try and play nice," I smirked.

PART III: EPILOGUE

DAY 400

H

ARANOR WAS ALMOST BACK TO its former glory, or at least to the glory I imagined, mixed with the stories I heard. We had rebuilt the defenses, widened the bridges, and many of the homes using the foundations that were already there. Nothing here could really be qualified as a home so much as just living quarters, considering how empty everything was. The larger buildings were used for meeting areas, mess halls, and we even established an infirmary. The smaller buildings we used as barracks and divided ourselves up by rank. I was the head of the city and shared a room with Erione that we had to ourselves. I felt I had finally found my purpose. The need the world had of me, as Eyvndir had proposed when I first awoke, I felt I had found what that was.

Jerum moved to Aranor with us, just as he promised. He and Arthur were in the building next to ours as the next highest ranks. We were not large enough to really constitute a whole army, as we only had ourselves and a few men who decided to stay with us to help us guard the city of Aranor. Abaven was still in direct service of the king as a scout for the border of the Arcane Ruins, and he would stop by on occasion to visit before returning to the capital.

Now that Jerum and I were here, the king had replaced his immediate Crown Guard entirely. I had not met any of the new members of the Guard. We had been given new roles that were equally as respected in the kingdom as the Guardians of Aranor. All of us here were currently under that banner, and as long as Aranor never fell again, we may as well still be members of the Crown Guard.

I found it curious that he never dismissed the army. I understood the Crown Guard as a symbol of power and, to a degree, an army, but he continued to amass soldiers.

Our days were surprisingly quiet. Not once did we ever encounter any of Ubel's army, but we also did not dare venture into the wastelands beyond the walls. Not yet. We sustained ourselves by clearing the area east of Aranor to start a farm and irrigating a stream to keep the new farming fields well-watered, in addition to our hunting and gathering in the forests. Aranor was a highly functioning fort, but it would be a while before it would be restored to its full status as a city of Haven. We had to convince people it was safe enough to move here. That was hard to do, considering there was no attack we could ward off. To the people, it just seemed like Ubel's army was scheming for revenge, and until we repelled that attack, it would never be safe here.

At the moment, however, the rebuilding of the city was the least of my concerns. Erione was giving birth in the room next to me. A few of the royal nurses came from Haven and had been around for the past month as we waited for the child to be ready. She sounded like she was in immense pain, but she was pushing through it all. The past few hours had been filled with her agonizing over the pain, and rightfully so. It felt like it was the worst possible day for this to happen, too. There was a thunderstorm right above us, and with each flash of lightning, a thunderous boom shortly followed, silencing the pounding rain on the rooftops.

The dim candlelight shone through beneath the door frame, and long shadows darkened it occasionally as nurses moved around the room doing whatever they needed to do. I was confident Erione was in good hands; the king was kind enough to send us whatever we needed. She had the best care. She had helped with delivering babies before, and as such, Erione had requested that I stay outside during the delivery.

"Am I too late?" Jerum asked as he barged in through the door. He was in simple clothes, and this was the one time I wished he had been in his armor. He was soaked to the bone with water, and the metal armor would have kept some of it off of him.

"No, Jerum," I said, guiding him to the hearth so he could dry off. "By the sounds of it, you still have plenty of time." There was still a lot of screaming coming from the room as Erione pushed through the pain.

After what seemed like ages, Erione's screaming stopped, and the cries of a newborn baby began. A nurse opened the door.

"Sir Horus, Lady Erione is ready for you now." He guided me through the door, being courteous enough to hold it open for me. In the bed at the center of the room, Erione was sleeping, exhausted from giving birth. Another nurse was holding the still bloody child with some clean cloths over her arm. "Just before she passed out, she said she wanted you to see the child before we cleaned him," the first nurse told me. "Do you have a name for him?"

"It's a boy?" I clarified. The child was crying and covered in enough blood to make me believe it had just been through a war.

"Yes, Sir Horus," the nurse holding my child said.

"We've had one in mind for a boy," I started. "Petrus."

"All right, Petrus," the nurse said in a loving voice to the child. "Let's get you all cleaned up." They had boiled some water in a small basin, and now it was a nice heat for the child. As the nurse put Petrus in the basin, she turned to me and asked, "Would you like to help?" I looked at Erione. The nurse noticed and said, "It will be a while before she wakes up; she did a lot of work today." I smiled, proud of my child and my wife.

"Gladly," I said as I rolled up my sleeves to prepare for the water. I sat on the ground near the basin and accepted a clean cloth from the nurse. I dipped the cloth in the water and wiped the blood as gently as I could from Petrus' crying face. The nurses took over from there, I assumed to make sure it was done properly, which was certainly for the best. After they were done, they swaddled Petrus in white cloth, and handed him to me to hold. He was heavier than I expected but still did not weigh much at all, not to mention he was all cried out. He slept as soundly as his mother. The nurses left me in the room with the child so that our small family could have our first few private moments.

A few hours passed with Petrus cradled in my arms when Erione finally came to.

"How is the baby?" she asked groggily.

"Petrus is doing just fine," I said. "He's sleeping." The lightning from the storm cracked again, and the rain continued to pour. The amount of noise Petrus was able to sleep through was startling. Erione took notice of that fact as well. "I wouldn't worry about being quiet, though," I remarked.

Erione woke up a little faster with the help of the storm and asked, "Can I hold him?"

I stood up and walked over to her and offered her the child. She accepted him into her arms and cried tears of joy as she adored his adorable face. I would proudly hold his cuteness over him for the rest of his life. "Do you mind if I bring Jerum and Arthur in as well?"

"After a moment," she said, "go ahead and get them ready to come in, but have them wait outside."

"As you wish," I said. I opened the door; standing right in front of it were Jerum and Arthur. Jerum was finally dry, but Arthur must have arrived recently, as he was still soaked. "Very well then," I said, examining Arthur, "you go stand by the hearth. Jerum, you can come in a moment." I looked back at Erione. She rolled her eyes and moved her head to indicate he was welcome. "Or now, I guess." Arthur seemed disappointed he would have to wait longer and Jerum was excited to see Petrus.

"Hello there, little guy," he cooed. "I'm a friend of your father. I'm Jerum." He pointlessly offered the baby his finger despite being asleep and was about to start tickling Petrus before I smacked his hand away.

"Don't wake him," I said. "I want to see how long Petrus can last in the storm."

Jerum shrugged, "That's fair. May I hold him?" I looked at Erione, and she was already offering him the child. He graciously accepted the privilege. "I promise I'll protect you with my life, Petrus," he told the sleeping child.

"I appreciate the offer Jerum. I don't know if that will ever be necessary, but as a witness, I expect you to keep that promise," I said.

"I will," he said. "I'll pledge my life for you and your family, Horus."

"Thank you," Erione said for us and put her arms out as if to ask for the child back in her arms. Petrus was being passed around a lot but still managed to remain asleep. Arthur walked in; he was still wet but no longer dripping on the floor.

"I just want to see him," he said. Erione held Petrus up so that Arthur could see his face, "The first citizen of Aranor," he said in awe. That had not even occurred to me yet. The rest of us were all here on duties for the king, essentially soldiers quartering in the city; he was the first real Aranorian. "What is his name?"

"Petrus," Jerum said.

"After Sir Petrus?"

"He did save my life," I said, "so yes. I hope to teach him all about Petrus' heroics in his life, and I might need some of you to help me with that."

"It would be my pleasure," Jerum said.

"Gladly," Arthur agreed.

"Now that Petrus is born, there is something else I have to take care of."

"Do you really have to go now?" Erione asked.

"Everyone here can help you take care of Petrus for the next few days, but I have to go see Princess Bellona."

"What if you don't come back? Jerum, you should at least go with him," she suggested, indicating with her chin.

"No," I said. "And I mean no offense, Jerum, but you would only slow me down. I want to discuss something with her. The fewer people I bring, the more likely I feel like she will have a discussion with me, especially if there is nothing to fight over."

"Just be quick," she sighed at my decision.

I smiled, "I'll be back soon enough." I went to my room, donned my armor to brace myself for the rain, and went over the stables we had assembled when we got here. I put a saddle on my horse, mounted it, then rode through the storm to Dracadere. I left my weapons back in Aranor, hoping to prove I meant no harm.

DAY 403

D

WE HAD A BIRD WATCHING over Aranor for any movement. When Horus left in the dead of night, it flew back immediately to tell us, or rather Bell, who was trained by her father to use the birds to track simple movements. She really was the best replacement for Ubel; they had so much in common. But unlike Lyss and her father, Bell had unfortunately not inherited the sense of humor in their family, which was the one downfall of having her rule over Dracadere.

All the bird was able to tell Bell was that a single rider had left Aranor and was coming straight for Dracadere, but we knew it had to be Horus. There was no one else would have the courage to do something like this. We left earlier this morning to meet him somewhere away from the castle but close enough that we could go back within less than half a day. With how outwardly he approached, it seemed he wanted us to know he was coming. He was unarmed, to our knowledge, but he also may have been saving his magic to fight us. He was approaching in the near distance, so Bell and I rode slowly up to meet him from where we were waiting.

"I think you are right," I told Bell as we rode our horses. "I think he has only come to talk. If he wanted a fight, he knows he has to bring that sword with him."

"You are armed, though," she asked, "right?"

"Always," I patted the hilt of my flame sword as it waited, unlit, for me to use it in my next fight. My bow was in the straps of the back of my armor. It had to be repaired after Horus' sword tore through me, my bow, my armor, and my cloak. "Do you think Lyss will be okay today?"

"Surprisingly enough, we still have the same skeletons we trained to deliver her," she said with wide eyes as she realized how long ago that was for her. "They will take care of her if she needs anything, don't worry about it. They may be dead, but they are good about bringing in new life. They've never failed."

"How many times have they done it?"

"Once with my mother and Lyss. And that turned out fine."

"That does not exactly establish a pattern."

"Don't worry about it, at least not right now. Here he comes."

Horus slowed down, stopped about twenty feet in front of us and dismounted. He put his hands up, saying seemingly relieved, "Mother Arinth, you're alive."

"Says the Arinthian who nearly killed me."

"I did what I had to. I'm glad she was able to save your life."

I gave a terse nod.

"I would like to speak with you, Drocan. I have news. And good afternoon, Princess Bellona." He bowed to Bell.

"You are unarmed?" I asked just to be sure.

"Of course," he stated.

I dismounted my horse, but Bell remained atop hers. "What would you like to tell me?" I asked.

"Aranor belongs to me, not Justain," he said plainly.

"What?" Bell interjected.

"What do you mean?" I asked.

Horus already had his explanation prepared. He filled us in on how after he claimed Aranor for the king of Haven, he decided to secede from the kingdom as an independent city from the kingdom that would still be an ally to Haven. Horus was apparently no longer under the king's direct orders but was now almost a monarch in his own right.

"I would like to form an alliance. I want Aranor to be a beacon of peace for the entire continent. War has divided it long enough. I don't want to carry the mistakes of the past to our present. I have a son now. I'll train him to be a soldier if I have to. He won't grow up as a citizen of Haven but of Aranor. If we make this alliance, I won't allow the king to send anybody to the west without your permission, nor will I allow you to send anybody east without his. Aranor will be our best hope for keeping any peace reasonable. If the king decides to attack you, then he declares war on both of us; I won't stand for a continuous war."

I was shocked. Bell had come along to offer the same kind of alliance so that we would not have to worry about any attacks. To have Horus be the sole ruler of Aranor sweetened the deal. Our only leverage was our offering of passivity, but he was offering us protection, not just neutrality.

"Horus," I started, but Bell stopped me for seemingly no reason. Then I remembered she was the one in charge of Dracadere now.

"Horus," she echoed, "we will gladly accept your allegiance. Is there anything else we can do for you?"

"There is one thing," he said, turning his attention toward me. "Drocan, to solidify this allegiance, I would like to offer you a place with us as a Guardian of Aranor. I leave the decision to you whether you accept it or not. I would be putting both of us at great risk, but I promise the king of Haven will have no control over you or your actions. I told him you were dead. Again, it is good to see that I was wrong. With that, if you were to make an appearance again, and the king of Haven was to find out, both of our heads would be on the line. I have enough loyal to me that if he does find out, his armies would not be able to best us, especially with you on our side."

"If I joined you," I said, "it would put another target on all Arinthians' backs again. I would rather stay peacefully here in Dracadere."

"I understand," he said while giving a few shallow nods. "If that's the case, I'll be on my way."

He had grown a beard since the last time I saw him, but he had been cutting his hair to keep it short. He seemed rugged, but he held himself in high regard and his confidence was showing in the way he talked as well.

"Stay safe, Drocan," he said, remounting his horse and turning it to the side as he prepared to go back to Aranor. "I hope to see you again." Then he rode off and never looked back at us.

I remounted my horse and looked at Bell, who seemed as equally as surprised as I was. "That was unexpected," I said to break the silence.

"I think you should have joined him," she said.

"What if it was a trap?"

"We both know it wasn't," she said. I wasn't sure. Our crows at Haven had shown us the king's army was still growing. He must be planning something. I could tell Horus was sincere about me joining him. He would be risking his life. "At the least it would have given us the chance to kill Justain for what he has put us through."

"That would only break the peace again," I said, steering my horse back toward Dracadere. "Let's go. I don't want Lyss to be alone with a bunch of bones for much longer." We rode for the next few hours in relative silence. The only sounds were the hooves of our horses and the clamor of her metal armor. We arrived at Dracadere just before nightfall, and I heard screams echoing through the halls. "She's started already?"

"Hurry up," Bell urged me. "I'll catch up, go be with her."

I rushed through the halls and followed the noise to one of the many spare bedrooms housed inside Dracadere. I swung the door open and saw Lyss screaming and sweating as she gave birth. She was pretty far along when I arrived. I went over to hold her hand as she pushed through the pain, but it was really her holding mine. Her grip was so tight it felt like my fingers were having their circulation cut off. I was happy to be by her side as she took quick short breaths then pushed with all of her might. Bell soon found the room, too, and helped supervise the skeletons. She took over as the main deliverer and urged Lyss to push more and soon held our daughter in her hands.

"She's beautiful," I said.

"Yes, she is," Bell agreed. Lyss was still awake and wanted to see the child, so she stretched out her arms and accepted the child from Bell.

"Kathryn," she said. "Just like my mother, so beautiful." Her voice was getting weaker with each word, making it difficult to understand her. "Take her, Drocan." The child was still covered in blood and crying, but I accepted her nonetheless. "Remember what you promised me," she said as she handed over Kathryn. "I love you, Drocan, Kathryn." I did not notice her arm fall nor the sound of it hitting the bed.

I was smiling as I took Kathryn into my arms, and I responded to Lyss with a question. "Why would you bring—" then my heart sank when I looked back to Lyss. "Lyss? Lyss?" I shook her shoulder, assuming she was asleep, but her chest wasn't moving at all, and I could not hear her breathing. It was almost exactly like the dreams I had before. I hoped that when they stopped months ago that it meant it wouldn't come true anymore, yet my worst fears were confirmed.

Bell had not quite noticed what happened yet, "Drocan, what's wrong?"

"Look at Lyss!" I told her. She obeyed and was about as appalled as I was. "No! I... I can't." It was hard for me to resist my own tears, "Lyss! I can't keep that promise. No! You can't go!"

I was trying to fight her death, but I knew I couldn't do anything about it. I held Kathryn close to my chest and shielded her from the sight of her dead mother. I was crying with her. It felt like a hole had just been ripped from my chest. It was so much more painful than Horus' sword. I felt like I had lost too much too soon. I was not ready for Lyss to go, but she must have seen it coming.

"No," Bell echoed, but she was holding herself together, fighting back tears and pain that I would have thought was impossible to resist. "Drocan," she swallowed. "Drocan, you can't blame yourself for this. I don't know if she ever told you how she brought you back."

"What does this have to do with her healing me?"

"It was her choice. She sacrificed her own life force to save yours," Bell said solemnly. "She said it was the only way to actually save your life. We thought she would have more time."

"No," I said in disbelief. "No, why would she do that?"

"I think the answer is clear. She loved you."

"Then she should stay with me!" I could not hold back the hot tears as they streamed down my face. "Take it back!" I fell as I cried out again, "Take it back!"

"She can't. She held on as long as she could have," Bell said, trying to comfort me. She took Kathryn from my arms and told the skeletons to clean her while I knelt at the bedside of my dead wife, holding her cold hand. Bell was standing next to me and reminded me again, "It isn't your fault."

I don't know if I would ever be able to believe her. I would never forgive myself for being alive at her expense, but I could live on for Kathryn. I would help her know the new world at peace. I may not have known my reason for being alive when I was created, but I knew it now.

ACKNOWLEDGMENTS

AS A DEBUT AUTHOR, there are many people I would like to acknowledge for their help in the completion of this book. First, I'd like to thank my parents and my eldest brother for being among my first readers and withholding their criticisms. Thank you also for your helpful and hilariously brief reviews of, "I thought it was good" and "I enjoyed it." Those reviews gave me something to put on the back of my first handbound copy. I would again like to thank my dad for encouraging me and helping in every way throughout the self-publishing journey.

Then to my other brother as well for helping inspire the story with the years we spent adventuring and for introducing me to some of my favorite book series. Then I would like to thank my other early readers, friends and professors alike, who made time out of their busy lives to read it and offer me feedback: Sara Say, Eric Oulette, and Dr. Hackett, author of *Outside the Gates*.

I would like to thank Matthew P. Smyser for designing the cover of this book and teaching me how to bind books, allowing me to see my book in a hardback form before the rest of the world.

Thank you to Alisha Dahl from "As the Page Turns Editing" for taking the time during the busy holiday season to edit my book and help me prepare it for publishing.

Lastly and certainly not least, would be to you, my new readers and friends. I hope you enjoyed the book; that's all I can really ask for.

Made in the USA
Monee, IL
20 February 2023

214e81c0-dc4d-4092-a9d0-6e1db20f3a3cR01